The Children of Jocasta

Also by Natalie Haynes

THE AMBER FURY

Non-fiction

THE ANCIENT GUIDE TO MODERN LIFE

Natalie Haynes

The Children of Jocasta

First published 2017 by Mantle
an imprint of Pan Macmillan
20 New Wharf Road, London N1 9RR
Associated companies throughout the world
www.panmacmillan.com

ISBN 978-1-5098-3615-4

1 3 5 7 9 8 6 4 2

A CIP catalogue record for this book is available from the British Library.

Printed and bound by CPI Group (UK) Ltd, Croydon, CR0 4YY

For Dan

ὁ γοῦν λόγος σοι πᾶς ὑπὲρ κείνης ὅδε

Antigone, Sophocles

Author's Note

The ancient Greeks did not think of themselves as 'Greek' (the word Graeci is a later, Roman invention). They were Hellenes. They prized opposites – when ancient Greeks wanted to describe the whole world, for example, they would split it into two: both Hellene and non-Hellene, or both freeman and slave. But they also, perhaps predominantly, defined themselves as citizens of whichever city-state they inhabited. Thebes had a dense mythical history, as did its environs: a surprisingly large number of unpleasant deaths in Greek myth happened on or near Mount Cithaeron, where Actaeon was turned into a stag and ripped apart by his own hunting hounds, and Pentheus was torn limb from limb by his own Maenadic mother. Perhaps the moral of these stories is that the countryside can be more dangerous than the city. But not always.

The Children of Jocasta

Prologue

The man looked across the room at his son, who lay shivering on the hard couch. He took a step towards the boy, thinking he would wrap a blanket more closely around him to coax the shivers away. But then he stopped, unable to persuade his limbs to repeat the actions they had carried out the day before and the day before that. He had kept his wife warm when the shakes ran through her; her body like an axe-blade, juddering in the trunk of a thick, black pine tree. And then he had kept his daughter warm until she too succumbed to the disease. What was it the washerwoman had called it? The Reckoning.

He felt his cracked lips stretch into a mirthless smile. What kind of a reckoning did the citizens of Thebes believe this to be? Punishment from the gods for a real or imagined slight? The temples rang out with the sound of prayers and offerings to every god, by every name. Most often they called on Apollo. Mindful of offending him, they addressed him by one name after another: Cynthios, Delphinios, Pythios, the son of Leto. Everyone knew that his arrows carried the plague on their immortal tips and that his aim was always true. But what possible grudge could the Archer have held against this man's daughter, scarcely more than an infant? Or his wife, who had made her sacrifices devoutly with each new season? The god could not have resented her, but she had died all the same. Two days ago, he had carried her body into the streets himself, struggling with the weight not because his sickness-ravaged wife was heavy – she was sinew and bones, the skin hanging loosely from her arms – but because the plague had left him barely able to lift hisown battered bones.

Carrying his daughter out the following day had been easier.

He looked over at Sophon again, and saw the convulsions ripple through his ten-year-old body. He felt a wetness beneath his eye and thought for a moment that he was weeping. But when he took his hand away from his face, he saw the raw crimson of fresh blood on his fingertips. The blisters were bursting, then. He had heard that men were losing their sight. Only a few heartbeats after he had silently cursed Apollo, he murmured a quiet prayer. Let me not go blind. A blind man was of no use to his young son. If the boy survived, he would not be able to take care of a blind beggar man. His prayers grew smaller: let me keep one eye, at least. One eye intact. And – they increased again without him noticing – let the boy live.

But should he really leave him to shake so? He had felt his own teeth drumming against one another when the shivering had consumed him a day ago. He worried he would bite through his own tongue. He paused, realizing that was not quite true; he had given no thought to his tongue when the fever rattled through him. Only afterwards, when the heat had broken and he lay spent on the ground, did he wonder how he had not injured himself. When the shakes came upon his wife, he had wrapped her up, and she had wrapped up their daughter. But neither had survived. He had placed all the blankets around them, so there was nothing left by the time he fell foul of the same cruel dance. Yet he was – so far – still alive. And so perhaps this was something he had learned about the Reckoning: it thrived in the heat. It might be driven out if it was denied warmth.

The boy moaned so softly that he wondered if he was hearing things. But he did not approach him, and he did not make him warm.

The Archer would take who he chose. But still, the man hoped – a tiny broken thing like a bird – that he would seek his prey elsewhere.

1

Sixty years later

I didn't hear him coming. I was in the old ice store, which lay at the furthest end of a forgotten corridor in a corner of the palace no one had used for years. Not since my parents were alive. My father loved ice, shaved with an iron pick from a block which dripped sullenly in this room, the thick walls protecting it from the constant sun which beat down on the white stone. How did it get here? I used to beg. Where did it come from? He would tell me a different answer each time: an angry river god had turned all the city's water into ice one day, and no one had ever found time to defrost this last chunk. It was an egg left behind by a huge frozen bird. Then it was Thebes's greatest treasure, and bandits had sailed across the oceans to invade the palace and seize it, like the Golden Fleece. This last story left me with nightmares of masked men, breaching one of the city's seven gates, climbing to the high citadel – fearless as they ran beneath the mountain lions which were carved into the stone gateway, golden stones embedded into their eye sockets to ward off our enemies – trampling along the colonnades and rampaging into the courtyard where we lived. My mother told him to stop frightening me. So the next time I asked him, he made me promise solemnly that I wouldn't tell her before explaining that he had won it in a bet with a Titan, who now cursed his name. I shouldn't be afraid of him, though, because he was fully occupied holding the weight of the sky upon his shoulders.

After my parents died, my uncle Creon had the palace extended and rebuilt. It needed to be more secure, he said, and grander. He added rooms and whole levels above the ground floor, so my home towered above every building in the city. The palace sat on the highest hill, and now it was the highest building too. Creon also insisted that the royal residence should no longer be kept ever-open to the city and her citizens, as my mother had liked it. There must be a space between us and them; we needed doors which could be bolted shut each night. Lessons had to be learned. And while all these works were being carried out, by teams of efficient and almost silent slaves, he decided this corridor might as well be abandoned. He didn't care for ice, the way my father did. So once the building works were completed, this room was no longer used for anything: it was too far from the new kitchens to be practical.

But it made a perfect place to read, on a bristling hot day. The light spilled in from two small slits, high up on the north- and east-facing walls. And with the door open onto the half-walled corridor outside, I could easily see to read the parchment roll I had taken from my tutor's office yesterday. I would return it as soon as I'd finished, like I always did. He didn't mind, so long as I placed it back on his dusty shelves in the exact spot from which I had removed it. I had learned to blow the dust across from either side to cover the tracks my fingers left on the wood. His eyes weren't as sharp as they used to be. The manuscript would be back in its place before he even noticed it was gone.

I often lost track of time in this room, which was one of its many advantages. The long days of summer were so hot and bright and dull. My uncle liked to say girls all across the city, across Hellas, wished to be in our place. But they must have imagined our lives to be other than they were, because no one would cherish these empty days. I longed to go down to Lake Hylica and swim with the frogs and the fish. But there was no one to go with, and I knew my sister would be annoyed if I took the maids with me. What if she needed them to help her change her dress or rearrange her hair? We couldn't all run around the palace like barbarians, she would say, not for the first time. I could almost imagine her petulant lower lip, protruding in annoyance at something I hadn't yet done.

The light only entered the ice store through thin strips, so it was easy to lose track of where the sun was in the sky. I would usually leave when I'd finished reading, or when I was hungry, or sometimes when I heard Ani or Eteo calling for me. They always knew that if I wasn't at lessons or in the courtyard, I'd be here. But no one was calling for me that day. It was always quiet in the palace in summer; anything important would be taking place in the public square at the front of the building. Perhaps that's what made me stand up and press my aching shoulders against the cool stone wall behind me. It was so quiet, I must have begun to think I was supposed to be wherever the rest of the palace's inhabitants were.

I heard his footsteps, I think, but I wasn't afraid. He wasn't walking like someone who had something to hide. I could hear heels striking the ground, a measured, easy pace. It didn't occur to me to be worried. Even so, I stashed the roll of parchment under my arm, in case it was my tutor, and covered it with the fine cloak I shrugged over my shoulders. I knew it wasn't his walk, though: he favours his right foot and drags the left one slightly. 'An old injury' is all he ever says if you ask him why. His eyes are dark and hooded, and they change if he doesn't want you to pursue something. The light disappears from them, and the subject is closed.

I walked out into the corridor, and the temperature rose pitilessly. Even wearing my thinnest cloak – a pale fawn colour, made of flax – I was too hot out here. I wished I could just wear a simple tunic, as I did when I was younger. But if my uncle caught sight of me dressed so informally, I would be in trouble. I could feel the sweat forming behind my ears and at the base of my spine. I almost turned straight back into the ice store. But I had decided I should go and find my siblings, so I kept walking.

With the increase in temperature came other reminders of the world outside the palace: grasshoppers scratching away beside the walls, darting sparrows chattering in their nests. Usually, a man with a long broom sweeps away the birds' nests from the walls, because their morning clamour irritates my uncle. But for some reason, they had been overlooked this year, and they chirruped away, gleeful at their reprieve. If the mountain eagles heard them, the sparrows would lose their fledglings.

The corridor twisted round to the left and then the

right, before it opened out into the family courtyard. My eyes were watering at the sudden brightness after the twilight of the ice store. I blinked away the tears and then licked them from my top lip. I realized I was thirsty; perhaps that was what had driven me out of my quiet corner. It must be Eteo I could hear, I thought, coming down the corridor to find me. Although he would surely be busy with his advisers at this hour. But the stride was much too long for Ani, and anyway, her shoes don't have those hard leather soles that slap the stones as you walk.

I followed the corridor around to the left, and saw the shadow of the man along the ground. Not Eteo, then, because this man was wearing a long cloak, and Eteo would be in nothing more than a tunic on a day like today. I heard a strange, metallic sound I half-recognized. And then I walked around the second corner and when he caught sight of me, the man stiffened, as though he were suppressing alarm. I had heard him, but with my feet bare, he clearly hadn't heard me. I was about to greet him when I realized his face was almost entirely covered, like the bandits of my nightmares. Only his eyes were visible: he had swathed the rest in a thin white fabric.

I tensed my arm against my side, to keep hold of Sophon's scroll. Behind the veiled man, I could see the courtyard, but it was empty. There was no sign of my siblings, my cousin, my uncle. I took a breath and decided I would rather run past him than walk. I am the second quickest of all of us: much taller than Ani, and Polyn – my oldest brother – would never deign to engage in a race with his little sister, so I would win against him by default. Only Eteo, with his long, lean physique, could outrun me, though my uncle would be horrified if he ever saw me hitching up my tunic to give my legs free rein. And when Eteo was busy with matters of state, there was no one I could prevail upon to accompany me somewhere quiet and spacious enough to sprint. So I was out of practice, but I still trusted my speed. Once I was in the courtyard, I could raise an alarm that a stranger was present in the family quarters. The household slaves must be somewhere nearby, surely.

I pushed my toes into the stone beneath my feet. I must have left my sandals in my room this morning: something else which would provoke my uncle to raise a weary eyebrow, if he saw me. I pressed forward and almost skittered past the man, but he stepped suddenly to his right, and I clattered into him. I felt a sharp jab under my ribs. He must have slammed the wooden end of the parchment roll into my side. I winced and said reflexively, 'I'm sorry.'

We were the exact same height, so our eyes met for a moment: his were a watery sort of grey, with two brown specks in the right iris. It made it look like a bird's egg. I should keep running into the courtyard, I thought, and then out the other side, and through to the next square where my brothers and my uncle would be. I could return the manuscript to Sophon and apologize for taking it without asking. He wouldn't mind. But even as I was thinking this, it occurred to me that perhaps my legs wouldn't carry me as far as the second courtyard. I was standing in the beating sun, but I was cold. The man looked past me for a second, though there was no one behind me, then his eyes met mine. Wordless, he turned and walked away. I thought perhaps I might sit on the ground for a moment.

I took a few more steps and fell to my knees, just before I was fully in the courtyard. A girl I didn't recognize – the daughter of one of the house-slaves, I suppose – was coming out of a bedroom, carrying a tray. The noise of me falling – my thick silver bangle crashing onto the ground – made her turn and she screamed, dropping what she was carrying everywhere. Hollow wooden things, cups maybe, or bowls. I heard them bounce and crash across the warm grey slabs. I hissed at her to be quiet, but she was too far away and besides, she was making so much noise herself, she wouldn't have heard anything I said. The light was so bright, it made me want to close my eyes. I saw the shadows of birds flying across the square, but I couldn't raise my head to see the birds themselves.

After a long time or perhaps no time at all, I heard voices, but they all sounded strange, distorted as though I was hearing them underwater. I blinked but my eyes wouldn't quite focus: there were guards and servants, and then my brothers, everyone running towards me. They were shouting – I could see from their flushed faces – but I could barely make out what they were saying. It sounded like, 'They've killed her.'

Killed who? There was only one person left in my family who they could possibly mean: my sister, Ani. Please don't let it be Ani, I thought. However much we argue, I can't lose her too. Please.

The last thing I remembered was looking down to see that Sophon's manuscript was completely ruined, covered in something sticky and red. I would have to apologize. It would be hard to replace. And then, of course, I realized they meant me. Someone had killed me.

2

As the pain coursed through her body, threatening to split her apart, Jocasta clawed at the bedclothes beneath her. If she could just get some air into her chest, she told herself, everything would be alright. Her lungs felt like an empty wineskin, trampled beneath a drunken soldier's boot. Yet she couldn't stop screaming for long enough to breathe. She felt Teresa's hand grabbing her own hard enough to squash the bones together. The secondary pain was so unexpected, she turned to look stupidly at her crushed hand.

'Breathe in,' said Teresa and counted her to four. 'And now out again.' The two of them counted the breaths, together but apart, because although Jocasta needed the older woman's help, she also knew it was all Teresa's fault that she was probably about to die, and she found that hard to forgive.

It had been Teresa's idea for the old king to marry. The city had gone too long without knowing its future. People were worried. If the king died without a son (even a daughter would be better than nothing), what would happen to the citizens of Thebes? They needed stability. Everyone agreed, the city had endured enough since the Reckoning had devastated them years before.

And it was strange, people said as they went about their business, that the king lived in a huge palace with courtiers, housekeepers, guards and cooks, but no family. He was past forty, past fifty almost: his habit of riding out into the mountains for weeks on end with his men – hunting deer or wild boar with their nets and short spears – was no longer as forgivable as it had once been.

Jocasta wasn't told how she was chosen. The whole thing must have happened so quickly: a group of men in a room lit by smoky candles, drawing lots to decide whose daughter would be elevated to royalty. One day, she had been at home – her parents' home, as she would soon learn to rename it – sitting in the women's quarters, thinking about very little. Five days later, she was standing in the public courtyard of Thebes's palace before an altar hastily dedicated to Ox-eyed Hera, pledged by her father to a man she had never met, before the eyes of a goddess who had ignored her prayers. She had no idea her father was considering marriage for her so soon, having expected to be at home for another year or two, at least. She was a dutiful daughter, careful at weaving and the other household skills her parents encouraged her to acquire. She would make a good wife. But surely not yet.

Her parents had acted with extraordinary haste. Jocasta felt foolish: she should have known what they were like. How else had they survived the Reckoning? Her father had a unique gift for profiting from situations that would fell lesser men. He had always been conscious of his standing: he was rich but he had earned his wealth, rather than inheriting it. Still he had earned plenty, and bought slaves enough to build a large house on the northern side of the city. It was not the most fashionable street (too far from the palace for that), but it was airy and the house was a grand stone affair, with the women's quarters tucked away behind the building's forbidding gates. His wife had slave women to do her weaving for her, though she still prided herself on the fineness of the cloth she used to make.

The particular pain of his behaviour this time came from the realization that he must have considered Jocasta – his only daughter, his first-born child – as nothing more than another problem waiting to be solved. It was one thing to be disliked by her mother – who had never tried to disguise the irritation she felt for her daughter – but another thing altogether to be rejected by her father, when he had always made her his pet, as if consoling her for her mother's indifference. After Jocasta's wedding – when she tried to defend him in her mind, so she could look back on some parts of her childhood fondly – she gave him credit for the fact that any father would be proud to marry his daughter to the king. Though she knew he had not thought about her, or what she might want, at all. Still, what man wouldn't seize a marriage connection to the king? And what father would jeopardize such a connection on the whim of his daughter? None. But he should have known she would have done whatever he had asked, if he had only asked. Instead of which, he organized the whole thing without telling her. The only possible explanation for such secrecy was that he knew how she would feel when she found out, and it saddened her that he had known but not cared.

He was a little drunk when he came home that night: the men had been drinking their wine too strong. Whoever had been master of the grape – pouring it into the krater and mixing it with insufficient water – had intended them all to get drunk before the flute-girls arrived. Jocasta preferred the euphemism to the word she heard her mother hiss: whores. But now she could hear her father whispering to her mother, who let out a sudden squawk of delight before the two of them began to laugh. Like children, she thought, in annoyance. She heard her brother murmur in his dream, and wondered if he would wake up. But as she stared across the room in the dim light, willing him back to sleep, he rolled over to facethe wall and his breathing levelled out once again. She moved her head slightly, trying to hear what her father was saying. But she couldn't quite make out the words.

Would it have made any difference if she had? Would she have argued with him? She did that anyway, when she found out the next day, but it had no effect. Everything was already arranged, and there was nothing she could do. Would she have run away in the night, if she'd known sooner? Where could she have gone? Thebes wasn't a large city, and her father knew everyone in it. Would she have tried to escape from the city altogether? But how would she have made it through any of its seven gates, all of which were guarded? She had never thought of herself as a prisoner behind the city walls. But that was only because she had never wanted to leave before.

Still, when she asked them the next day what all the fuss had been about, she wished she had known sooner. Her father smiled luxuriantly, his pleasure slowly revealing his yellowing teeth, greying now at the gums.

'I have done the best deal of my life,' he told her. 'And you are to marry the king.'

The second sentence was so incongruous following the first. She had been waiting for him to say that he had discovered a new trading partner in the Outlying, Theban slang for Boeotia, the territory outside their beloved city, or to produce some rhyton that he had bought from a shipping merchant: her father loved the most ornate drinking cups. His favourite was a pointed vessel made from rock crystal, with smaller polished green crystal beads, wrapped in twists of gold, for a handle. She felt her face rearrange itself, from congratulatory to perplexed.

'What do you mean?' she said.

'King Laius needs a wife,' her mother explained, condemning herself forever in her daughter's eyes. 'You're very lucky.' Her father nodded.

'The king is an old man,' Jocasta said. 'He must be more than fifty years old.'

'Half-dead, then,' said her father, his eyebrows raised in a parody of amusement. 'He's only ten years or so older than me, you little brat.'

'So why would I want to marry him?' she continued. 'Instead of someone who isn't older than my father?'

'Sometimes,' her mother sighed, 'I think you take pleasure in being wilfully obtuse. I really do. So let me explain to you in words that even your little brotherwould understand: Thebes needs a powerful king. Laius is getting older, and people are growing nervous. What if something happens to him when he's away from the city? What then? The Elders will fight to succeed him. Thecity could fall into chaos.' She reached over to Jocastaand grabbed her shoulder, next to the fabric knots which formed the top of her daughter's tunic. She allowed her nails to rest on Jocasta's skin. 'That can't happen,' she said. 'The king needs a son. And, before that, he needs a wife, a young one, who could act as regent until the child comes of age, if something happened to him.' She shook Jocasta's shoulder with each alternate word. 'And that is going to be you, because your father is clever and lucky, which is exactly why I married him. Do you understand?'

Jocasta nodded, and her mother let go of her arm. 'It's an honour, you ungrateful little bitch. You'll be queen of the city. So run along to the temple of Artemis and dedicate your doll. And do it nicely, so she doesn't curse you, as you deserve.'

The ritual should have been only a part of Jocasta's proaulia: the time between betrothal and marriage when a bride prepared herself for her new life, but there was little time (and, on Jocasta's part, no enthusiasm) for more. When Jocasta was born she had been given a small clay figure of an Amazon girl, wearing brightly patterned leggings and a tunic top. She had played with it so much that the paint had rubbed away, only the odd fleck of red or green remaining from what had once been a parade of colour. The doll's left eye was still black, but the paint on the other had cracked, allowing the faded orange terracotta to show through. But married women could not have toys: she must take her doll to the temple and dedicate it to Artemis, praying for her to give Jocasta strength, like the warrior woman. After the dedication, the next temple she would enter would be sacred to Hera. Artemis would have no time for her once she was married.

Traditionally, a girl's family and friends accompanied her when she offered her doll to the Virgin Goddess. It should have been a party, a feast, an occasion for joy. But Jocasta's parents were too angry with her – and she with them – so she went alone, save for the slave girl who followed two paces behind her, to the temple only a few streets away.

She placed the doll in a small brown leather bag, and walked quickly along the dusty road, her feet reddening from the dirt that clung to the bottom of her shift. The rain would not come again for another month at least, and the sharp-pointed acanthus leaves at the side of the road were beginning to droop in the heat. She hitched her skirt up a little into her belt, but the disapproving stare of an old woman sweeping the steps outside a nearby house made her blush and drop it back to graze the dust once again. The temple would be cool inside, and she climbed the steps grateful to escape the glaring afternoon heat beneath the grand columns that ran along the front. She turned to her mother's slave and told her to wait in the shade beneath the temple portico.

Jocasta stepped inside and blinked into the darkness, but no one else was present. She took the doll from her bag and walked up to the large statue of Artemis – her serene face expressing mild pleasure in holding her bow and arrows – feeling oddly self-conscious. She knew she should issue a formal prayer as she left her toy for the goddess, but with no priestess to help her, she couldn't find the words. So she placed her doll carefully at the divine foot, propping it up against the cold stone. She murmured, 'Keep me safe', and turned to go. As she walked through a shaft of sunlight, her eye was caught by an angry red weal on her shoulder. Her mother's thumbnail had broken the skin, and when she raised her arm she saw four more gashes – the skin around them pink and inflamed – on the back of her shoulder.

She stopped and knelt on the ground, not wanting to go home again while her mother sat in the women's quarters, emanating spite. Her brother would be at lessons with his tutor, and her father would be in the market square, clutching the hands of florid men as he accepted their congratulations. She could see the gold rings which pinned back the flesh of her father's fingers, so they spilled fatly above the metal. He would consider this a very good day.

As she sat on her heels, she tried to imagine what it would be like to live in the palace, the citadel of Thebes. She had been there a handful of times when she was younger, always for festivals. She tried to separate the building from the occasions, but it was difficult. She could remember the overpowering smell of charred meat, tinged with cloying incense and the vinegary tang of wine. She heard the clamour of a crowd, all eating and drinking their fill. The priests in their finery, leading Thebes in their sacrifices and prayers. She had a sense of a big open courtyard, but she couldn't fill in any details of the rest of the building: the colour, the scale, nothing. Were there trees? She had half a memory of reaching up to touch silver-grey bark with her fingers. Above all, she could not place the king in his palace. She tried to remember whether he was clean-shaven or bearded, whether his eyes were light or dark, whether his hair was black, like most Thebans, or fair, as some were. Whether he was stocky or thin, tall or beginning to bend forward at the neck, like a tortoise. She bit her lip when she realized that whatever colour the hair had once been, it was probably grey now, or white. Or perhaps he was bald. She tried to suppress the sudden sourness she felt rising at the back of her throat.

She looked up at the statue of Artemis. The goddess sat placidly on her throne, her hair neatly plaited behind her head, a bow in her hand and a quiver at her side. The latter was decorated with deer, running between trees in bright green leaf. 'Please,' Jocasta said, looking up at the figure and reaching out to hold the cold stone hem of her robe. 'Don't let him touch me. Please.'

She stared at the painted eyes but received no reply. Zeus nods, Thebans said. If he assents to your request, he nods. But did Artemis nod too? Perhaps if she stared straight into the goddess's eyes and didn't blink at all, Artemis would understand how important this was. She held her gaze for as long as she could but eventually tears formed and she could no longer force her eyes to remain open. Did she imagine the head moving? She wiped the tears away with her small, pale hand. 'Thank you,' she whispered, just in case.

The dressmaker came the next day, her grey hair combed back so the bright sunlight picked out every wrinkle in her creased brown face. She had brought two bolts of fabric with her, in two contrasting shades of red. Jocasta wondered if her mother had chosen the cloth, which would make a thick, heavy chiton to wear on a warm summer day. Certainly no one had asked her. But she didn't question the dressmaker, in case it was all the woman had. Perhaps there hadn't been time for the dyers to begin work on new fabric. Besides, it was an unspoken rule of living in Thebes that no one complained about shortages. Everyone knew that the king and his Elders were doing their best to ensure supplies came into the city. But with the Sphinx in the mountains – right outside the city walls people sometimes said – no one could be surprised if there were interruptions and delays. She tried not to imagine herself in the shade of saffron she would have preferred, tried not to think how hot she would be dressed in fabric the colour of blood.

And at least the dressmaker's second bolt of cloth – for the cloak and the veil – was thinner and lighter, so she would not struggle to catch her breath. She said nothing, and stood obediently on a small wooden stool, while the old woman held the material around her waist and pinned the edges together. She kept the pins between her thin lips, her mouth puckering to keep them in place. She reached for each one without looking, but never scratched herself.

It was the first dress that had been made especially for Jocasta. Her other clothes had all been worn by a different girl before they came to her. She thought about how much she would be enjoying this process if the circumstances were different and she were not so afraid of what was to come. The dressmaker tapped her leg. 'Stand up straight,' she said. 'Or the hem will be uneven.' Jocasta pulled her ribcage towards her spine, and looked at the wall opposite. Their house was large by Thebes standards, built around a small courtyard with herbs and flowers growing feebly in the burning sun. But it felt cramped to her now, as though the building were readying itself to be rid of her.

The following day, the old woman came back with the finished dress. Had she been up all night, sewing? Jocasta shrugged it on, and the dressmaker's frown eased slightly.

'You'll do,' she said. 'Think of me when you're buying new clothes in future, won't you?' Jocasta felt suddenly awkward. It was the first time anyone had treated her as though she had something they might want.

'How did you make it so quickly?' she asked.

The old woman shrugged. 'I had to,' she replied. 'You need it tomorrow.'

*

When Jocasta awoke on the morning of her wedding day, she wasn't sure if the sun had risen or not. Weak light filtered through the thick curtain which covered her window. She peered round it to see if she could tell how early it was without waking her little brother. The sky was pale grey and there was only a faint trace of light, hinting that the clouds had built over the lake in the night, and the sun might not burn through until later. She could smell the fruit on the sweet almond trees outside, almost ready to be picked.

She lay back down for a moment, testing how she felt. At least she would make her journey across the city in the relative cool. But she would be too queasy to eat before she left. She could hear muffled sounds coming from her mother's rooms. They needed to set off early today, to travel up to the palace. She lay completely still for five more breaths, feeling the cool sheet wrapped round her calves and ankles, the warm, squashy pillow beneath her head. Then she sat up, placing her feet quietly on the floor in the hope of being alone a little longer. But she crept out and almost walked into her mother who had been preparing herself for the day ahead since well before it was light. Her hair was tightly plaited, then twisted into a once-fashionable style, and her eyes were lined with thick black paint. Her mother had perfected a way of talking to Jocasta without looking at her at all, so Jocasta had learned to do the same in return. She fixed her gaze instead on her mother's white dress, edged in bright blue stitching. The dress folds were too wide, puffing out from the thin leather cord that bit at her mother's waist and broadened her across the hips, but she knew there was no value in offering to rearrange it. The cord had been dyed specially to match the new embroidery on the dress, and Jocasta could see that it was already leaving a faint trace of colour on the sun-bleached white cloth. Her mother would be furious when she noticed. Perhaps she would have to have the whole dress dyed blue to hide the marks.

'We'll need to leave shortly,' said her mother. 'The slaves will help make you presentable.'

Jocasta nodded, but did not reply. Her mother's maidservants had never offered to help her, taking their cue from her mother. So the morning of her wedding was the first time anyone had assisted her with her clothes since she had been old enough to dress herself. Jocasta disliked the women's hard, dry hands on her skin. She tried to banish from her mind any thoughts about the hands of the king – which would also be old and dry – touching any part of her.

A short while later, she was wearing her new dress – a simple red tunic with a plaited brown cord to draw it in – and her dark hair was loose. The red made her pale skin look paler still, but the dressmaker had made the stitches small and even. If she had worked the cloth by candlelight, she had not allowed it to affect her stitching. And even Jocasta's mother had once said her daughter had beautiful skin, never disfigured with blemishes or browned by the sun. The maid pulled Jocasta's hair into a knot at the back of her head, twisted it three times and bound it into the bright ribbons which held the style in place. She stuck a silver-and-ivory-tipped ebony pin into the back of Jocasta's knotted hair, jabbing it into her scalp as she did so. Jocasta winced, but she could see the woman knew her job: her hair would now remain fixed in place. For one terrible moment, she thought the woman would try to paint her eyes like her mother's, but the maid preferred to save herself the trouble, so Jocasta dipped her fingers in the rose-scented olive oil her father had recently given to her mother, in a lovely aryballos in the shape of a ram, his horns curling around his ears like ringlets. She fixed the stopper into the ram's patient head, and was about to return it to her mother's dressing-room. Then she reconsidered, adding the bottle to her own bag of clothes and other belongings.

She hurried to the front of the house where the rest of her family were waiting. Her mother looked her up and down, and said she supposed that would do. She gestured irritably at the doorway, hurrying her daughter along. Jocasta walked through the warped wooden door, noticing for one last time the tiny cracks between the panels where the wood had shifted apart. She had expected to feel wretched as she left her home for the last time, but instead she felt nothing at all except a faint pleasure at the thought of the little terracotta ram nestled among her things.

Across the city, she could see its outer walls glowering down over the rest of them. The palace sat atop the highest hill in Thebes, like a watchtower. The grandeur was undeniable, but it resembled a temple or a treasury, both of which it had within its walls; it was difficult to imagine anyone living there, impossible to imagine herself among them. Her little brother was hopping from one foot to the other. He was torn between the excitement of the trip across town, and the promise of a ceremony – a feast and dancing delighted his five-year-old self beyond measure – and a growing uneasiness at the incomprehensible idea that his sister would no longer be living with him.

'I'll come and visit every day,' he had said, throwing his arms around her neck, when she had explained to him that the marriage meant she would be moving away. She had nodded, pretending it was true. Jocasta was surprised to see a small carriage waiting outside the house, attached to a pair of truculent horses. Her brother was eyeing them with the wariness born of having already attempted to pet one.

'This is a fitting mark of the king's respect,' said her father.

'It isn't the best he has,' her mother replied, eyeing the carriage balefully. The king's household had, it seemed, forgotten that four of them would be travelling, and it would be a tight squeeze to fit them all behind the dark curtains which swung down from the wooden roof. Jocasta's father spoke briefly with the driver, and together they tied a strong-box to the carriage roof next to the bag containing her possessions: her dowry. She wondered how much of the weight was the thick wooden box and how much was the precious metals within. Would she be permitted to wear the jewellery, or would it go straight into her husband's treasure-house?

She climbed into the carriage, and sat herself down on the far side of the seat. Her brother ran around to sit opposite her. Jocasta felt a sharp stab of relief when her father pressed in beside her: at least she wouldn't have to look at his treacherous face all the way there. Her mother was much easier to ignore. She lifted herself up for a moment and rearranged her dress, trying to make sure the back wouldn't crease too much as she sat on it. But the driver was in a hurry, and he clipped the horses to a trot. As the carriage swayed into reluctant motion, Jocasta sat heavily back down. Her brother fell forward into her lap, and giggled.

The road made her teeth judder with every one of its many holes as they meandered down the long hill. Her stomach turned over and she found herself glad that she had eaten nothing. Even her brother – who had been so excited when he saw the carriage – realized it was barely quicker than walking when they reached the lowest point and began to go uphill again. Thebans usually reserved wheeled vehicles for transporting heavy goods around the city, and Jocasta hoped she wouldn't be expected to travel by carriage from now on. At least with her feet on the ground, however dusty it was, she could avoid the deepest troughs in the road. The carriage cracked over another one so aggressively that she wondered if the axle beneath her seat would survive the journey. She half-hoped it would not, that one of its wheels would crack and roll back down the hill behind them, so she would have an excuse to get out and walk. It was stiflingly hot, even with the curtains tied back, something her mother had finally agreed to after her brother had appealed to her twice.

They had crossed through the lowest part of the city, which was always busy unless the winter rains had caused flooding. Today, it seemed unusually quiet, though Jocasta knew the floodwater was long gone. When they finally reached the bottom of the palace hill, she thought she might recognize some of the buildings. But things looked different through the window of a swaying carriage than they did when you were on foot. It too appeared deserted, though it was surely now late enough for people to be bustling around the city. Many of the shop-fronts were shuttered, though their painted signs suggested that the food stalls and taverns would be opening later. As they climbed the hill, the buildings grew larger, and people finally appeared on the streets, though there was something strange about them which Jocasta couldn't place. It was her brother who noticed. 'Look,' he said, tugging at her wrist and pointing. 'Everyone is walking in the same direction. Isn't that odd?' And she realized that he was right: everyone she could see was walking up the hill. The further they went, the more the street began to surge with people. Men and women bustled through the crowds, giving a purposeful air to the city.

By the time the driver brought his horses to an exhausted halt, the sun was blazing high above them. It had burned through the clouds, just as she had known it would. Her brother pushed his fingers past the curtains and touched the roof, before drawing them back in exaggerated pain. Jocasta was desperate to get out and walk however far was left to travel, but her mother jabbed at her with one carefully filed nail. 'Wait here, and don't let your brother get out,' she said. She clambered down with Jocasta's father who never saw a crowd without wanting to stand in front of it. What could he possibly sell them today?

But the crowd wasn't looking at her father. They were staring behind him, at the dark carriage window, trying to see through the curtain which had swung free when her parents climbed out. It took her a moment to notice they had something else in common: everyone was wearing their best clothes. Torn cloaks had been patched and repaired, white tunics had been bleached to a brightness they didn't usually possess. She imagined them all stretched over rocks, their colour gradually eaten away by the harsh noon light. Leather shoe-straps had been tied symmetrically, and red dust had been brushed from feet and ankles. Those who wore jewellery had polished it: dark stones glinted in bright metal. These weren't simply passers-by, gawping at a carriage. They were, they must be, wedding guests.

'Come on,' she said to her brother, covering her face with her veil so no one could accuse her of impropriety. 'Let's get out.' His eyes glittered as she opened the curtain and let him step down. Her parents were deep in conversation with a small cluster of men. Jocasta blinked in the bright sun, and looked around.

She was standing right outside the palace, she now saw, at the top of the citadel. She wanted to stretch her arms and her neck, which were knotted up from bouncing over every uneven stone, but she was too self-conscious with so many people watching her. She looked back at the way they had come. A bumpy path curved up off the main street and formed a loop around a big square – Thebes's marketplace – outside the palace gates, where they now stood. There were more people than she had ever seen in one place before, even at festivals. Her brother, usually desperate to see and hear everything at once, was suddenly shy.

The palace was less imposing now she stood next to it. Its bright perfection was not so perfect up close: just like her doll, its paint was cracked and fading, and the ground beneath her feet was broken open. It was even bigger than she had remembered, though. She could not see all the way round it: only along the front wall, until the angle shifted and it disappeared from view. The palace must sit with its back on the hillside, in front of the olive groves and the vines which grew on the sloping rocky soil. Twisted old apple trees lined the walls, and while they must provide welcome shade for those inside the palace – and those waiting outside today – their roots had forced their way through the paths, leaving the stones cracked and distorted. The dark mountains which covered the miles south of Thebes rose high behind the palace, dwarfing it. Jocasta had never been close enough to see the individual pine trees on their higher slopes: they had only ever been a blanket of blackish green before.

She heard an odd sound, a rippling noise. She looked over to the palace, and saw it came from the crowd. They were clapping, more and more of them. Her mother turned sharply to find out what was happening, and began looking around to see what had prompted the sudden applause. Her eyes followed the eyes of the crowd, and saw that her daughter had disobeyed her instruction to stay inside the carriage. Jocasta felt a brief surge of alarm that she was about to be shouted at, humiliated in front of all these people. And then she realized that none of the wedding guests cared what her mother thought, or did. They were interested only in her, and there was nothing her mother could do while they were watching. She looked up and gazed intently at her mother for a moment – jolting her into eye contact at last – before turning to smile and wave at the strangers who applauded her. She could not change what her parents had done. But she would not be afraid of them again.

*

Jocasta would have almost no recollection of her gamos. The wedding faded from her mind almost as it was happening. She remembered the things which didn't matter: the dark berries which had fallen from trees and stained the ground with their purple juice. An ornate hair decoration made of spiralling gold and studded with blood-red stones worn by a wizened elderly woman which she longed to have in her own hair, where it would shine against her darkness instead of sparkling feebly against the old woman's thin white strands. The procession of unmarried girls – bright crocus-yellow ribbons tied into their hair – dancing around her in celebration of her arrival, and the dark, watchful eyes of boys the same age, admiring every step the girls took. Her father's tangible aura of self-congratulation. The smell of charred meat as the priest made his devotional offerings. Her mother's silver and gold bangles clanking together as she ostentatiously wiped away a non-existent tear.

But the gamos itself, the moment where she was sworn to Laius – a vulpine man with sparse white hair and ill-tamed brows – and presented with a slender gold diadem as a mark of her newfound status? The crowds of Thebans cheering their new queen as the priests mixed wine and water in a huge ceremonial krater? The taste of the wine she and her husband drank from a large kylix to seal their vows to and before the gods? She recalled none of it. In the years that followed, she would try to remember if they had stood on the north side of the courtyard or the south. If they had poured wine to the gods at the main altar, or one of the smaller ones. If the afternoon sun had streamed over the portico as the day dragged out, or if evening rain had fallen on the assembled crowd. She never came close to being certain of anything that happened between leaving the carriage and walking in through the front gates and the moment when she found herself alone again, many hours later, in what was now her bedroom.

Jocasta spent the day dreading the night. She knew something of what her husband would expect from her: she was not a fool, and nor was she completely naïve, even though she had been brought up in seclusion from boys, except her own brother. Girls talked, nonetheless. She was not wholly averse to this aspect of marriage. But she had always assumed that any man whose bed she shared would be one who was not so old that thick wiry hairs emanated from his nose and ears without warning. One whose skin glowed gold as the late afternoon sun caught him, and who could move without a percussive chorus of cracking joints and exhalations. Instead, she found herself able to think of little else but how his body repulsed her. An old man, one among many old men at the wedding party who winked and elbowed one another with delight at her evident discomfort. She hated them all.

The afternoon turned into evening, and the party continued. The old men – including the king – were drinking a great deal of wine, poured by slave boys all wearing matching charcoal-grey tunics. Jocasta was torn between wanting to ask questions of these boys – the only people her own age who treated the palace as familiar – and not wanting to look stupid in front of what were now her own slaves. She wondered if she would feel more confident if she too drank some wine. But the thought of tasting something sour and acidic made bile rise in her throat.

It had been dark for many hours when people finally began to leave: the torches had been lit for so long they were beginning to sputter. Jocasta had her arms and cheeks squeezed and prodded so many times that bruises were starting to form on her edges. No one, it seemed, could leave without touching the bride: they believed she would bring them luck. People believed all kinds of stupid things. Across the courtyard, she saw her mother teetering towards her father, and realized they, too, were leaving. Jocasta hurried towards the colonnade which ran around the outside of the square, stopping behind one of the broad columns so she could watch unseen as her family began to look for her. Her throat thickened at the sight of her little brother, crying when he understood that they really were leaving without her. But she stayed where she was, nonetheless. He was too young to understand anything she could say to him. It was kinder to leave him to her parents now, and hope he still remembered her in a year or two.

One of the boys dressed in grey caught sight of her, and walked towards her, carrying two silver rhytons. She had never seen such ornate cups: raised dolphins jumped around the base of each one, beneath painted azure waves which curled all the way up to the rims. She wanted to hold one and run her fingers over the design.

'Can I help you, Basileia?'

Jocasta looked around to see who he was talking to, this boy who might have kicked a pebble across her path a week ago, hoping it would bounce off her sandal and force her to look up. She would have blushed when she saw it had come from a boy she did not know, and looked back at the ground as she scurried away, so he did not see her smile.

'Basileia?' he repeated.

'Why are you calling me that?' she hissed. She might be the wife of the king, but she felt a long way short of being a queen. The word sounded ludicrous on his tongue. The boy frowned, and looked down at the cups he was holding.

'Would you like something to drink, Anassa?' he asked carefully. Perhaps the less formal title would please her. 'I can get you anything you like.'

'I don't want anything,' she snapped. 'Thank you.'

'Yes, Anassa,' he said. 'I'm sorry for disturbing you.' He began to turn away.

'Wait – do you work for my – ?' She couldn't frame the thought. 'For the king?' she asked.

'Yes, my lady.'

'Will everyone dressed like you call me Anassa?' she said. The boy nodded. His face remained solemn, but she saw a trace of amusement in his eyes. 'Once I tell them it is your preferred title,' he said.

'I should get used to it, then. That's what you're thinking?' she asked.

'I wouldn't presume . . .'

'Don't be stupid. Stop talking to me like I'm my mother. Or your mother.'

He looked at her steadily. 'I'm talking to you as though you were my queen.'

'I'm so tired,' she said, pressing one hand against her ear as if trying to expel the sound of revellers and musicians. 'Do you think they will leave soon?'

'I don't know,' he replied. 'Parties are usually all-night affairs at the palace. I mean, I think they are. We haven't had a wedding before. Obviously.' He blushed. 'I'm sorry.'

'What for? I'm sure it all seems obvious to you. But it isn't to me. I lived on the other side of Thebes until this morning. I don't know anything about the king, or the palace or the way you do things. I don't even know what you'll do if I ask you something.'

'I will do whatever you wish. Everyone will,' the boy said.

'Find me tomorrow. I want to know more about . . . well, about the palace and the citadel. The customs of the household. And whatever I ask, you have to promise now to tell me the truth.'

'Yes, Anassa.'

'You're not to laugh at me behind my back with the other slaves for not knowing. Swear it.'

'I would never laugh at you,' the boy said.

'Do you feel sorry for me?' she asked.

'Sorry?' His eyes bulged. 'No, of course not.'

'Good. Tell me where I'll be sleeping,' she said. 'I'm too tired to stay awake any longer. Can I go to bed, do you think? Before everyone leaves, I mean.'

'You're the queen,' the boy said. 'You can do whatever you want.'

Jocasta slept badly, and woke many times. She felt as if she were falling, although she was sleeping in the middle of the largest bed she had ever seen. When she finally came to the next morning, groggy from the interrupted night, she looked around the room in surprise. The flickering torches the night before had given her the idea that the room was dingy and oppressive. But now the light streamed in through lofty windows, she saw that she had been mistaken. The walls were a pale yellow colour, with a blood-red pattern of interlocking squares painted along the highest part. She had been tricked last night by the height of the lamps which were hung low, so the torches could be lit and extinguished without a ladder. A large, ornately carved wardrobe stood on the far wall, its doors a labyrinth of twisting inlaid lines.

Jocasta had not removed the bag from the roof of the carriage yesterday, where the driver had lashed it before they set off from her parents' house. But here were her dresses anyway, hung up carefully by someone else. There was no sign of her dowry, but she was not surprised by that. At least she had her diadem, which shone even without the torchlight to reflect back at her. She stopped for a moment as she reached out to pick it up: was she so vain that all she cared about was her jewellery? Jewellery which, for the most part, she had never worn, had not even seen before yesterday. She gripped the diadem until its sharp edges drove into her soft fingers. The gold was thick, not pliable. Jocasta might be new to the palace, but she was not so foolish as to think gold was a trivial matter. It was beautiful, certainly. But if things were ever so terrible that she needed to run away, jewellery would be the only thing she could bargain with. The delicate little crown represented more than her regal status.

There was no sign that the room had belonged to another person before she arrived last night. Had it been empty for years? A wooden dressing-table stood beneath the windows, a cracked, blackening glass offering her a view of herself: slightly puffy-eyed from sleep. Her hair was tangled, and she tugged it straight, before noticing a fine-toothed ivory comb in front of her. She picked it up, and tidied herself a little.

The room was large and well-appointed compared with the one she'd slept in at home. Although she had to stop thinking of it as that. This was her home now. She had always imagined that a room of her own would be wonderful, an impossible luxury not to hear the breathing of her brother – who whimpered through his nightmares and woke her – all night long. And now she seemed to have just that. Because one thing her bedroom was missing was the man who was now her husband. Not only was he not present himself, there was no sign a man had ever been in here. There were no men's clothes anywhere, not even a single robe. She had expected her husband to sleep in a room of his own, of course, just as her father did. But surely not on his wedding night?

There were three doors on three walls. The one behind her she had come through last night. It led to an open-sided corridor along the edge of a small courtyard which must once have contained a formal garden. Even by torchlight she had been able to see that the plants had run wild, sprouting up between the paving stones and forcing their way through the miniature walls designed to contain them. She had caught her sandal on the edge of a broken stone, and turned her left ankle over. She had said nothing, though, not wanting the boy in grey to know that she had tripped. She tested the ankle again now and felt only a small twinge. No harm was done. The door in the far corner of the right-hand wall was locked. She turned the handle quietly, but nothing happened. The door on the left-hand side of the windows led, she discovered, to a room containing a pump and several large bronze basins. Was it possible this was all hers? There was another door into it, from the corridor, but it too appeared to be locked. She tried the pump, and the water flowed freely. She washed her face and hands, before noticing a battered bronze cup on a narrow wooden shelf. She filled the cup, and drank. The water was cool and fresh, as though it came from somewhere deep underground.

She was nervous at the thought of leaving her room: the palace was quiet and she could hear no one outside, not even servants talking to one another. She was beginning to think of this corner of the huge building as hers, she realized: her table, her wardrobe, her bed. But she couldn't stay in there for the rest of her life, and the longer she waited, the more anxious she felt. She should go now, before it became unmanageable. She dressed quickly in a plain fawn-coloured linen dress. It hung shapelessly to her knees, and she belted it with a twisted length of undyed leather she found on the floor of the wardrobe. Combing her hair back behind her ears, she pinned it in place with the ebony pin she had worn yesterday. Jocasta took one last look in the dressing-table mirror and reminded herself that even today, away from everything she knew, she was the same person who had worn the pin before. She should not be afraid. She opened the door into the main corridor.

It was deserted. Was it really possible that all last night's guests had disappeared so completely? Or did the noise simply not carry this far through the palace? She still could not imagine its scale and layout. She stood for a moment, listening. She could hear nothing but the twin chirrups of birds and cicadas. She looked around one more time, making sure she knew which door led to her room – she paid close attention to the precise shape of the cracks in the shattered stones beneath her feet – so she could find her way back to this one familiar place without embarrassment. She turned to her left, wishing she knew where she was going. She soon found herself in a second, larger, equally empty courtyard, which she couldn't be sure she recognized from last night. Was this the way the boy in grey had brought her? There were frescos on the colonnade walls: horses riding towards centaurs who rode towards satyrs who ran towards wood nymphs who hid behind trees. They might not have been illuminated in the torchlight last night. Or perhaps she had come a different way entirely.

She decided to retrace her steps, and went back to the first square. This too had frescos, now she began to pay proper attention, but they were faded older paintings, this time of once-bright blue dolphins and fish. Was there another way out from this square? She could see a small doorway in the far corner: perhaps that led somewhere. But wasn't that the opposite direction from the main courtyard from last night? The disorientation vexed her. Where was everyone? Could a whole palace have lost its inhabitants overnight? Were they playing a cruel trick on her? Finally, she heard a brushing sound behind her. Someone was sweeping a floor somewhere in one of the courtyards, or in the corridors around it. She walked back to the colonnade between the two squares and stood still, trying to hear exactly which direction the sound came from.

Was it further away now? It seemed to come from the opposite side of this second courtyard, so she crossed it, and found herself looking onto the main square through decorative metal gates. This was where the party had been in full swing when she escaped to bed last night. There were several women at the near end of the courtyard, cleaning tables with wooden brushes and water. One of them looked across and saw her, then called out. The boy from last night appeared from a corridor on her right. The smart grey uniform was gone, and he was dressed today in a plain tunic, just like her.

'Forgive me, madam,' he said. 'I didn't realize you were awake.'

'Why should you?' she asked. 'Where is everyone?'

The boy looked at her face, but not her eyes, as he chose his words. 'Everyone is gone, ma'am. The guests all left around daybreak. The king and his escort have gone hunting.'

'Hunting what? Where?' She knew no one who hunted.

'In the lower reaches of the mountains,' he explained. 'They will be gone for around a week, I believe.'

'They go outside the city?' Like many Thebans, Jocasta had never left the city gates.

'Yes. They're out to catch a wild boar. The king has been trying to capture this particular one for some time,' he said.

'The king does this often?' she asked.

'Whenever the weather allows it,' he said. 'His retinue go with him, and most of the Elders go too. Those whose families can spare them.'

'He travels with a large party, then?'

'Yes, ma'am. The king is quite safe.'

She nodded, as though the king's safety was of any interest to her. He had made no effort to speak to her once the ceremony was out of the way. He had not said goodbye before he left. It seemed he had left no message for her.

'And you are part of the king's retinue,' she said.

'Yes,' the boy nodded.

'So why didn't you go with him?'

He smiled. 'You ordered me to stay, ma'am. Last night.'

And though she was affronted that the king had behaved so rudely, Jocasta thought she might hate her husband marginally less the morning after her wedding than she did the night before.

3

I didn't notice the pain at first, because I was too distracted by the thirst. My mouth felt like a piece of old dried-out parchment. My lips cracked as I separated them, tiny fissures of pain. I half-opened my eyes, though they were gravelly and itched so much I wanted to shut them again. But I didn't know where I was, and I needed to find water from somewhere. Everything was so bright. I lay on my back, trying to persuade my eyes to focus.

I turned my head to see Ani, my sister, sitting on a small wooden chair beside me. I was in my own bedroom, a large, high-windowed room on the west side of the palace, away from the city, overlooking the hills behind Thebes. She was working a small tapestry of some sort – I could see the light glinting off her needle as she took it up and down through the fabric. I wanted to ask her for water, but my throat was too dry and no sound would come. I tugged on the sheets to try and get her attention, though it fired pain through my left side. Eventually, I pulled hard enough to move the thin top sheet, and the rustling sound forced her to look up.

'Oh!' She put her hand to her chest. 'You're awake!' She leapt to her feet, and shouted, 'Isy's awake! She's awake!' She ran to the door to announce her news further afield. This was not what I had been hoping would happen. I heard quick feet padding towards me. My brother Eteo – king, for now – tall, dark-haired, always with a slight frown. He looked down at me and smiled. He looked at me for a moment, then stepped back. When he returned, he was holding a battered bronze kylix of water in his hand.

'You must be thirsty,' he said. 'Let me help you up so you can drink something.' If I had not been so desiccated, I would have wept.

He held my arms, and pulled me up and forward, stuffing an extra pillow in behind me. I felt another jolt of pain, but I didn't care. I reached out my hands and took the cup. I peeled my lips apart and took a sip, forcing it into every corner of my mouth before I swallowed. My throat hurt, and my tongue was swollen. I tried to drink it all, but Eteo reached over and took my hand.

'Easy,' he said. 'Don't drink it too fast. I'll get you some more in a moment.'

Ani ran back in with my oldest brother Polyn. 'Look,' she said, elbowing him hard in the gut. 'I told you. Why don't you ever believe me?'

'Well done, Isy,' Polyn said. He was stockier than Eteo, and his hair was a lighter, muddier brown. His eyes were light brown too, where Eteo's were so dark they were almost black. Without looking at his brother, Polyn reached over and ruffled my hair. 'We thought we'd lost you.'

'No,' I said, finally able to get the words out, now the water had released my voice, croaky but audible. 'You just misplaced me for a while.'

Eteo laughed. 'It was a while, Isy. You've been unconscious for three days.'

Three days. No wonder I was thirsty. 'What happened?'

Eteo opened his mouth to say something, but Polyn grabbed his arm. Eteo recoiled from the unexpected contact, but he said nothing. Ani reached over to the bed and picked up the sewing she had dropped when she saw I was awake. She fed the needle carefully in and out of the corner of her cloth to hold it in place, and stuffed it into the pocket of her green dress. She almost always wears green, to match her eyes. Virtually no one meets her without remarking on their extraordinary colour, so her strategy works. My sister has no intention of going unmarried, no matter what people say about our family. She knows that will be my fate, and she pities me, but not enough to condemn herself to the same thing.

Eteo took the cup from my hands and went to the table opposite my bed to refill it from an old jug painted with a faded harvest scene: men holding scythes and carrying sheaves of wheat. Polyn adopted an expression which was meant to convey, I think, fraternal concern: head tilted, lips slightly pursed, creased brow. And a moment later, the door swung open again, and my uncle entered the room. Four guards followed and stood just behind him. The clanking sound which accompanied them told me they were armed, even though they were inside the palace, inside the family quarters. This would never have happened before. We have always tried to keep the areas of the palace distinct: the public courtyard at the front, the royal courtyard in the middle, the family courtyard at the back. My uncle is solidly built: he never forgets that all adult men have an obligation to fight for Thebes, if any army declares war upon us. That is why my brothers and my cousin have been training with weapons since they were six or seven years old. Creon has always kept himself and his family in the proper condition to fight. Nonetheless, it was disconcerting to see his soldiers in my sleeping quarters.

'Isy,' said Creon. 'It's good to see you awake. We were worried . . .'

'Thank you,' I said. I didn't want to hear any more about people's worry. It was making me afraid for myself in the past, a position I could already see Sophon dismantling as foolish.

'You're safe now,' he continued. 'There are guards at either end of the corridor.'

I wanted to ask why, but there were so many people in the room now, I couldn't bear to tell them all that I didn't remember what had happened to me, and how I got hurt.

Then I heard the voice I always wanted to hear. 'Is she alright?'

My cousin Haem ran in, one hand pushed back through his hair to keep it out of his eyes. He wasn't looking at me. He was looking at Ani, of course.

'She's well,' my sister said. If you didn't know better, you would think they were talking about me.

'I'm glad to see you're recovering,' Creon said, ignoring them both. 'We have missed you at dinner, Isy. No one tells stories when you aren't there. I've been waiting to find out what would happen next with the Medusa. If you had slept through another day, I would have had to send someone to read your dreams and tell me what becomes of her.'

'That's why I woke up,' I told him. 'I knew you couldn't wait any longer.'

'Well, we shall let you rest now,' he said, smiling. 'Perhaps you'll feel well enough to continue the tale tomorrow or the next day.'

My uncle loves stories and songs. It is something we share. I learned to play the phorminx – a small lyre – when I was seven years old. Eteo plays too, but he rarely has time for such pursuits when he is ruling the city. Polyn has never played any instrument: as soon as Eteo showed interest in music, Polyn decreed it a worthless pursuit. Ani prefers to make things – sewing, weaving – but I have never had the gift for that kind of work. It requires a patience and attention to detail which I do not possess. She says the same is true for playing the lyre, but she is mistaken. Playing has never required my patience, only my concentration, which I give freely to music. My uncle loves songs about heroes and monsters, gods and men. I have played them for him after dinner for as long as I can remember, composing a little more of the story each day, or playing old songs for him again.

Creon beckoned Haem to follow him. My cousin flashed a pained glance at my sister and they withdrew, taking the guards with them. The room was suddenly huge, empty and safe.

'I don't know what happened,' I said to Eteo.

'What's the last thing you remember?' he asked.

I thought for a moment. Bright sun and blood on the papyrus.

'Someone stabbed me.'

'Yes,' Eteo replied. 'But we'll find him, Isy. I promise.

I have men interrogating everyone who was in the palace that day. Someone knows something and we'll soon catch him.'

'If I were king, the wretch would have been run through with my own sword a day ago,' said Polyn.

'Because you would have killed every man in sight, irrespective of whether he was involved or not,' Eteo snapped. 'Or tortured them until they named someone – anyone – to make you stop. How would that make our sister any safer?'

'Stop it,' Ani said. 'You can see you're upsetting her.' She shook her head. 'It's been so awful,' she said. 'I don't understand how someone could get into the palace to attack you. How are we supposed to stay safe if strangers can enter the palace unheeded?'

'But I'm alright. I mean, I will be.' I thought I was stating a fact, but as the words came out, I realized I was asking a question.

'Yes, you will be,' Eteo replied, his anger ebbing away. 'The blade caught your left lung, Is, so you ran out of air. The girl who found you was hollering for help – she made an extraordinary racket. She frightened the birds out of their nests: they all flew up in a great clamour over the palace. It was lucky she was there – and Sophon came running. He moves quickly for an old man, doesn't he? The moment he saw you, he knew what to do. You weren't in danger for long.'

'He was most worried about a fever,' Ani added. She would have enjoyed the drama of it all, I thought, even though she loved me. She would have enjoyed being the sister of an almost-murdered girl. I could imagine her tying her dark hair back, frowning and calling for hot water, with no real idea of what she might use it for. 'He stitched you back together and said we would have to wait and see what happened.'

I wondered what I would say to my tutor when I saw him. Should I thank him for saving my life? Apologize for bleeding all over his papyrus? It didn't seem right that another person had seen the inside of me, laid eyes on a part of my body that I could never see. I struggled to imagine his gnarled hands pushing a needle through my skin. Once Ani had mentioned stitches, I could feel a pulling sensation, quite separate from the pain of the wound. My fingers itched to explore it, to test how much it hurt and how neatly Sophon had sewn it up. But I knew I could not. The old man was right to fear an infection more than anything else.

'You were lucky, Isy,' said Polyn. It was true, even though I didn't feel very lucky. I felt like someone who was nursing a hole in her side, grit in her eyes and a sore throat.

I nodded, suddenly tired. 'I think I might rest for a while,' I said. 'Would you ask Sophon to visit me later? I want to thank him.'

'Of course,' said Polyn. He sounded relieved. 'We'll see you later.'

Eteo squeezed my hand, and followed the other two out. I did want to thank my tutor, of course. But not as much as I wanted to ask him what more he knew, about my injury and about the attacker. My siblings – even Eteo – tended to treat me like a little girl whenever something bad happened. But Sophon always told me the truth. He understood when you have grown up as I have, there is no security in not knowing things, in avoiding the ugliest truths because they can't be faced. There is only an oppressive, creeping dread that the thing no one has told you is too terrible to imagine, and that it will haunt the rest of your life when you find out. Because that is what happened the last time, and that is why my siblings and I have grown up in a cursed house, children of cursed parents.

4

Jocasta had assumed, from everything her mother and father had told her, that she was marrying the king because he wanted a wife. It now seemed to be the case that he did not, in fact, want a wife, or that if he did, he did not want her. It was oddly painful to be rejected by someone she didn't know. Had he decided on the hunting trip the moment he saw her? Before he saw her? She swept her hands down her dress, as if she could brush off whatever defects she apparently possessed. Because if he didn't want her, where was she supposed to go? She could hardly return home. She corrected herself, go to her parents' home. They could not take her back, even if they wanted to. She would be disgraced: a married woman running away from her husband. It was unthinkable. And anyway, she remembered her mother's claws in her arm. Even if her husband died (the only respectable way for her to cease being married to him), she would never go back to her parents. Begging on the streets would be preferable.

But she was getting ahead of herself. If she couldn't go anywhere else, she could at least explore the palace, and examine her new surroundings. It was easier if she forgot about the idea of home for now. The palace was where she was. The boy who had stayed behind – the one who had obeyed her – would take her into the marketplace later, with a maidservant in tow, so her propriety could not be called into question. And it would give her a greater sense of belonging, she was sure, when she knew the palace neighbourhood. But she would spend this morning trying to map out what stood where in the palace, so she didn't feel so lost.

She now knew, having walked through them in daylight, that the palace was made up of three courtyards of decreasing size from front gate to back walls. The huge public courtyard was the first square she had entered yesterday. As its name implied, it was open to any Thebans who had business in the palace. There were altars and a small temple enclosed on the west side, which – as she had seen last night – was the religious focus of the royal house. There were priests who came to the palace each day to maintain the sacred precincts and accept offerings from any citizens who brought them. The animals were kept in small pens near the back of the temple, ready to be sacrificed. On the east side were the king's treasurers, who also arbitrated in any disputes which arose outside in the market. As she peeked out at the bustling space, Jocasta saw two bearded men – so alike they must have been brothers, their black beards mirroring one another, and their curled hair bobbing in harmony – arguing in front of one of the treasurers, so loudly that she could hear them from where she stood, in the second courtyard, looking through the gates which sealed the public out of the rest of the palace. Or did they lock her inside? She tested the one on the right and found that it opened. But she did not dare to go out alone. The king might be absent, but the queen should avoid causing a scandal on her first morning in the palace, she supposed. She couldn't go wandering about in public without any kind of chaperone. She wasn't entirely sure what her duties would be – there was no sign of a loom anywhere in her quarters, so no one was expecting her to sit weaving all day, at least – but she knew it was her responsibility to behave respectably.

And there was plenty more to see in the two courtyards which were open to her. The middle square was a smaller copy of the public courtyard, with white stone paths bisecting each side and criss-crossing from corner to corner. They met in the centre of the square, which was dominated by a statue of the king atop his horse. Jocasta wondered if Laius had ever looked as tall and muscular as the sculptor had rendered him. She doubted it. But the sculptor had been clever; there was just enough in the statue's colouring to make it clear that it was intended to be the king: the brown curls of hair into the nape of the neck, the pale irises, picked out in a light blue stone. And perhaps he had been tall once, before his old man's spine began to curve in on itself. It was possible.

But this square wasn't filled with shrines or temples. The east and west colonnades were punctuated with closed doors. Some were obviously storerooms, but Jocasta could hear the sound of men's voices behind others. From what she could work out, as she stood eavesdropping in the colonnades, this was where the king's work was done in his absence. Or more politely, on his behalf, while he was off hunting. The corridor which housed the gates between the second and the main courtyards was also home to the kitchens. She could smell bread baking, and a sudden twist in her stomach reminded her that she hadn't eaten for more than a day. She walked towards the heat, and peered in to the dark room, her eyes taking a moment to adjust from the bright morning sun outside. 'Excuse me,' she said to a girl scouring dishes, when she saw she had found the main kitchen. The girl squeaked and ran out of another door in the far wall, reappearing a moment later with a pink-faced older woman. The woman was short but sturdy, and perhaps forty years old. Older than Jocasta's mother, but not by very many years, she wore her grey-brown hair tied back in a plain, unadorned knot. Her eyes darted around her domain: Jocasta could almost hear her counting the faults as she noticed them, one after another. The kitchen girl would be in trouble later. Jocasta was sure of it.

'Yes?' said the woman, wiping floured hands on her apron, before she looked to see who was bothering her.

'Could I please have something to eat?' Jocasta asked. The woman finally turned to see who was asking for her. Her hands moved up to push loose hairs behind her ears, a gesture which looked inappropriately girlish to Jocasta's eyes.

'Of course,' said the woman. 'Forgive us, we would have brought you something earlier, but no one knew where you were.'

'I was in my room, I think,' Jocasta said. 'And then I came looking for someone.'

'Oh, you were in your room?' said the woman, as though this were unlikely. 'Well, we'll know to bring food to you there tomorrow. Would you like to go back to your quarters, and I'll send something after you?'

'Would you mind if I stayed here?' Jocasta asked, looking across the kitchen to a large wooden table with several small stools sitting beneath it. She didn't want to admit that she was lonely, on her own in this strange new place. But nor did she want to go back to her room and sit there eating alone. Besides, her stomach was groaning at the smell of food, and the last thing she wanted to do was leave before she had consumed anything.

'Not at all,' said the woman, gesturing to the girl who pulled a stool out for Jocasta. 'I'm Teresa,' the woman added. 'I'm the housekeeper. And you're Jocasta, and we haven't even been introduced.' Her tone made it sound like this was Jocasta's failure of courtesy, though Jocasta couldn't see how the woman had arrived at that conclusion. The housekeeper should have been at her door this morning, summoned by the slave girl who should have been sent to help her dress. Teresa should have introduced herself to her new mistress and offered to show her around the palace. But Jocasta did not want to start her new life arguing with the king's servants and their lax manners.

'I'm sorry,' said Jocasta, taking the woman's hand, which was hard and dry, as though it belonged to a wooden statue. 'I didn't know where to find anyone this morning. It was all so deserted.'

The woman clicked her tongue against her teeth. 'We're not used to having anyone here when Laius goes away. But to forget all about you, when you only got here yesterday. You must think we're very disorganized.' Jocasta shook her head. She knew she had been set a test, but she couldn't tell if she had passed or failed.

'I suppose if I'd shown you to your room last night,

I wouldn't have forgotten,' Teresa said. 'Who did take you, if you don't mind me asking?'

Another woman's daughter would have missed the subtle change in tone, from apology to interrogation. Jocasta did not. 'One of the king's bodyguards showed me to my quarters,' she said. 'I didn't ask his name.' She did not mention that she had seen him this morning. She wasn't sure if it was him she was trying to keep from getting into trouble, or herself. But she knew it would be wise to say no more than she had to.

'Oh, that's Oran,' said Teresa, the tension slipping from her posture. 'The king left him behind to keep an eye on us all, I think.' This statement was so evidently ridiculous to her that she was smiling. Jocasta smiled too, anxious to keep on her right side, at least for now.

Blackened pots and pans were hanging from hooks above her, all around the table. Jocasta imagined her little brother leaping onto the stools so he could bang them all together to hear what sort of noise each one made. She pressed her lips together to quash the thought before missing him brought her to tears. Teresa bustled into the room she had come from and returned with two griddled flatbreads, one covered in olive paste, the other piled high with spiced chickpeas. Jocasta thanked her and began to eat. The bread was warm and fluffy inside, and the olive paste was dark and salty. 'You're half-starved,' said Teresa, watching her. Jocasta must be eating too fast.

'No,' she said, putting the bread back on its plate, though all she wanted to do was stuff the rest of it into her mouth. 'It's just that it's so good.' She hoped Teresa was susceptible to flattery.

The housekeeper smiled. 'I'm afraid we've been so busy clearing up after the wedding party, we quite lost track of you. It takes a lot of time to sort everything out when the king goes away, I'm sure you can imagine. But I promise we'll make up for it now. You must come and eat with us tonight – unless you prefer to be alone?' She raised an eyebrow, and Jocasta was reminded once again of her mother, who also liked to ask questions which weren't questions at all.

'No, I'd prefer to meet everyone and get to know you all,' she replied.

'That's good,' Teresa continued. 'We'll all know each other better by the time Laius gets back. He'll be delighted.'

Jocasta agreed, and listened as Teresa told her more about the palace staff she would meet, both slave and free. In addition to Teresa and Oran, there were various maids and gardeners and cleaners and cooks. She tried to keep track of the names as Teresa rattled through them all, but she could not. So she nodded and carried on eating, and wondered why Teresa's first action had been to lie to her. The housekeeper clearly controlled the household and it was inconceivable that she could have forgotten something as important as a new queen coming to live in the palace. So why pretend that she had?

*

It was something she wanted to ask Oran that afternoon as they set out for the marketplace. But the presence of a slave girl who accompanied them both – hovering behind her, holding a simple woven reed basket as though she had never been trusted with something so valuable before – made her wary of beginning a conversation about anything to do with Teresa. Instead she asked him about the public square, since they were walking through it.

'You mean the Great Court?' he asked.

'Is that its name?'

He nodded. 'It's the oldest part of the palace. It was here when this was just a citadel. The other courtyards were built later. That's why we're on the top of a hill, you know. It's the easiest place in Thebes to defend.'

'You don't believe all that?' she asked, watching with satisfaction as he reddened at her tone. 'That the oldest part of the city was built by dragon-men, sacred to Ares? And that we live here because an ancient hero followed a cow until she lay down and decided to build his city where she had indicated was the most propitious location?'

'Of course I believe it,' he replied. 'What do you believe?'

She looked at him in surprise.

'Forgive me, your majesty,' he added.

'I'm not angry,' she said. 'You needn't apologize. I don't know what I think, really. It just doesn't seem very likely that warriors rose from dragon's teeth and built a city. It doesn't even seem likely that a cow would wander up a steep hill of her own accord. A goat maybe. But not a cow. I've never seen anything like that happen. And don't pretend you have.'

'The plane trees were planted many years ago,' he continued, pointing to the gnarled branches that sprang up at irregular intervals along all four walls of the courtyard.

'By a dragon?' she asked, smiling.

'By a gardener, I imagine,' he replied. They walked towards the front gate, and Jocasta could hear the hubbub of the market on a trading day: stall-holders, bargain-hunters, gossip-mongers, butchers and fish-sellers, leather-workers, dyers, shoe-makers and smiths all vied for space. Chickens squawked and beat their wings against the bars of metal cages. Rabbits – crammed together in wooden boxes – looked fearful, and dogs barked as though they knew she was a stranger.

She felt as though she had been hiding in a back room, waiting for a festival to begin. The smell of freshly fried lentil cakes enticed her one way, but the sound of a flute being played in another direction made her want to go there instead. One stall was piled high with wooden crates that held pomegranates of such an urgent pink that she could almost taste the seeds. On another stall, her eye was caught by piles of clothes in every colour: bright dresses which she longed to touch, every shade of red between orange and pink, every shade of yellow between saffron and unripe lemons. She walked into the thronging aisle and reached out to feel the deep blue fabric of a simple shift dress. It was crisp and unworn and would be the right length without alteration.

'Nice colour on you,' said the owner, barely looking. 'I'll do you a good deal.'

Jocasta smiled and nodded. 'I'll be back later,' she said.

'You do that,' said the woman, her interest immediately switching to another potential customer. Jocasta wished she had brought something to trade, though she wasn't sure what the value of her possessions would be. She had entered the palace with a dowry, but that was technically her husband's gold now.

'Do you want it?' Oran asked.

'Yes,' she said. 'It's a pretty colour, and it would suit me.'

He jerked his head at the slave girl, who scurried up to the clothes-seller and spoke a few words. The dress was folded and handed over, and the girl placed it carefully in her basket. The clothes-seller bobbed her head to Jocasta as she walked away. 'We're here every day, ma'am. We make anything you want to order. Any colour, even the darkest purple. Come back whenever you want the highest quality fabrics in the city. We're always here.'

Jocasta now felt her own cheeks darken. Foolish, to be thinking of which of her pathetic belongings she might trade for a new dress. She was married to the king. And as soon as the locals learned to recognize her, she would be able to have whatever she liked.

*

Jocasta had been in the palace for nine days, and there was still no sign of the king. Teresa never mentioned him, unless to reply to a particular question. It was peculiar, Jocasta thought. It must take more effort not to talk about the man whose palace they all dwelt in, and in whose employ everyone but Jocasta worked. He was the centre of their world, but they all pretended it wasn't odd that he was always absent. And perhaps for them it wasn't. Jocasta had vague memories of her father complaining that the king was shirking his duty (spoken quietly in the privacy of his home, when no slaves were around to overhear, of course). But why had that been? Jocasta tried to bring the memory to the front of her mind, but she could never quite catch it.

Oran was not as discreet as Teresa. If Jocasta asked him about the palace when no one else could overhear, she sometimes learned more. That evening, Jocasta wandered into the family courtyard – as the slaves called it, though the only person sleeping in any of the quarters was Jocasta – and thought she would sit a while in the darkening evening. She told the slave who was hurrying ahead to prepare her room that she could go on without her. The girl scurried away and moments later, Oran appeared.

'Are you well, Basileia?' he asked. She rolled her eyes.

'How many times must I tell you?'

'I'm sorry, madam,' he said. 'Did you need anything? Water? Wine?'

'No, thank you,' she replied. 'I have everything I need.' She drew a new stole – spun from the finest wool she had ever touched, a dark purplish-red – around her shoulders.

'You're cold,' Oran said.

She shook her head. 'I just like wearing it.'

'It looks well on you,' he said.

'Yes,' she agreed. 'Why don't you sit down?' She patted the wooden bench which she had chosen. Oran walked to its far end and sat there. She turned and lifted her feet up, so her back rested on a cushion which she propped against the wooden arm, and she was facing him, curling her toes against the warm, smooth wood.

'It's not at all like I imagined,' she said. 'I thought it would be busier. People everywhere, rushing about, ruling the city. Instead it's almost deserted.'

'The Elders are keeping everything in order,' he said. 'They always do. It doesn't take much rushing about.'

'The king is away a lot, I gather,' she said. He nodded. 'It doesn't seem even a bit strange to you?' she continued. 'To go away the morning after his own wedding?'

'Well, no, of course not,' he replied.

Her eyes glinted in the half-light. 'Why is it obvious to you, when it seems so opaque to me?'

'Let me get you some wine,' he said.

'Please don't be so rude as to ignore me when I ask you something,' she said. 'Or to assume I am so stupid that I will forget my questions the moment you wander back with one of those beautiful terracotta jugs, covered in – what will it be today? Horses? Kingfishers? And by the time you have asked me to admire the intricate designs, and told me about the craftsman in the dark corner of Thebes who paints them, and how he sells them to the winemaker in exchange for all the wine he can drink so his wife must work for their children's food, and suggested we visit his shop one day, on the backstreet behind the hill up to the marketplace, our original conversation will have disappeared with the tail of Helios' chariot.'

'I could fetch another torch,' he said. 'If you are worried about the dark.'

'I am not worried about the dark. And as you well know, if you fetch a torch, we will soon be surrounded by insects. And then you can tell me you're worried I'll get bitten, and suggest I go inside, out of their reach.'

'I only asked,' he said.

'You avoided my question. Why is it clear to you, but not to me, that the king would leave the palace the morning after his wedding? Are you trying to humiliate me? Is it obvious he would leave because that is what kings do, and everyone here knows that except me, because I am a foolish girl from the other side of the city? Is it obvious he would abandon the palace because I am too ugly to be his wife? What, precisely, is clear to you?'

Oran looked hard at the darkening ground. 'It is obvious, madam, because the king is not interested in girls. In women. I thought you knew.'

'Not interested? Then I don't understand.'

'He prefers young men,' Oran replied.

'No, I understand what you are saying,' she said. 'Perhaps I haven't made myself clear. If the king is not attracted to women at all, I'm sure you can see that I might be perplexed as to what I am doing here. Men who don't like women don't want wives. At least, that has always been my understanding of it.'

'Men want heirs,' Oran said. 'All men need heirs. Or who will look after them when they are old?'

'Laius has a household of – what? – fifty slaves: cooks and maids and housekeepers and administrators and guards and grooms and the gods know who else,' Jocasta replied. 'I'm sure some of them will look after him when he's old. He's old now, and you're all still here.'

'But he needs a child,' Oran said. The small night-flies were descending on them as the darkness fell. 'Someone to guard his memory after he dies. No one can be immortal if their descendants decide otherwise. Or if they have none. He needs someone who will put up a statue commemorating him and listing his achievements as king.'

'Well, I'm sure if someone gave you a chisel, you'd give it a try,' she snapped.

'I am loyal to my king,' he agreed.

'Then perhaps you can explain something else to me. If Laius wants an heir, enough to marry, I presume he understands that he will have to spend at least some time in the same room, in the same bed, as his wife. Don't start blushing again. You're not a child.'

'That's not necessarily true,' Oran said. 'He wants an heir. It doesn't need to be his child.'

Jocasta tried not to allow her shock to show. A man would bring up another man's child? 'What are you saying?' she asked. 'That he expects me to . . . ?'

'Yes,' said Oran. 'He's waiting for you to become pregnant. It would be better, for him, if that happened sooner rather than later. So he can claim that the child was conceived on your wedding night.'

'And who exactly does he imagine I am cavorting with?' she hissed. She wished now that she had agreed to Oran fetching a torch. At least then she would be sure that no one was listening in to their conversation. But as it was, the colonnades were in almost total blackness, and anyone could overhear her, so long as they were quiet. Oran said nothing.

'You?' she asked. 'That's why he left you behind.'

'You asked me to stay,' Oran replied. 'I told him, and he was delighted. He'd rather you bore the child of someone you had shown a preference for.'

'Would he?' Jocasta asked.

'Don't be like that,' he said. 'Please don't. I promised him. He's my king. And he's your king too.'

'Hardly,' she said. 'We've barely even met. And what if I refuse?'

The silence was as wide and long as the night.

'You won't, will you?'

'Would it matter if I did?'

'It would matter to me.'

'But you would still obey your orders?'

'They are orders,' he said. 'I serve the king. I would have no choice.'

5

I felt pain again under my ribs when I lifted myself out of bed: duller now than it had been. When I placed my fingers gently on the dressing Sophon had used, I could feel the heat of the injury. But not the different, more intense heat of an infection. I knew when I peeled back the bandages in a day or two that the skin would be shiny and red, not swollen into the almost bluish-pink that characterized an infected wound. He had recommended I stay in bed for another day or two, but no one had come to visit me since yesterday afternoon, and I had woken far too early this morning, when I rolled onto my side and the pain jolted me awake. But if I were to tell Sophon that, expecting sympathy, he would smile and say that if my sleeping self had forgotten I was hurt, my waking self would follow in a day or two.

I would rather have taken the risk of ripping open my stitches than spend another hour on my own. I padded over to a wooden chest, and found an old shift dress the colour of freshly churned cream. The slaves had taken advantage of my period in bed to wash and mend all my clothes: I scarcely recognized the dress as mine. It was cut wide enough for me to lift it only a little way above my head. I twisted my neck to slide myself into it without using my injured muscles more than I had to.

I splashed water on my face to convince myself it was morning: my mind was still fogged from having woken too early. I couldn't reach down to put on my soft leather sandals, so I walked barefoot towards the door, relishing the cool stones. I could hear a faint murmuring from outside, and I was sure it was Ani. As I opened the door onto the colonnade at the side of the family courtyard, I saw her sitting by the fountain, its sides painted with leaping dolphins, holding hands with our cousin Haem.

My mother used to say that this was her favourite part of the palace. She didn't usually enjoy telling stories, it was something she preferred to leave to our father. But occasionally you could persuade her to talk about her life before she married him, before us. When she came to tuck me into bed at night, I would ask her to tell us a story about what the palace was once like. She would resist, saying it was time for me to go to sleep, or that she was tired. But sometimes, she gave in. This courtyard – she would say – was bare and sad when she first laid eyes on it. Scarcely any living plants in the ground, no water in the fountain. The frescos on the walls were faded, and chunks of the plaster had fallen off. Some of it still lay on the ground, like half-chewed lumps of meat. She didn't even think about how dilapidated it looked, she said. Until she met my father, who had spent so much time outside the city walls. He had grown up loving flowers and trees, she explained. Ask him to tell you the names of all the plants in the garden, she would say. He knows them all. When she saw him looking at the sad, dead courtyard one day, she realized she wanted to give him a proper garden. She found a gardener to fill the flowerbeds and repair the fountain. He brought three other men and they came at night, so it would be a surprise.

And so one morning, she and my father woke to the sound of the water, tippling down the sides of the long-parched ornamental stone. It was worth the effort, she said, just to see my father's face when he realized the gardens were filled with herbs and shrubs and new fruit trees. When you asked my father about the same day, he offered up a detail my mother always missed out: the first morning he looked at the thyme and rosemary, freshly sprouted from the new black soil beneath them, he claimed he had spotted the first butterfly seen in the palace of Thebes in hundreds of years. I always believed him. It took years before the almond trees first produced their fruit, or the figs. My parents never lived to eat them.

My sister looked so much like our mother: the same dark hair plaited around the sides of her head and bound at the back, the same pale skin. And the same tendency for dramatic gestures: every time my sister placed her hand on her heart, I wondered if she was copying our mother deliberately. But it never felt like the sort of question I could ask. She loved to sit by the fountain because she knew it was the perfect place for private conversations. No one could approach you from any side of the courtyard without being seen. No one in the colonnades could hear what was being said in the centre because the sound of the water masked the words being spoken.

Haem noticed me before she did and he pulled his hand away from hers. Only a small distance, just so you couldn't say they were holding hands. He knew – even if my sister pretended not to – that I wanted more than anything to be sitting where she was. His hair was a dark gold colour, lighter when he let it grow long and curl into his neck. And although it was many years since we had played together in this square – him carrying me around on his back, pretending to be a horse while I squawked with glee – I could still remember exactly how his hair smelled: clean and somehow warm, like spiced wine in winter. But of course he only cared for Ani. And now we were no longer children, he barely saw me.

I waved to them both as I walked along the colonnade. I wanted somebody to talk to, but I was too embarrassed to stop and speak to them now. My sister waved back and smiled.

'Are you going back to lessons already?' she called. I nodded and kept walking. I could make it to Sophon's study, surely.

I was the only one who still visited our tutor. Polyn had finished lessons when he turned fifteen, Eteo and Haem the year after when they reached the same age, both boys resenting that final year, when Polyn was spending his days with men as they were left to feel like children. Ani had never been interested in the classroom, unless my cousin was in it. She called Sophon a dry old man and said he had nothing to teach her. But once it was just him and me, Sophon began talking about more interesting ideas – history, philosophy – almost as if he had been waiting for the others to leave. I had never dared to ask him if he had deliberately bored them into removing themselves from his lessons, one after another. He was almost the only person who spoke about my parents at all (everyone else preferred to pretend they had never existed, even my uncle), and I wondered if he wanted someone to remember them to, as much as I wanted to hear them remembered. He was nearly seventy years old, and had lived through the Reckoning, when he was a boy, then through my mother's reign, and so far – he would say – he had survived my brothers. He liked to say that he planned to hold on till I became queen, and then he'd die happy. I would laugh, knowing this was a promise to live forever: as the poets would sing of me, I am the youngest of four siblings, cursed daughter of cursed parents. My brothers will marry because they are kings. My sister will surely marry Haem. But I cannot expect such a future for myself, and Thebes will never want me as her queen.

I knocked on Sophon's door and found him sitting in the thin early morning light on a battered old chair by the fire. It was cold in the courtyards at the beginning of the day. The sun took its time to clear the mountains behind the palace, and until it filled the open squares, it was never really warm, even during the summer. The hairs on my arms were standing up: I should have asked Ani if I could borrow a cloak or a shawl. My own cloak had disappeared. I asked one of the servants about it, and she told me that they had scrubbed and scrubbed but couldn't get the blood out of it. I was relieved to see that Sophon was also feeling the cold. He used to say the heat went out of him when he was thirty, so he had spent the last forty years lighting the fire.

His room was my favourite part of the palace. Its walls were lined with shelves, which were filled with carefully rolled papyri. There was nothing you couldn't find here, if you had the time and the inclination. Sophon didn't play favourites with the manuscripts he had acquired overthe years: astrology and astronomy were next to each other, history and biography, agriculture and household-economy, and – most numerous and my favourite – stories about great heroes of the past.

The fireplace was on the far wall, surrounded by the shelves. Sophon's desk was under the high windows, but he preferred to sit closer to the heat. He was white-haired, balding on the top. He had a neatly trimmed white beard, and I never saw him wear anything which wasn't brown. I had asked him once why he liked brown so much, and he said it was easier. Long ago, before the Reckoning, he was a doctor, and lived at the temple of Asclepius, son of Apollo, down in the belly of the town. People would travel from all over Thebes and the lands outside to be treated by him. But he moved up to a house near the palace when he met my mother and she asked him to be Polyn's tutor. She couldn't think of anyone better, she said.

'Isy – you look cold. Come and sit here.' Sophon waved at the chair opposite his, and I hurried over and sat down, trying not to wince. 'I'm not sure you should be up yet, should you?' he asked. He pointed to the back of the chair, where there was a woollen blanket. I pulled it down and wrapped it around myself.

'I woke up so early,' I told him. 'I was bored.'

'You wanted something to read, I imagine,' he said. 'This might be what you're looking for.' He stood up with a suppressed groan and walked over to his shelves. He was a cacophony of bones: a joint creaked or snapped with every step. He reached up without a moment's hesitation and picked out a new papyrus from the crammed stacks.

He gave it to me, and I saw it was a replacement copy of the one I had been reading before. The one I had covered in my blood.

'I'm so sorry I ruined it,' I said.

'Isy, it doesn't matter,' he replied, though his eyes were filmy, as though it mattered very much. 'And the scribe was pleased to have the work.'

'Thank you.'

'Is there any news on your attacker?' Sophon asked, as he sat back down. I looked across at him. His chair was in front of the window, so it was too bright behind him for me to see his face in more than silhouette.

'I don't know. Eteo is searching for him. What have you heard?'

'I've heard your brother will find him,' he said quietly.

'I don't understand.'

'I believe your attacker will be found shortly. It has taken several days now, long enough to make it appear that it has been a difficult job to track him down.'

'You're not saying that Eteo . . .'

'I don't think so, Isy, but I can't be completely sure. I think someone else is responsible, but – as far as I can tell – Eteo is as much their target as you.' The fear must have leapt across my face because he corrected himself. 'Not a target of an assassin. The target of a plot. Someone is trying to destabilize his kingship. Killing you would have been an extremely effective way of doing that. The king can't be responsible for keeping his city safe when he can't even keep his own household safe. Do you see?'

'But Eteo will only be king for one more month,' I said. 'Then it is Polyn's year.' My brothers alternate the kingship. In other cities, Polyn would have become king, because he is the eldest. But the age gap between my brothers is very small: barely more than one year. And my uncle decided that sharing the kingship would be a better solution for our city. He believes in prophecies, and he was persuaded by a fortune-teller that our city could easily descend into civil war otherwise. The king of Thebes, whoever he is, is cursed, Creon believes. Lots of Thebans believe it. So by splitting the power, he hoped to divide the curse. And half a curse can't possibly be as bad as a whole one. One day, I would like to ask him if he really believes this or if he just believes he should pay heed to it in public. My uncle is not an easy man to read.

'Yes, that's the most confusing aspect of things,' Sophon said. 'Only a month . . .'

'What do you expect to happen next?' I asked.

'I think they will find someone who appears to be guilty. But if he is the perpetrator – which I doubt he will be – he will only be the most visible element. The real plot is still hidden from view. You must be careful.'

'I was careful before,' I said, although I knew this wasn't true. I hadn't been expecting a masked man to infiltrate my home. We have guards everywhere. I thought I was safe and I had behaved accordingly.

'I'm not blaming you, Isy. I'm trying to protect you.'

I nodded. I had come to Sophon to try and feel better, and if anything I now felt worse. I wanted to go back to my room, but my side was throbbing too much for me to stand.

'Do you have any old parchment?' I asked him. 'That you aren't using?'

'Yes, I think so,' he replied. 'Are you too old for wax tablets now? Your words need some permanence?' He smiled. 'How old are you today?'

'Fifteen,' I reminded him. He knew perfectly well when I was born.

'It feels like a year or two at most since you were a baby,' he said. 'It's only because you've grown so tall that I believe you when you say that.'

He opened a cupboard door beside the desk and pulled out two small rolls of parchment. 'Here you are,' he said. 'Will this be enough for now?'

'Yes. Do you have any ink?'

'There's ink and everything else you need in the cupboard over by the door,' he said. 'You can pick it up when you go back to your room. Save me walking over there.' He crunched his way back to his chair and sat down again.

I thought of something Eteo had said, about Sophon running to help me, when I was stabbed. The man who supported his way round the room leaning on the furniture could not really have run, surely? Not even if there was a fire behind him. But my brother has never been prone to exaggeration: like me, he prefers to leave that to Ani.

'What do you intend to use it for?' Sophon asked.

'I want to keep a record,' I told him. 'Of what's happening. When we talked before, about history, you said I must always bear in mind who composes it. And I thought about that a lot when I was in bed. I thought about how my story would never be told if I didn't tell it.'

Sophon said nothing.

'An official history of Thebes would mention my

brothers and my uncle. It might even mention Ani, because she will end up marrying Haem.

Sophon nodded. 'Yes, I think she will.'

'But no one will remember me, the youngest daughter. I don't matter, do I?'

Anyone else would have told me I mattered very much to them. Sophon sighed. 'No, Isy, I'm afraid you don't.'

'So I should compose my own history, shouldn't I? Or it will be lost forever.'

'Yes,' he agreed. 'You should.'

'Is it better to start at the beginning?' I asked him. 'Or to start now and work backwards?'

He thought for a long moment. 'You should try to compose it in your head first,' he said. 'And then you will know how to begin when you write it down. I think, perhaps, you should start now, and then try to understand what will happen in the light of what has happened so far. Do you see?'

'Everything that is to come has been decided by what has already occurred? You sound like Creon: the gods decide everything, and we are their playthings.'

'Not the gods, Isy. The gods do what they will. I doubt they have much time for us: why would they? Don't they have more important things on their minds than the fates of a few mortals?'

'Of course they do. You know I think the same. That's why I don't understand what you're saying.'

'Because events are decided by other events. Aren't they? If someone ran in through the door now, and shouted that a pack of wild dogs was tearing through the main courtyard, what would happen?'

'We would shut the door and lock it. We might push some of the furniture against it, too. Then if the lock doesn't hold, the chairs might keep them at bay.'

'And if no such messenger arrives, what happens to the furniture?'

'We leave it where it is.'

'So the fate of the chair today is decided by the decision of a pack of dogs that have – at this moment – never set eyes on it. Who could not begin to understand that it even exists. Do you understand?'

'Yes. I think so.'

'No one would believe the gods had nothing to do with what happens to us, Isy, but we surely can't believe they would intervene in the existence of a simple chair, or even a dog.'

'And a human life is more complicated than the life of a chair,' I said, wishing I had thought this through for myself.

'Of course. Can you even begin to count the myriad ways in which your life might be affected by the choices other people – people you have never met, whose existence is utterly hidden from you – are making every day?'

'So how can I write my history, when there is so much I don't know, which might cause a profound change to things I think I do know?'

'Well, that is the difficulty of writing it,' he said. 'The ink is by the door. I told you, didn't I?'

He closed his eyes. This is typical of our conversations. I end them knowing more than I did when they began. But I am somehow less sure of things.

6

Jocasta had been in the palace for almost a month now, and the king had yet to return. She often woke in the night, disturbed sometimes by random noises of a large household but more often by the sense that someone was nearby, wishing her ill. She had no proof that this was so, but she knew it to be true. Her bedroom door had a lock, but no key. Or if there was a key, she did not have it. So many doors in the palace were locked to her, but not even in sleep could she close herself off from anyone who wanted to walk in. She had asked Teresa about the absent key, but Teresa had blinked slowly, and said she wasn't sure she had ever seen it. It was at this moment, when Jocasta thought she would reach out and slap the woman right across the face, when she wondered if she might be pregnant. She didn't know what made her think of it.

Oran still visited her every night. He took his duty seriously. And although she knew he didn't need to, he tried to make her happy. He told her she was pretty and that he liked the way her hair – released from its daily plaits – flowed across the pillows, like seaweed on the lakeshore. He had tried never to hurt her, and if she expressed any pain, he stopped. But still she stared into the darkness when she wanted to fall asleep: this was the boy she had believed her only friend and ally in the palace, and he too chose to obey the king's perverse whims.

Her days were less terrible than her nights, though the sleeplessness left her blurry and exhausted. She liked to walk around the agora with her slave girl and look at all the stalls and the people who came to buy. If she had married anyone else, this would have been her daily routine: carrying a basket to fill with fresh onions and lettuces, cheeses and bread. But she had no such responsibility. The palace was managed entirely by Teresa and their food was managed by the cooks. So Jocasta wandered the market aimlessly, stopping to look at whatever she pleased. She chose dresses in pale colours, knowing she would never have to worry about keeping them unmarked: whoever was in charge of the laundry was someone she would never meet. And if a dress was damaged, she could pick something else in a different shade, perhaps this time with serried lines of contrasting embroidery around the neckline and shoulders. The stall-holders soon recognized her, and kept aside their best cloth for her. Though she liked the market, she wished that the palace was not quite so high in the city. It meant there was only ever one road she could take, and that was down and into the bustling streets, when she would sometimes have preferred to go somewhere quiet. Not contained, tamed quiet: she had quite enough of that in the palace. But she would have liked to visit the lake or wander out past the city graveyard onto the hillsides, and hear the goats and sheep bleating as they grazed. She would have enjoyed walking around the hill beneath the back of the palace, but she had not yet found an exit from the palace into the wasteland outside the city walls. She wondered what would happen if she announced to Teresa that she wanted to visit her husband in the mountains. But she didn't wonder for very long.

One morning she planned to go to the market as usual, but when she woke, she felt feverish. Her room was cool, but her hair was pressed damp against her scalp and the sheets were sticking to her back. She wiped the sweat from her forehead and realized she was also queasy. She refused breakfast, in the hope that the nausea would pass. She sat for a while in the shade, too uncomfortable for the bright sun. She ate only an apple for lunch, and noted Teresa's beady pleasure in her sickness. Of course Teresa knew about Oran. Jocasta had no doubt that the whole thing had been the sly housekeeper's idea.

Eventually, she decided that she would go out in spite of the shakiness which radiated from her belly to her feet. She summoned her slave and insisted they go to the market now, even though it was the hottest part of the day. The girl said nothing, but picked up her basket and followed her mistress through the courtyards. With every step, Jocasta knew she was making a terrible mistake. The sickness threatened to overwhelm her. But she could not lose face in front of this girl, in front of the palace. She put one brittle foot in front of the other, and wished that she had a parasol. She decided she would search for one among the stalls.

She didn't recall seeing parasols in the market before, but then, she hadn't been looking for one, and sometimes these things slipped past the eyes of the uninterested. Perhaps she had half a memory of a vendor of curved sunhats, made from elaborately woven straw. That might do. She took a different route through the square, hoping to notice them again. But although she wanted to give the stalls her full attention, she soon realized she needed to concentrate on her feet, kicking their way through the sandy dust beneath her sandals. She felt a small piece of grit wedge itself between her foot and her shoe, and the pain was as intense as if someone had driven a sharp metal blade into her heel. She grabbed at the foot, and fell heavily onto her knees. The maid stood behind her, useless.

A dark-haired man, greying at the temples, rushed out from behind piles of papyrus, and reached down to help her up.

'Fetch me my stool,' he cried, and another stall-holder brought the man's folding wooden seat out into the aisle behind her.

'Here,' said the man, and lifted her onto the seat. 'Try to take deep breaths. You—' he barked at the slave girl. 'Fetch water, now.' The girl ran off.

'Is she entirely hopeless?' he asked Jocasta. 'Or does she do what she's asked?'

Jocasta thought for a moment. 'She usually does what she's asked,' she replied. 'Though she might have been quicker if we'd told her where to get the water from.'

The man pursed his lips and glanced across at the stall-holder – a middle-aged woman with stringy nut-brown arms – and asked a wordless question. She produced a flask and poured water into a small wooden cup which she held out to the old man, who took it and brought it to Jocasta's lips. He tipped it carefully towards her mouth, and she felt its coolness wash into her.

'Thank you,' she said, to him and the woman who had given her water away.

He looked at her, lips still pursed. 'You'll be well again shortly,' he said. 'But you need to rest. How far did you walk to get here?'

'From inside.' She waved at the palace behind them.

'Hmm,' he said. 'I'll take you back there in a few minutes.'

She sat watching dully as he engaged the woman at the next stall to keep an eye on his papers and scrolls. He picked up an old leather bag which he swung over his shoulders, and offered her his arm. She smiled at the kindness, in spite of the sweat she could feel crawling over her scalp.

'Thank you.' She took his arm and they walked slowly back to the palace. They were entering the front gates when they almost walked into the slave girl, who was carrying a small kylix of water, most of which she had already spilled.

Teresa caught sight of them as Jocasta entered the third courtyard. She hurried over, frowning.

'What's going on?' She pointed at the stall-holder. 'Who's this?'

'Are you her mother?' asked the man.

'I – no.' Teresa wasn't used to being questioned, Jocasta saw. And certainly not by someone who wasn't afraid of her.

'She needs rest. She shouldn't be on her feet, especially in the afternoon heat. Where can she lie down?'

Teresa was torn between telling him to leave, and wanting his help to move Jocasta into her room. Need won out, and she took Jocasta's right arm while the man continued to support her left. Together they walked to her room, and led her to bed. The papyrus-seller reached behind her, rearranging her pillows with one efficient hand.

'Take off her shoes,' he told Teresa, who obeyed him in silence. He helped Jocasta to sit back on the bed, and placed more cushions beneath her legs.

'I'll check back on you tomorrow,' said the bookseller, once he was satisfied. 'Until then, don't go further than you have to.'

'Thank you,' Jocasta said.

'You're comfortable?' he asked. She nodded. 'Good. Tomorrow, then.' He strode off, walking far more quickly now. Teresa shot a baleful glance at Jocasta, and hastened after him.

By the time the king heard this story, on his return from the mountains, Jocasta had no doubt that it would have been Teresa's idea to find a doctor to keep an eye on her. As her pregnancy became more visible, so did the king. But she never saw him alone, and he barely spoke to her, even when others were present. Every man in the palace would toast her and Laius, and wish health to his heir. 'A son!' Jocasta grew weary of hearing. She secretly wished for a daughter, just to serve them right. The king looked no more enthusiastic at the prospect of a son than she felt, though he never spoke about it to his wife. 'So long as the child is healthy,' he would announce to whoever asked, trying to avert the evil eye. 'I wouldn't mind at all being the father of a daughter.'

She almost preferred it when he ignored her, or went

back to the mountains, because the alternative provoked a black-eyed, wrathful stare from Teresa, who resented any time he spent with his bride at all. Jocasta tried to puzzle it out, but could not: if the housekeeper was so devoted to Laius, who had no interest in Jocasta, why had Teresa not married him herself? She could have had children once: no one was born old. So why had she not done so, instead of embroiling Jocasta in the whole hateful deceit?

At least Jocasta had found Sophon, the man who ran the papyrus stall. He had been a doctor for several years, before deciding to indulge in his primary pleasure of reading and dealing in manuscripts. But he was happy to have one more patient: he began to visit Jocasta, checking up on her, answering her questions about the dizziness and the sickness. He brought herbs which quelled the latter and advised rest to battle the former. As the weeks dragged by, and her body felt more treacherous with each day, she asked him if he would be there when she gave birth.

'Of course I will be nearby,' he replied. 'But you know a midwife will attend you. You need someone who has been through it herself.' Jocasta asked Teresa if she would find someone, and the housekeeper nodded.

'Of course,' she said. 'It's all in hand.'

*

After seven months of persistent, sometimes crippling nausea, Jocasta was desperate to be rid of this parasitic child which persecuted her from within. She was not precisely sure when she had conceived it, but she knew it must be due some time in the next few weeks. She was terrified of what was to come. She was barely sixteen years old, slightly built, and afraid her body would soon be split in two by an infant who cared nothing for damaging her, but whose only determination was to be born. She wanted to ask Sophon the one question she could not: was it rational to hate a part of your own body? And what if it wanted you dead? For the last time in her life, she wondered if it was too late to send a message to her mother. But she could not bring herself to do so. News of her pregnancy must have spread across Thebes by now. And yet she had not heard a word from her family. She lay on her bed, propped up by cushions, wishing the whole thing was over. And then, of course, it was.

The pain was indescribable, and more than once she found herself pledging every possible offering to the divine Eileithyia if it would abate. When she understood that it would not stop until the baby was out or she was dead, she screamed into the uncaring air that she would give anything, everything she had if the goddess would ease her pain. She reflected, between the worst pains of contraction, that this particular goddess – a daughter of a vengeful mother – should be her ally, above all others. But still the child of Hera did not come to her assistance.

She asked and asked for Sophon, but no one could find him, or even guess at where he might have gone. Jocasta was so upset that one of the palace guards brought in the woman who looked after the stall next to Sophon's. She said he had received a message from home yesterday which required an immediate response, and he had yet to return. Looking over at Jocasta – who was red-faced and gasping for air, her hands clawing at the sheets she was lying on – she asked if she might be excused, and ran from the room. A dead mother was a bad omen. So in the end, it was just Jocasta and Teresa, as the housekeeper must have always intended it would be.

Teresa was solicitous, pushing Jocasta's hair out of her eyes and behind her ears, murmuring that all would be well. Jocasta soon lost track of time: she wasn't sure if she had been struggling for hours or days, and Teresa would not tell her. Shutters were drawn across the windows and she found herself dozing in the half-light, waking up anguished and confused. In the whole awful process, it never once occurred to her that anything could be worse than the pain. And then eventually, after time had slowed or perhaps stopped, after she had pushed and struggled and panted and wept, she made one final impossible effort and heard Teresa exhale loudly as the pain receded a little.

'Is it a boy?' Jocasta asked. In a single moment, she found she no longer hated the parasite which was trying to kill her. She had a baby, and she wanted nothing more than to hold it in her arms and keep it safe. She had survived the birth. She had lived to be a mother.

Teresa replied that yes, it was indeed a boy, and Jocasta was so happy that she didn't notice Teresa's expression or hear the warning tone in her voice. Jocasta knew Teresa had little time for her. But she had never seen a look of pity on the woman's face until now.

'Give him to me,' Jocasta begged. There was something purple in the woman's hands, like offal at a sacrifice. Where was her son? And why didn't he make a sound? Babies cried, didn't they?

Teresa turned away from her, and walked out of the room.

'Give him to me,' she shouted, though her lungs ached and her throat was scratched raw. She tried to get up and follow Teresa, grab her baby and hold him tight. But her legs wouldn't support her, and she simply lay there for what felt like forever. When Teresa returned, she was holding nothing. She looked at Jocasta and shook her head.

'He wouldn't have let you keep a boy, even if the child had survived. Do you understand?'

Jocasta shook her head, wordless.

'The king cannot have a son, only a daughter. There is a prophecy which said he would be killed by his son. He won't allow that to happen. So I couldn't allow it to happen either.'

Jocasta thought she must be hallucinating from the exhaustion. A prophecy? Was Teresa mad? It was one thing to pay reverence to the gods who controlled the affairs of men, but another thing entirely to believe that they gave out messages for the future. To their priests and most devout followers, perhaps, but to ordinary men? Even to kings? It was almost blasphemous to suggest it.

The rational part of her mind, if she could have reached it, knew that after the Reckoning, plenty of people had sought meaning in messages from the gods. They had preferred to see it not as a disaster, but as a warning, or something foretold. People wanted priests and fortune-tellers, entrail-readers and diviners to prove that they had seen it coming. Most of all, the survivors wanted to believe that they had been saved because of something, or perhaps for something. Blind chance was too frightening for anyone; who could feel safe if their survival was simply down to luck? And who could grieve for the crushing losses they had experienced, if none of it held any meaning?

'The king believes in prophecies?' She was clutching at sense.

'Devoutly,' Teresa nodded. 'He refused to have a child, for years. Eventually, he was persuaded that he could have a daughter, because the prophecy said he would be killed by his son. I hoped you would have a girl, you see. Because I could only have sons and I couldn't leave a third one on the hillside to die.' Jocasta gazed at her, wondering if she was hearing the housekeeper's dulled tones correctly. Had Teresa borne healthy sons and then exposed them on the mountain to avoid a prophecy? The woman must be quite mad.

'I want to see my baby,' said Jocasta.

'He didn't survive.' Teresa looked at the floor. 'He was too small, and the cord was wrapped around his neck. He went too long without air. It happens often.'

'I need to see him.'

'It wouldn't help,' Teresa said quietly. 'Your doctor will be back tomorrow or the next day. He'll say the same thing. There is nothing to be gained by holding a dead baby, and wishing life into it. Believe me.'

And with this, she walked out. Jocasta was too bloody and exhausted even to cry.

7

I now felt uncomfortable only when I reached upwards, though I still couldn't twist my body: if someone called my name, I would feel a stiffness under my ribs as I tried to turn. Even moving my neck pulled out echoes of leftover pain below. But the stitches were gone, leaving me with a puckered red triangle beneath my ribcage. I stood in the sunlight beneath the high windows of my bedroom, and raised my arms to shoulder height. Ani ran her fingers across the scar, and said doubtfully that it would probably fade over time, and that no one but me would ever see it anyway. I didn't tell her that I liked it: I was drawn to its symmetry and the way it marked me out as someone who didn't die when they were supposed to. It was like the tattoos of an Amazon warrior, the mark of the victor. But I was alone in perceiving it that way. Only when the stitches were gone did everyone stop behaving as though I were a breakable object. I saw myself as bronze while my family viewed me as a delicate piece of terracotta which had already broken once and been carefully glued back together. It was hard to feel like myself again until everyone stopped treating me like someone else.

I had begun to think about composing my history, and decided it would be best to begin the story with what was happening now. In a few days, Eteo would be giving up the kingship to Polyn. It was a huge occasion every year, when Thebes gave thanks to her ruling family for providing the city with not one, but two kings. Thebes, Sophon says, is an anxious city: she always fears for her future. It is the only place I've ever lived, so I don't know if things are different in other cities. And it seemed reasonable to me to fear for the future of Thebes, but that was because her kings were also my brothers, so my fate was woven into the city's well-being.

The dual kingship was my history as well as my future. My mother was queen of Thebes for many years. When she had two sons, and then two daughters, everyone has always said the city gave a sigh of relief. The ruling family was in place for another generation. It was only when I came to think about this for my history that I realized it was strange that Polyn had not yet married. He was almost twenty; it was more than time. He and my uncle must be considering potential brides. Perhaps they were waiting until Polyn was king again to give the city a royal wedding she would enjoy: a formal ceremony with a grand sacrifice, a feast and songs through the night and into the next day. And then Eteo would marry the following year, and he would never be here again, splashing in the fountain with me in the warm summer evenings. He would be with someone else, a stranger I might not even like. And then there were further consequences to us having dual kings: whose son would take precedence? Polyn's, because he was older? Or Eteo's if he was king when his son was born?

I had set myself the task of writing about the past, but it seemed I could only think about the future.

—

Eteo had asked us all to stay inside the palace grounds until my attacker was caught. Polyn scoffed at the idea that he should modify his behaviour for any reason. Ani went wherever Haem was, wherever they could meet in private. So although we were all supposed to be in the same place, the family quarters were deserted except for the increased number of guards and slaves. I understood why Eteo was worried, but I was growing bored of being stuck here on my own. I found myself peeking through the gaps in the outer walls, trying to imagine myself on the hillside, sitting beneath the shady pine trees that dappled its lower slopes. Or, looking out the other way, I could just make out the edges of Lake Hylica from the east wall. I could see children diving in, their muscled bodies like dolphins against the glinting water.

How I envied them. But I couldn't sneak out to join them, even if I hadn't made a promise to my brother to stay in the palace. Sophon would never forgive me if I swam with a still-healing wound. And though he was right to tell me I had to keep it dry and clean, I wanted to feel the weeds beneath my feet and the cool water on my skin. It was so hot in the palace: dipping my toes in the fountain made little difference. The water was too shallow, and it soon grew warm in the afternoons. Besides, I wanted to see the kingfishers and frogs, hear the insects buzzing around me. I wanted to watch the water-skaters dancing across the surface as they tried to escape my splashing arms.

And on top of the boredom was the strange atmosphere in the palace. Usually, we marked the changing of the kings with celebrations. Preparations took several weeks, as the public square was decorated and a calf was sacrificed every day in the temples. The priests burned incense to the gods and the whole city participated. But something was different this time. Instead of a sense of excitement for renewal, Thebes was like a snake sloughing off its old skin too soon, and crawling – still soft and vulnerable – into the light. We were fearful rather than exuberant. Nothing was safe.

Even my uncle, who was usually so calm, had been touched by disquiet. The day before, he had had a statue delivered for his rooms, which were across the courtyard from ours. He had decided to redecorate his quarters, as part of the new year celebrations. It was the second delivery of this likeness, because when it first arrived, it was a rather nondescript representation of him: plain, almost austere. Even the stone looked to be of lower quality than the other statues in the palace. The marble was veiny and held a strange pinkish colour. Creon was disappointed with the piece, even more so when Haem snorted at the likeness.

My uncle had obviously expected something more impressive. So the sculptor was commissioned to improve upon the original before bringing it back. The man painted detail into the clothes and hair – applying a handsome pattern of interlocked blue squares around the hem and neckline of the reddened tunic – which had left the face strangely bare in comparison. Creon still felt the statue failed to reflect his status, as well as his appearance. So the sculptor agreed to make further improvements on site rather than carting the statue back to his workshop a second time. He decided to replace the blandly painted eyes with ones made from lapis, which is extremely prized in our city and all across Hellas. He must surely have believed that my uncle could find nothing to complain about then.

The sculptor could not find two pieces of the bright blue stone which were large enough to use in their entirety, so he smashed several smaller stones onto a palate covered with adhesive paste to create a glittering blue that he could paint over the irises. He stood on a ladder – the statue was slightly larger than life-size – and coated the dead stone eyes of my uncle's likeness with a layer of sparkling blue dust. When he came down the ladder and looked up at his work, he wasn't quite satisfied with the symmetry of the result. He climbed back up and pulled a chisel from his belt, to tidy the right eye which offended him. At this precise moment, Creon walked in from the courtyard, and saw the sculptor jamming a metal shaft into the statue's eye. My uncle – who never shows weakness or fear – gave a horrible cry and ran out of his rooms, out of the courtyard altogether. Palace guards came running from the second square when they heard the awful sound and marched the offending craftsman away.

The statue was removed, but no one knew where. Sophon has asked around but even he cannot find out what happened to the sculptor.

*

And then one day, they found my assassin. My would-be assassin. When everyone called him a killer, they seemed to have forgotten I didn't die. He was one of the new young recruits for the palace guard. Sixteen years old, the same age as Ani. The recruits live in dormitories, with twenty boys to each room, in the barracks down the hill from the market square in front of the palace. Their training-grounds and gymnasium are all part of the same complex. They are taught to defend the king, his family, and each other, in that order. They spend many days learning drills and practising with their weapons. They start with wooden swords, just like my brothers did when they were first taught to fight. Only when they have proved they won't injure themselves or their comrades are they given the heavy bronze swords they have earned. It is a source of enormous pride to be the first boy to graduate from his practice-weapon to a real one and a corresponding shame to be the last.

The evidence was easily found: this boy had not progressed yet to the bronze. He was still practising every day with wooden sticks. Yet he had a knife, a real one, stashed beneath his blanket which he had folded to use as an extra pillow on his pallet. The blood – my blood – was still visible on the blade, a dark rusty coating which he should have known to wipe off.

He was marched up the hill to stand before the king and explain himself. The rumour raced around the palace more quickly than the guards could drag him though to the main square, where cases of treason are heard. Thebes's traders were hard at work in the agora in front of the palace, so the guards lost time going around the outside. If not, I wouldn't have been able to squeeze my way through the crowds which had formed when my brother and his advisers strode out into the main square to sit as judges. I knew if Eteo saw me, he would be angry that I had ignored his request to stay in the secluded part of the palace. But surely he would understand that I had to see the man who had tried to kill me. If I didn't, I would forever be plagued by the nightmare vision of a masked man. I needed to see the face which had worn the mask.

The crowd were jeering and shouting so loudly I could scarcely hear what was being said. The accused boy had the same difficulty. He was too frightened to speak until he was punched hard, once in the ribs and once in the side of the head, by one of his erstwhile trainers. Eteo sat in front of him – his advisers on both sides, my uncle in the most prestigious place to his left – and asked the boy to explain himself. The boy could not. He had never seen the knife before, he didn't put it there, he didn't know who had, it hadn't been there last night or this morning, he hadn't ever been to the palace, he would never hurt a member of the royal family. He wept as he gave his answers. Perhaps he was younger than Ani after all.

My uncle leaned over to advise my brother, and the men huddled together for a moment. Eteo nodded and turned to the boy. The crowd fell quiet.

'Thebes finds you guilty,' said my brother in a stranger's voice. 'The sentence is death.'

There was a scream but it didn't come from the boy. It came from a woman in the crowd. She was his mother, I suppose. Her cries were quickly hushed by her neighbours.

I didn't see the boy's face until the guards turned to march him away. I had pushed myself around the edge of the crowd to catch sight of him, and I knew from a glance that they had the wrong man. He was nowhere near tall enough, he must have been a hand's width shorter than me. The man who attacked me had been my height, and his eyes were grey. This boy had brown eyes, like a calf about to be slaughtered by a priest.

I pushed my way through to the front and shouted to Eteo.

'I need to speak to you,' I called. Annoyance and worry flashed across his face, one after the other. But he knew why I had come.

'I'm not glad to see you, Isy,' he said, stepping down from the wooden platform so he could hear me. 'I wish you'd stay inside, where you're safe.' I watched him realize the folly of his words. The palace was the place where I had been least safe.

'It isn't him,' I said. 'He's not the one.'

Eteo looked at me so sadly that I wanted to reach over and hold him. 'I know, Isy. But there's nothing I can do.'

'You can't mean that. He's innocent. You're sending an innocent boy to his death.'

'It's him or me, Isy. Not just me, us.'

'The man who did it is still out there. Out here.' I waved my arm at the dispersing crowd. They had seen executions before, but many of them were still wandering out of the courtyard towards the barracks where the boy would be killed: strangled, probably, or bludgeoned by his former comrades.

'I know,' my brother said. 'Stay beside me until we're in the second courtyard. The guards will escort us back inside. You have to trust me. It's better this way.'

8

A year after her baby had died, Jocasta looked at her hair in the blackening, pock-marked mirror, and wondered when she had begun to look so haggard. One day she had been ripe, her belly stretched taut like a peach around its stone. After that, she had ignored her reflection as the days slid into months: her torn skin and rent garments were nothing she wished to see. And now, after a year, she saw that somehow she was no longer young. And although this seemed like a minor loss after everything else, she felt the pain of a fresh wound rushing up from her gut to her throat and she opened her mouth to scream.

*

Two years later, Jocasta wondered if Teresa would replace the mirror which (having hated it for as long as she could remember), she had finally smashed against the hard stone floor of her bedroom. The housekeeper, often so quick-tempered, had not even shouted when she saw the floor covered in dark shards. Slaves had come running from every corner of the palace courtyard; even Jocasta had been startled by the noise it made as each piece sprang free from its bonds. She laughed as she watched the glittering angles spin around her feet. It was not until later, when Sophon was picking splinters of glass from her legs with a pair of small silver tweezers, that she even realized she was injured.

*

The following year, Jocasta spent every day kneeling before the shrine which Teresa had arranged to have built in the courtyard. Laius had refused his wife, when she had petitioned him, but the housekeeper had eventually persuaded him that Jocasta would be quieter if he gave way. Laius was himself a pious man, and he made his offerings in the temples in the main courtyard of the palace. But his wife was no longer able to walk among the people of Thebes to pay her devotions: the eyes of strangers overwhelmed her and she was swiftly reduced to tears. Even the women turned away from her, fearful that her ill-fortune might be contagious, might afflict their own future children. Once, she saw a woman make the sign to avert the evil eye. She would have sworn she had no evil in her, but at the same time, she knew she must have affronted a powerful god; why else was she punished so cruelly?

*

After three more years, Jocasta no longer trusted she would one day see a grave marker for her son. She had dedicated years of her drawn-out life to pleading with Teresa but the woman was obdurate. She insisted there was no grave, no stone to signal the place where Jocasta could take a lock of her hair to her beautiful boy, and pour wine into a wide, shining dish for him. Jocasta did not believe her: how could she have simply disposed of the boy, as though he were nothing but refuse, like mouldering cabbages thrown away from a too-warm kitchen?

She demanded to see her husband and ask him the same questions. But Laius, who had long since given up speaking to his wife, and now avoided the palace almost entirely – preferring to live out on the mountains in all but the harshest weather, rather than find himself within earshot of Jocasta – had no consolation for her. He either did not know or did not care what had become of the baby. Once it was dead, he was satisfied. The opposite was true for his wife, who would never be satisfied again.

*

In the eleventh year after her son's death, Jocasta began sending messengers to the Oracle. Although Delphi lay several hundred stades away, across territory which was rarely safe, she had concluded that the Pythian priestesses offered her the only comfort she might find. Making offerings to Apollo in her home was no longer sufficient. The wine was poured, the entrails were burned, but she was no closer to happiness. Fear and revulsion still coursed through her whenever she thought of her own body almost tearing in two. The mere sight of a pregnant woman left her panting for breath. She longed for her missing child, but she could not imagine having another. Even Teresa had stopped suggesting it. The grief it caused was too disruptive for the whole palace.

The Oracle returned Jocasta's interest with gnomic utterances but only occasionally. There was no certainty her messenger would survive the journey there and back:

bandits, robbers and mountain lions all fed on her slaves from time to time. And those who did return brought messages whose meaning twisted away from Jocasta, like snakes in her hands. She would take the message gladly, and when she first heard it, she felt better, somehow lighter. The Oracle was benign, it offered sage advice.

Then, over the next day or two, she would reflect on its hidden meanings and on the Oracle's possible motives. How could she truly know what it meant when it was so vague? Was it really saying that her son was alive, when it referred to him as 'cursed'? Or was his death the curse itself? That she too was cursed she had no doubt. Almost more cruel than the loss of her child was the terrible, suffocating uncertainty. After several days, she would demand that another messenger be sent to request clarification. But the clarification, when it came, if it came, was no less vague than the previous message.

*

By the fifteenth year, she was given a new mirror, and was shocked to see she had grown old. She had a mesh of fine lines around her eyes that she had never seen before. Her mother had died that spring. When her brother arrived with the news, he had been tentative, not wishing to add further grief to a sister bowed down by the weight of what she had already borne. But, if anything, Jocasta had been relieved. She had taken the carriage across Thebes to attend her mother's burial: it would have been impossible to do anything else. And as she cast the damp earth over her mother's grave, murmuring the ritual words to grant her mother safe passage to Hades, she felt no grief. She said the words again, beneath her breath, for her dead boy, and cast an extra handful of dirt over his imagined corpse.

*

The following winter, her father followed her mother into the boat of Charon and across the River Lethe. Again, Jocasta scattered earth and poured offerings to his shade. Although she conducted the rituals as was proper, she rent her garments and tore her hair because custom and the gods demanded it, not because she felt any fresh pain. In her own mind, she had been orphaned fifteen years earlier, when they gave her to the king. And then orphaned again when her baby died. Why was there a word to describe the child of dead parents, but no word to describe the mother of a dead child? The question had plagued her for years: there should be a word for her, for what had happened to her. Yet there was not.

*

It was sixteen years since her son had died, and only Creon existed as the bridge between her past life and her present existence. She found her brother's visits both reassuring and difficult. Firstly, there was the problem that he had grown up. He was twenty-one now, and she found it disconcerting when he arrived a stranger: taller, darker, his face lengthening and hardening as he left childhood behind. Only his voice stayed the same: calm, deep, measured. His voice and his pale blue eyes.

Jocasta wished her brother would move into the palace

and keep her company all the time, so she would have someone to talk to, someone who connected her to a time in her life when things had been easier, happier. But he wouldn't agree to it: on his last visit he had mentioned a girl he was hoping to marry. Perhaps once they had married, they might consider moving nearer to the palace and the hub of the city. Jocasta thought he should hurry: Creon was no longer a boy. It began to look peculiar if men went unmarried for too long.

She thought she would send a messenger to ask him to visit her. But were the only reliable slaves all away in Delphi? She could not think when she had last received an oracle. Perhaps one was due back today. Or perhaps he had been due back yesterday or the day before, and she had lost another man to the perils of the Outlying. The anxiety rose in her: if her messengers kept dying, she would soon have no one left to trust. And then what would she do? How could she find someone else who wasn't in Teresa's pocket, telling Jocasta not truths which emanated from the god, but stories which came from the old housekeeper? How could she be sure the slaves she had already sent were loyal to her rather than Teresa? She could not.

Her hair had grown wispy and lifeless. It hung down behind her ears, when once it had – she was sure – curled over them. Realizing she hated it, she opened one dresser-drawer after another until she found what she needed. She bundled the hair in her left fist, and hacked into it with a blade that should have been sharper. She placed the offending hank on the table and immediately wished someone would take it away, so she couldn't see it any more. Once it was no longer attached to her, she was revolted by it.

*

Two days later, when a messenger, a foreigner, arrived and asked to see the queen, the palace staff were perplexed. There must be some mistake. Did he want to see Teresa? She was in the agora somewhere, and would doubtless return before nightfall. She had left no instructions for what they should do if someone asked for Jocasta. No one ever did except her brother, Creon, and they all knew him. But the man – or he was really nearer a boy – stood firm: he must speak to the queen, immediately.

There was some quality in his manner, his urgency, which spurred them into an action they did not want to take. Two slave women – who usually acted as Jocasta's maids – hurried him through the courtyards, each one noticing that the messenger had clearly travelled in haste: his boots were mud-spattered, his cloak had a small tear on the lower back, as though he had caught it on a branch, and wrenched himself free. They entered the private courtyard and found Jocasta kneeling before the shrine, as she often was these days. She was murmuring something to herself, a prayer to the god who tormented her.

'Forgive me,' said one of the slave women. She had the wit to know Teresa would probably have them both flogged if she found out that they had allowed a stranger into the company of the queen. Looking across at her fellow slave, she jerked her head in the direction of the kitchens. They should disappear into the bowels of the palace and then they might be able to deny their involvement later.

'Excuse me, madam, but this visitor needs to speak to you.'

Jocasta turned. Her eyes darted to the stranger and she noted his dishevelled appearance. She reached one hand to the altar, to support herself as she stood. Then she bent down and brushed the dust from her dress. 'What is it, sir?' she asked.

'It is the king,' he replied. 'I'm very sorry, madam. He is dead.'

'Dead?' Jocasta asked. The messenger nodded, his face a mask of mute sympathy. 'Good,' she said. 'So what happens now?'

9

It was the morning of Polyn's coronation and, getting dressed in my room, I could hear the preparations taking place throughout the palace. The market stalls had been removed from the agora outside the palace gates, and the sand had been swept into a racetrack. Once the ceremony had taken place in the throne room, fifty youths – who were known as the aristoi, the best of Thebes's young men – would be competing in the celebratory games. They were all Polyn's age or thereabouts. Many of them had been his friends for years. They were the sons of Thebes's leading families, and Polyn, Eteo and Haem would compete alongside them: Polyn and Haem in the wrestling and Eteo in the foot-race. It was a chance for my brothers and my cousin to show off, and Thebes would be disappointed if no one from the royal household won an event.

I was making my preparations alone. My sister and I would both be wearing crocus-yellow dresses: the colour worn by girls at Theban ceremonies. It was a colour which Ani said suited me, bringing out the golden tones in my usually mousy hair. My sister was far less happy about wearing it herself, saying that yellow made her look sallow and plain. She wanted to wear a beautiful blue-green dress – the colour of the lake we never visited any more

– which she had recently acquired (a gift from Haem, I imagined), but she could not prevail on either my uncle or my brothers to let her disregard the traditional colour and wear what she chose.

She was so angry that – to placate her – I suggested she had the slaves help her to make herself presentable (she would allow no more than that, in such a horrible dress). My sister has never looked anything but beautiful to everyone else. The intricate hairstyle she was planning required at least two women to plait and wrap. I reassured them that I could dress myself without assistance – as I did most days – and Ani threw her arms around me with gratitude. She knew my hair would look the same no matter how many people tried to ambush it with combs and pins. But that was not why I preferred to dress myself. I could not bear to hear the slave girls gossip. The palace was buzzing with details from those who had watched the boy – my supposed assassin – die. Everyone except Eteo thought I would want to know what had happened. It was meant to reassure me: no more danger, now the man who attacked me was gone. Instead, hearing them was like joining a conspiracy. The soldiers had beaten him to death, before carrying his bludgeoned body to a wooden pole in front of the palace gates and stringing him up as a warning to other criminals. Even by staying away from the main courtyard, it had been impossible to avoid him: the smell, sweet and rancid, permeated the palace. I wondered how long they would leave him there, beckoning the crows and wild dogs to ruin him completely.

When I refused to go and look at the broken boy, Polyn laughed and said I was too squeamish. But I could not stand to see another person dead. My parents died within hours of each other, years ago. I was five years old, Ani was almost seven, Eteo nearly nine and Polyn ten. And the only thing which comforts me, when I think back to that whole terrible day, has been the certainty that my parents loved one another in a way that most couples do not. If one of them had to die, it was better that they both did, because neither of them could have survived without the other.

No woman has ever gazed at her husband with the urgency that filled my mother's face whenever she looked at my father. When he left a room, even if it was just for a brief time, her whole body slumped, as though her soul went with him and she could do nothing but sit and wait until he returned. It might have been pitiful, had he not loved with equal fervour. If he had to go somewhere without her, you would see him almost sprinting across the courtyards on his return, just to get back to her a moment sooner. When the aristoi run in their foot-race today, each competing for the glory of victory over his peers, not one of them will have such focus in his eyes as my father, hastening across the palace to my mother. She used to wait for him like a dog, her head lifting every time she heard footsteps that might be him, coming home. This never struck me as odd, because it was all I knew. If I thought about it at all, I just believed everyone's parents were like this: anxious when they were not together. As long as my mother could hear us playing, she was content. The sound of her children was sufficient for her to know we were safe. But with my father it was different: she needed to see him, to touch him, as though only then could she persuade herself that he truly existed.

So when she died, the idea that he might live without her was unthinkable. His heart broke on the spot, so people used to say, and he simply gave up and died himself. As a child, this seemed to me not only plausible, but necessary. But now I can no longer resist the knowledge that people rarely die of broken hearts, except in the stories poets sing.

I have only the most fractured memories of the day they died: the rest I know from my siblings. My parents were buried over by the city walls, a little way down the hill from the palace. I remember the funeral because so many people were crying and tearing their clothes. I didn't understand why my uncle was weeping and holding Haem so tightly in his arms. My brothers had tried to explain to me that our parents were gone and would never come back, but I still thought they would walk into our rooms at any moment, holding each other and laughing. Once it became clear that no one thought this except me, not even Ani, I indulged in this belief only when I was alone in bed. I cried when my uncle snapped at me that they were dead forever, and then Ani would cry too, because she hated to see me cry and we both hated to hear what he said. So on my own, in my head, in the darkness, I would imagine their return: how we would hear two sets of sandals clipping the stones in the courtyard, how the splashing water would be interrupted when my father ran his hands through it and splashed it into his face to cool off. How they would block the light for an instant when they stood in my doorway and smiled at me. I knew exactly how it would be, but it never happened.

I still remember the smell from the temple grounds where offerings were made after the funeral: the pungent incense – pricking my eyes with its sweet, suffocating smoke – which the priests burned in their honour. There were gleaming white calves with fillets tied around their heads which were sacrificed to the shades. Their small clean hooves clattered against the cobbled ground as the blade cut through their undefended throats. I remember that too.

But so much is lost to me. I have always felt that if I had been even a little bit older, I would have known more. No one ever spoke about my mother after she died. Perhaps they believed that we would forget about her if no one mentioned her. In fact, the opposite has happened. She seems more real to me now than ever, as though I could walk through the door into her bedroom and see her sitting up with pillows all around her, patting them for me to spring up and kiss her, even though I would now be taller than her. I still wake up sometimes, thinking I can hear her shutting the door as quietly as she can, having checked I am safely asleep.

There is one more memory I have from that day, one I am certain of. One I cannot forget. My mother was carried across the palace on a stretcher by two men, one much taller than the other. They had placed a sheet over her, as a sign of respect. But as they hurried through the square, the disparity in their heights meant that my mother was tilting downwards. The cloth shifted as they shuffled along, and the one at the front could not see: he was facing the wrong way. So he didn't notice when the sheet uncovered part of her face.

Ani and I were standing in the colonnade, trying to understand what was happening: so many people – slaves, guards, our uncle, Sophon – had been rushing in and out of our mother's room. We knew something was wrong, but could not imagine something so terrible. And even when we saw the stretcher, we didn't think it could be her, because why would our mother be lying on a litter with her face covered? That wasn't how she behaved at all. Even when I saw what I now know must have been her face, I didn't realize it was our mother because it was not her: the person I saw was purple and puffy and broken, barely a person at all. Then our father walked out into the courtyard and caught sight of her. The sound he made – a wordless howl of anguish – is one I could still hear now, if I allowed myself to do so. He ran over and flung himself onto the stretcher, crashing with her down to the ground. Within moments, my uncle had intervened and my father was lifted away from her.

I have tried and tried to remember what happened next, but I cannot. Nonetheless, I am as certain as I can be that this moment was the last time I saw my father. And how am I supposed to compose my own history without including this part of my story? I am the daughter of a king and queen, the sister of two kings, but I will remain unmarried and will grow old alone. What Theban family would ally themselves with one as cursed as mine, unless real power and wealth was at stake?

Perhaps I should leave here one day, and settle in another city, where the curse is not common knowledge.

But I doubt if even Eteo would agree to his sister wandering Hellas like a vagabond. My parents were disgraced and died in so short a time. I was the same child from one year to the next (or the changes I underwent were minor: a little taller, my hair a little longer), yet I metamorphosed from princess to burden in the cessation of a heartbeat. No wonder the philosophers say that a river is always in flux, never staying the same. So a person cannot step into the same water twice.

10

The messenger looked at the queen and then back at the slave woman who had accompanied him through the palace. But the woman said nothing, her eyes fixed on the ground in front of her feet. He turned towards the queen once again.

'I worry I may not have made myself clear, highness,' he said. 'I was trying to convey to you that the king of Thebes is dead.'

'You made yourself perfectly clear,' she said. 'It's hard to imagine you could have been any clearer. Laius is dead. I understand. My question, which you perhaps misheard in your quest for clarity, was: what happens now?'

'What happens now?' The messenger was flummoxed. 'Well, the king's body will be brought back to the palace, I should think, and then –'

'I'm sorry.' Jocasta flashed him a gleaming smile. 'You seem to be struggling to comprehend what I'm saying. What I mean is, am I in charge now?'

'Er . . . yes, I would imagine so,' said the messenger, trying to dispel doubt from his voice. 'Yes.'

'Thank you,' she said. 'My husband had financial advisers, didn't he? And political ones? Where are they? They didn't all die too, I suppose?' Her voice was almost wistful, and the messenger looked more perplexed than ever.

'No, I don't think so,' he said. 'If they were the men who journeyed with their king, they are now accompanying him back to the city. He travels in state, of course.'

'It can't make the slightest difference to him now, whether he travels in state or not,' Jocasta said. 'You could tie him facedown to the back of a mule for all he'd know about it.'

'Madam?'

'Unless he isn't dead at all? Are you sure he's dead?'

'Madam, I regret to say that I am completely sure. He was stabbed by one of the Sphinx, and then . . .' His voice tailed off as he saw that Jocasta was only half-listening.

'The Sphinx?' she said. 'I can never quite remember who they are.'

'Why, they're . . .'

'No, don't tell me,' she said. 'I have enough to worry about without thinking about things that can't be changed and don't affect me. You will stay here, at the palace, I hope. Put him up in the guards' barracks,' she said to the slave woman. 'And when the late king's advisers arrive, which will be tomorrow? The next day? We'll have to see how eager they are to reach me, won't we? When they arrive, you will please show them to me in . . .' She turned to the servant again, 'Which of those rooms in the second courtyard would be the right size? I'm sorry, I don't know your name.'

'Phylla,' said the woman.

'Which room did the king use for his most important meetings? One of the big ones in the second courtyard?'

'Yes, madam. The blue room, on the east side.'

'You will show them to the blue room when they arrive,

please. Then you will fetch this gentleman and bring him to find me in the private courtyard. He will escort me to them. Understand that I will accept no excuses if you fail to do precisely as I have asked.' The girl nodded. Teresa could not punish her for obeying explicit instructions from her mistress. Jocasta turned back to the messenger.

'You will be my ally in that meeting, do you understand?'

'Yes, madam,' said the messenger, confusion still playing across his face.

'For every day that they are behind you,' Jocasta continued, 'I will give you a plain gold ring.'

The messenger blushed, greed suffusing his cheeks along with the colour. 'Thank you, madam.'

'Do you know why?' she said, and he shook his head. He was not confident about anything the queen was saying. 'Because the longer they take, the more it proves that you were trying to reach me as soon as you could. The more it proves that you were hurrying here to make me the ruler of this city, while they dawdled behind you, excusing their indifference to me behind their proper respect for the dead.'

The messenger thought for a moment, and decided it would be better for him, at least economically, if he agreed. 'Yes, madam,' he said.

Jocasta turned to walk away to her room. She seemed taller than usual, Phylla thought, when she lifted her gaze from the ground. Perhaps her strange haircut had added to her height, with spikes of hair sticking up at every angle.

'Excuse me,' the messenger called after her. 'Please

don't go. I didn't introduce myself, madam. And I have only told you half of the story.'

Jocasta slumped a little. This was the longest time she had spent speaking to a man other than her brother since – she couldn't remember. Oran? But she didn't like to think of him. She was growing tired and fretful, and wished she could scratch at her forearms with her nails, because they were beginning to itch intolerably. Nonetheless she turned back to face the stranger and raised her eyebrows.

'In your tongue, my name is Oedipus, ma'am,' he said, and she looked at him properly for the first time. He was young, this boy, with beautiful long dark hair and glinting brown eyes. His mouth was set in a serious line, but she couldn't shake the thought that he normally laughed a great deal. He was tall and slender, and though his clothes were torn, his skin was golden from the sun, rather than brown from the dust. He reminded her of ripe apricots.

'Have you worked for my husband for long?' she asked.

'I don't work for your husband at all,' he said. 'I am not from Thebes, madam. I come from another city.'

Phylla gave a small choke, and covered her face with loose fabric from the top of her tunic.

'Don't be ridiculous,' said Jocasta, brandishing her arms about her. 'There hasn't been an outbreak in over twenty years, for hundreds of stades in any direction. Not one. And anyone can see this man isn't sick. Look at him.'

Phylla did as she was asked, but she didn't remove the cloth from her mouth. 'Leave then,' Jocasta shouted. 'If you're so afraid. I will direct him to the barracks myself. Or perhaps I will invite him to stay in our guest quarters.' Phylla scurried away.

'Come and sit down, sir,' Jocasta said, gesturing to a bench. She sat beside him, and smoothed her hair with an anxious hand. She found herself suddenly wishing she hadn't cut it all off two days earlier. 'I'm sorry,' she said. 'I just assumed you were one of Laius's boys. You look like them.'

'No, I'm sorry,' Oedipus replied. 'I should have made myself clearer from the outset. I came across your husband and his men in the mountains. They were pegged back by the Sphinx – is that what you call them?'

'I think so,' she said. 'I've never really known very much about the land outside the city. Just enough not to believe that every other city in Hellas is afflicted by the Reckoning, except ours.' She jerked her head in the direction the maid had left. 'They think Thebes is special. Blessed. They don't understand that it is the opposite.'

'Have you lived here all your life?' Oedipus asked, gesturing around them.

'In Thebes? Yes. In the palace? No. I've been here for almost seventeen years. But I lived on the other side of the city before that. My father was a trader so I was brought up not to fear the Outlying.'

'So you've never been to the mountains? That's a shame. They're beautiful in the summer.'

'Are they?' It had never occurred to Jocasta that the mountains were beautiful at any time. As a child, she had thought of them as an impassable green wall behind the city. As an adult, she had seen them as her husband's territory. She had never thought of them as an actual place, with characteristics of their own.

'Where do you come from?' she asked.

'Corinth,' he said. She looked blank. 'A trading city on the other side of the mountains.'

'Is that right? What do you trade?'

'All sorts of things. Minerals, metals, oil, grain: whatever you need. We trade with everyone. We're well located, on the isthmus.'

She nodded, but he could see she didn't know what he was talking about. 'We're on the sea,' he explained. 'So everyone comes to us.'

'And you're a trader?' she asked.

'Not exactly.' He smiled at her. 'My father is an important man. He wanted me to stay in Corinth and learn the trade. But I wanted to see something of Hellas first. And the mountains are less dangerous at the start of the year, so they say, so I decided to try my luck. My parents know I can take care of myself.'

'And they are right, because here you are,' Jocasta said. It took a moment before she remembered that he had probably been about to tell her of her husband's death when they got sidetracked, talking about the mountains and distant trading posts. She wondered if he had just realized the same thing, for his golden confidence dimmed slightly, while he tried to find his next words.

'You found my husband and his men in the mountains?' she reminded him.

'Yes, they were in a bad way,' he said. 'They were pinned into a dead end. The mountain is full of them, you have to learn where they are. I don't know how they got themselves into such a position. His scouts should be hanged, if any of them survived.'

'You're not very forgiving,' Jocasta said.

'No.' He shrugged, unapologetic. 'They led your husband into a trap. They were either incompetent or treacherous. There is no excuse for either.'

'But you tried to help?'

'I think I did a bit better than that.' He smiled again, the sudden anger of a moment ago disappearing. 'The Sphinx are very much less terrifying than people make them out to be, in their stories. They aren't a mythical fighting force, they're just a gang of mountain men. They know the paths and secret routes through the peaks better than anyone alive. But they aren't an army; they have no discipline. If one of them is hurt, the others panic, or they get angry. Either way, it makes them weaker. People say they are numberless, but I doubt they are more than forty altogether. They seem to come at you from all sides, but that's just because they know shortcuts that are hidden from the ordinary traveller. Of course they do – they have been born and raised on the mountains, they are practically goats.'

'And how do you know the mountains so well?' Jocasta asked. 'I thought this was your first trip to Thebes.'

'I don't know the mountains all that well, but there are other mountains nearer Corinth which are not so different, and which are home to similar men. So I have the good sense to move carefully on unfamiliar terrain. And I don't travel with a huge retinue, making a racket and drawing their attention. Your husband – forgive me, madam – was practically begging to be attacked by brigands.' She waved his apology away. 'Besides,' he admitted, 'I had something more important than knowledge on my side. I had luck.'

'What do you mean?'

'I came up behind the Sphinx, completely by accident. Their attention was focused entirely on your king. No one was keeping watch behind them, because they were embroiled in a skirmish ahead. Your husband's men outnumbered them, even though they weren't well prepared for a fight. So the mountain men had their hands full, fighting. It was easy to pick a few of them off, one by one.'

'But people say the Sphinx can't be killed,' she said.

'People say all kinds of nonsense,' he replied. 'I told you, they're just men.'

'So if you killed the Sphinx, what happened to my husband?'

He coloured. 'That is harder to explain, madam.'

'Perhaps you might try,' she said.

'It was an accident,' he replied. 'Your husband was distracted by the carnage around him. He saw one man after another fall. And he was injured himself. He had taken a knife wound to the right shoulder. You can't imagine how that must feel. His whole arm would have gone numb.'

'You know a lot, for someone so young,' she said.

'My city is not as civilized as yours, Basileia.'

'Don't call me that,' she snapped. 'And my city is a great deal less civilized than it appears to you.'

'I'm sorry,' he said. 'But I'm afraid your husband was disorientated. He was slashing at anyone who came near him with a knife. The sweat was pouring into his eyes; I doubt he could see very much.'

'So what happened?' she asked again.

'I approached him to tell him that the threat was over, that many of the mountain men lay dead, and the rest had run away. He lashed out with his knife.' The boy raised his left hand and she saw a long cut down the leather guard he wore on his forearm, the bare skin beneath it flaming red. 'Lucky I move faster than your husband, or I'd be bleeding out in the mountains instead of talking to you now.'

'He tried to kill you.'

'Yes.'

'So you killed him.'

'Not intentionally,' Oedipus said. 'I shouted at him to stop, but he wasn't listening. He backed away from me to prepare for a second attack. And he lost his footing.'

'He fell?'

'Not very far, but he landed horribly. Like I said, he couldn't see. He broke his neck – it would have been very quick,' he finished.

'And so you came here to tell me that you are responsible for my husband's death?' Jocasta asked.

'In a manner of speaking,' he said. 'I saw his men collect his body and decide to bear him home. That's how I found out he was the king: I was watching them from the rocks above. If he'd stayed with the main party, he would still be alive, Basileia, I swear it.'

'I said not to call me that,' she said. 'Did you not think it was a risk? Coming here to a strange city to tell me you'd killed the king? What if I decided to have you executed?'

'From what I overheard, madam, your husband's men didn't seem to think you would be unduly saddened by his death. They seemed to think you could be removed from the palace quite easily.'

She nodded. She had never been popular with her husband's men. Of course they would want to replace her.

'And I suppose I took a chance. Your husband deserved to die, madam. He was foolish and vain. He should have been more careful and he should have hired better scouts, and treated the mountains with more respect. But I couldn't see that you had done anything wrong. I thought I would ride ahead of them and tell you what had happened. So you could prepare yourself.'

'That was kind,' she said. She reached over and touched his arm.

'And then, when I told you he was dead, you said I was your ally.'

'I thought you were one of his boys,' she said again.

'It doesn't matter,' he said. 'Just, when you said it, I decided it was true.'

'My hair doesn't normally look like this,' Jocasta said, wishing she had not hacked it off with a blunt blade two days earlier.

'I don't imagine it does,' he replied. 'It suits you, though.'

11

The flutes were playing a loud, clear song, regal and imperative. They had rehearsed for many days to prepare for the coronation. There was no longer any hope of ignoring it: I opened my door and almost stumbled over my sister, who had found a way to wear yellow which did not make her appear sallow. Her dress was paler than crocus, closer to the shade of ripening lemons. Only the sash was the crocus colour of my own dress, and I wondered how she had managed to change it. Her hair was woven into plaits which spiralled around her head, and she had rubbed perfumed oil on her limbs so they shone white, like an alabaster statue. She looked me up and down.

'That's a pretty dress,' she said. 'You look lovely, Isy. You'll catch plenty of eyes, especially if you stand up and stop slouching.' She noticed one of my uncle's guards walking through the courtyard behind her. 'Not that you would want to,' she added, her eyes following him. 'Your only desire is to be an ornament to your brothers and the royal house.' And as she spoke, she winked at me. My uncle would be too busy today to listen to tales from an eavesdropping guard.

I put my arm through hers, and we walked through into the second courtyard, which was full of our brothers' many advisers and associates, all scurrying around trying to look important as they went about the palace. There was an air of anxiety about these men each summer, when the kingship changed hands. Half of them worried they would lose whatever influence they had cultivated under Eteo when Polyn took over. The other half were hoping that was true, and that they might be able to grease their own way into a position of greater authority. It was this dynamic of constant unease which appealed to my uncle: if the king was permanent, Creon was sure the administrators would grow lazy and complacent.

We walked across to the gates on the far side of the square. The main courtyard was a clamour of noise and colour: every citizen of Thebes must have been there. The guards at the gates smiled and stood aside for us to pass. They held silver-tipped spears, having exchanged their usual weapons for ceremonial ones in honour of the occasion. A thick cloud of perfume surrounded us: it was being poured in offerings around the square. Thebes liked to honour all the gods on coronation day, so none would ever feel slighted and turn their immortal wrath against the city.

Ani and I were just in time. The doors to the throne room – a small, gilded corner of the public square, which was kept locked except for this day each year – had been opened. The room shone like a statue of Zeus himself, as the sun caught its chryselephantine adornment. My brothers, both sweating in their ceremonial robes – bright red and trimmed with so much golden embroidery that they were stiff, like wooden mannequins – were waiting for us. My uncle and Haem, similarly attired though with a little less pomp, were already seated to the right of the throne. Ani and I climbed the steps and took our seats on the opposite side of the altar which was placed directly before and below the throne. Finally, the flutes reached their high note, and were silenced. The ceremony could begin.

Muttering priests surrounded us: my uncle loved a religious ceremony. It was not enough to have a feast and a ceremonial handing-over of the crown. He wanted vows to Zeus and Apollo, followed by multiple sacrifices and offerings of wine. He enjoyed sitting in the sweltering heat hearing the prayers and nodding his solemn promises to guide the new king as he had guided the old one. Ani, I could see, was focusing most of her attention on Haem, who was studiously trying not to look at her. He must be hoping his father was unaware of their increasing closeness, though that seemed unlikely. My uncle might have been pious, but he wasn't blind.

I was only half-listening to the priests. We had done this ten times before: we knew when we had to bow down before the majesty of Zeus and when we could stretch ourselves back up. We could have completed this ceremony while half-asleep, which was fortunate, given the heat. I was grateful to be in a simple linen dress – its belt kept loose to allow a little air onto my damp skin – rather than the formal garb the men were wearing.

Finally, the droning ended, and the priest reached his right hand into the pocket of his white robes. He was nearly finished. The crowd looked on, bored now of the excessive religiosity. They wanted more music, they wanted the meat to start cooking and the wine to start flowing, not just for the gods but for them too. And most of all, they wanted the games to begin. Although the chariot-races, the sprint and the wrestling were sacred to the gods, there would be many men who wanted to place bets on the outcome, discreetly enough to avoid the attention of Creon and his priests. An abundance of property would change hands before the sun set this evening. Bottles of oil, terracotta figurines, weapons and jewellery: no one could be certain who would take treasures home tonight.

The priest removed his hand from his pocket and held it aloft, as an acolyte brought the calf – too docile for this noisy occasion, as though he had been drugged with the leaves the priests were always chewing – to the space in front of the throne room. Perhaps they had stunned it with a quick blow to the head before bringing it outside. They would deny it – sacrificial offerings were supposed to have their wits about them when they went to the gods – but religious men are not always honest. The priest took the calf tenderly, holding its head by the nascent horns. As he brought his hand down to its neck, the sunlight reflected off his gleaming silver blade. And then everything became impossibly loud, as though every word and shuffling footstep were happening all at once, next to my ears.

Then my sister was holding me around the wrist, squeezing it tightly. Her nails jabbed into my arm and brought me out of the noise and back into my skin.

'We'll get you out of the sun in a moment, Isy. These endless prayers and offerings. It's too much, almost blasphemous,' she said.

I wanted to tell her that the heat wasn't what was making sweat pour down my back, nor the dizziness threatening to knock me to the ground. It was the knife, and all the blood. Somewhere in this huge gathering was the man who had stabbed me. I could feel his eyes on the priest, assessing the efficiency of his blade, and the elegance with which he drew it across the neck of the beast, whose huge eyes gave no sign of the spurting horror beneath them, though his legs kicked frantically at the ground. Out there in the crowd was a man who had looked at me in the same way as we looked at the dying calf. A sacrifice for a greater good.

That was why I was shivering in bright sun.

The ceremony was finally over. Polyn had sworn to protect Thebes for the duration of the year to come, and Creon had lifted the crown from Eteo's head and placed it on Polyn's. The crowd cheered wildly, more because this was the end of the formal ceremony than because my oldest brother was more favoured than the other. The mass of people poured out into the market square, which was unrecognizable today. Every stall had been folded down flat, and wheeled into tight-packed rows by the city walls. Fresh sand had been swept into a racetrack which was marked out with round white stones. There were wooden benches on every side of the course for the spectators quick enough to reach them. Palace guards stood at either end of a raised bier with individual wooden seats placed in a neat row upon it. This was where Creon, Ani and I would be sitting. On the other side of the square, workmen had erected a temporary palaestra, where the wrestling would take place later in the day.

The aristoi were already preparing themselves in the palaestra. They had stripped naked, and were covering themselves in oil and the red dust that keeps their skin from burning in the harsh sunlight. The sprint would be the first competition today, and Eteo was running as always. The crowd was humming with excitement. The priests were still attending the remains of the sacrifice inside the palace courtyard, and spectators were taking advantage of their absence to mutter their bets. By the time the eight competitors lined up at the starting rope, people were jostling one another for the best view of the finish line.

At the crucial moment, the two slaves who held the starting rope dropped it to the ground. The youths sprang over it, and pelted down the track for one complete circuit. The dust sprayed up so high it was impossible to tell which boy was which: all of them were dark-haired from the oil which they had slicked over their bodies before wiping their hands through their curls to keep their hair out of their eyes. All were red-skinned. Only when they cornered the furthest bend and began to sprint back towards us could I see it was Eteo ahead of the others, running with all his might. He took a long, loping stride which looked almost effortless. I saw how hard he was pumping his arms: he was determined to win. There was a boy on his heels, but my brother ran so easily, it must have crushed his rivals. The second boy was frantically trying to keep up, his arms and legs splaying in every direction, as though he were frightening the birds from the crops before the harvest.

The other boys clustered behind them, running as a pack. The one at the front of their group was a friend of Polyn's, I thought. He usually ran a faster race than this: he and Eteo had been competing in the sprint since they were both children. Perhaps he was holding something in reserve for the final straight, hoping Eteo and his rival would tire each other out and he could race past them and take the crown. Eteo had done exactly that to the boy last year, and he was surely hoping to take his revenge now. But he had misjudged the race and it would cost him the victory: Eteo was extending his lead, and showing no sign of slowing down, or even struggling to maintain his pace. The boy just behind him, to his left, looked like he was about to pull back. His face was almost as red as his dust-coated limbs.

But as they turned the last corner, the boy in second place suddenly tripped and fell forward, his arms tangling themselves in Eteo's legs for just long enough to knock my brother off balance. Eteo was too graceful an athlete to fall, but he lost momentum as he was forced to extend his arms to stay on his feet.

'I thought we'd have to wait for the chariot-race tosee this sort of thing,' shouted one man, laughing. The charioteers often fell from their cars when their horses clattered into one another on the tight bend of the racetrack.

Eteo saw his chance was gone, as the loss of speed had allowed his rival to spurt past on his way to claim the victory. So confident was the boy of his win that he took an almost comical zigzag route to the finish line, laughing and raising cheers from the spectators. Meanwhile, Eteo stopped to offer his comrade a hand up. The crowd cheered this kindness almost as loudly as they cheered the winner. The royal prince would cross the finish line in last place, but his honour would be intact. My clever, kind brother.

The boy couldn't lift himself at first: Eteo's arm was too slippery with oil for him to get a good grip. Seeing him struggle, my brother reached out two hands and heaved the boy upright. But when the boy stood, his left leg buckled immediately. He grabbed at it, crying out in pain. Mingling with the orange sand beneath his feet and the red dust on his body was the unmistakeable crimson of blood, dripping from the boy's foot onto the sand beneath him. Eteo reached down and picked up a sharp iron spike, which must have been hidden beneath the surface of the sand. All the boys ran barefoot, so whoever placed it there knew he would injure one of them.

A gasp went up from the spectators, followed by a groan when my uncle declared that the race result would not stand. No one would receive the crown of olive leaves. The winner began to protest, but seeing the anger of the crowd as their bets were nulled, he sensibly decided to accept things without making more fuss. The slaves who had set up the track were summoned before my uncle, who ordered them to stand in a line, remove their shoes and walk across every finger-width of the course.

The limping boy was helped off the course by Eteo, and Creon signalled to the charioteers that they would compete as soon as the course had been checked. The atmosphere improved as the spectators realized their pleasure was merely postponed rather than cancelled. The charioteers checked their horses' hooves, and readied themselves to race, each one tying himself to his car with leather straps. But it was hard to concentrate on their preparations when the injured boy was trying to clean his wounded foot, and bind it closed. The gash was huge, right across the sole, so it would tear open again whenever he took a step. Eteo summoned one of his guards and sent him away: a short time later he returned with a stick which the boy could use as a crutch. But the bandages still reddened as the day wore on.

The crowd were so involved in their next series of bets that they had already lost interest in the injury and how it might have occurred. Had one of the boys laid a trap for his rivals? Was it an attempt to hurt Eteo? Everyone knew he was quick: he was likely to be at the front of the sprinting group. I tried to dismiss the thought of sabotage.

But what else could it have been? The slaves found four more sharpened iron spikes wedged into the sand at different points on the course. It was pure luck that none of the other boys had been injured. Or perhaps the boy who won the race had known which parts of the track to avoid. Perhaps they had all known.

12

Jocasta had never enjoyed being married to her husband more than at his funeral. She loved everything about it. She ordered a dress to be made in a dark reddish-purple – the most expensive dye she could have chosen – knowing that if anyone suggested it showed insufficient respect for the dead, she could simply remind them that she married Laius wearing crimson. There was no more fitting tribute than wearing a more flattering shade of the same colour at his funeral. She had her hair neatened into a simple style which made her look younger. She had ribbons plaited into it, so it appeared more ornate for the funeral. And – once the slaves had polished it to its former shine – she placed her wedding diadem on top, lest anyone forget who she was.

The prettiness of her dress and hair were only a small part of her delight, however. She radiated pleasure at having seen off her husband's friends and their attempt to depose her. Not realizing that Oedipus had ridden ahead and told her everything, the men made no hurry in returning to Thebes. They were three full days behind Oedipus and even – this was their crucial mistake – one day behind Laius's guards. The commander of the guard was happy to swear loyalty to Jocasta, as were his men. She bribed them all with nuggets of silver – mined in the Outlying many years ago – which she had found in one of the store-rooms next to the treasury, opposite the formal reception rooms in the second courtyard. Perhaps she had known before that it was there, and had simply forgotten. She couldn't now remember. So much from the past seventeen years had lost its separateness, as though it had been written on papyrus which had suddenly rolled itself back up so individual parts of the text were lost within the whole. But the presence of Oedipus, so determined to help her fight off the threats he had overheard in the mountains, focused her attention on matters of importance.

So – in the three days between Oedipus's arrival and the return of her husband's body – she hunted around in the state rooms of the royal courtyard, most of which she had never previously entered. She didn't wait for Teresa to tell her what to do, and she didn't wait for word to come from the Oracle. For the first time in as long as she could remember, she gave very little thought to what the Oracle advised at all. After all, it hadn't forewarned her about Laius dying, or Oedipus arriving. Perhaps it was less powerful than she had thought.

In Laius's bedroom, she found a small wooden box filled with keys, all in their own divided spaces. These turned out to be everything she needed to open the treasury and a host of other rooms which had been hitherto forbidden to her. Had she really lived in such a small part of the palace for so long, trotting between her bedroom and the shrine and occasionally the kitchens? It seemed ludicrous to her that the keys had been here all along – presumably Laius had always left them behind – and she had never gone looking for them. But then, what would she have done with them before the king died? Teresa would never have let her walk into Laius's rooms while he was alive. But the announcement of the king's death (so welcome to his wife) had devastated his housekeeper. Teresa withdrew to her quarters for two days when Phylla gave her the news. Had she known that the messenger had come from abroad, and was now staying with the queen under Hellene rules of guest-friendship, Teresa might have postponed her grieving. It was one thing to offer food and a warm bed to a stranger for a few nights, as the gods demanded, but it was another thing to allow him to stay in the family courtyard, in a room which had only ever been occupied by the queen's brother for a few days each year. But Phylla never thought to mention what she perceived as these less important details, and by the time Teresa reappeared in the palace, her previously unassailable position was too damaged to be repaired. The stranger had wormed his way into the queen's trust.

Jocasta smiled to herself as her husband's corpse – tightly wrapped in white linen as was respectful – was carried out through the three courtyards of the palace, in a long, slow procession. As she walked at the head of the procession – head bowed appropriately, crown glinting in the dawn light – she remembered the insufferable smugness of his closest friends and advisers, each one arriving back in Thebes determined that he was the man to replace Laius as king. Perhaps if they had all been less ambitious, and had thrashed out a compromise before they returned, they would have been more dangerous. But much as they disliked the queen, none of them wanted to see his rivals promoted. And they didn't have the discipline to set aside personal gain for the good of their factions.

She had welcomed them coolly when they arrived, then instructed Laius's guards to carry his body into the palace where it would lie in state for one day, not from a lack of respect but because the delay in bringing him back to the city meant that he now needed to be buried as soon as possible. She had immediately assumed a position of religious authority: who was responsible for the delay, if not these men who had made such slow progress to the city? The gods would not forgive Thebes if the king lay unburied for days on end. He must go beneath the earth, and offerings must be poured. While they dallied along the lower reaches of the mountains, her husband's shade was stranded on the banks of the River Lethe, unable to pay Charon to carry him across. The men shuffled awkwardly, eyes fixed anywhere but on their queen. They could make no defence against the charge of religious impropriety.

And then Jocasta told them to leave. Surrounded by the armed guard, who had appeared in full ceremonial dress to pay their respects to her late husband, the queen was not the woman that they had spoken of so scornfully over her husband's still-warm body. She thought she might interview one or two of them in a few days, and see if they could be civil. She might need advisers herself, after all.

Throughout all this, the boy Oedipus remained with her. She gave him, as she had promised, three small gold rings for his arrival three days before her husband's men. But although Oedipus had his reward, he seemed in no hurry to leave. In fact, he appeared to relish his new surroundings. His eyes gleamed when Jocasta found the keys to her husband's treasury, filled with serried ranks of gold and silver, bronze and jewels, tapestries and perfumed oils. Oedipus offered to help her make sense of what she owned and what she needed. He only left her to go to the market outside, from which he returned a short while later, carrying a fine leather string, which had been dyed a vivid magenta. He fed it through the treasury keys – one for the door to the main room, one for the door to the treasury itself – tied it into a knot, then stood behind her to place it carefully over her shorn head.

'So no one can take them off you,' he explained, his warm breath raising the hairs on her neck as he sounded the first word. Jocasta wondered when anyone had last thought about what she wanted, or worried about her safety.

Teresa had always been quick to act as an intermediary for her, with the Oracle. But now that Jocasta thought about it, the Oracle had rarely made her feel better about anything. That was not what it was for, of course. It spoke the truth and saw the future. But she couldn't shake the sense that it had been better at seeing her future when it was unchanging – as it had been for so many years – than recently. Her mind returned to its suspicions: if the Oracle was all-knowing, it should really have predicted her dramatic change in circumstances. And of course she knew that oracles were riddlers, only to be understood by those versed in their opacity, like the priests, or Teresa. But it had said nothing about the king's death, not even when

Jocasta thought back to its recent utterances with the clarity of hindsight. She could scarcely remember why she had wanted the shrine to be built. Or had it been Teresa's idea?

It was built soon after the death of her baby; that she could remember. Her poor dead son was still now beautiful in her imagination. She had watched him grow up in her mind: heard his first words, seen his first tumbling steps. She had taught him to count and draw, she had watched him go to his tutor in the early mornings and come home each afternoon. It had become harder to imagine his voice cracking into adulthood, as it surely would have done last year. But she had kept him alive nonetheless in this dual existence – a dead baby she had never set eyes on, a living son she saw every day.

Teresa had realized that Jocasta was spending a great deal of time alone, with her child. She had proposed the shrine as what? An alternative to a grave marker? Jocasta had asked Teresa, in the beginning, where her child was buried, but Teresa refused to give her an answer. She lost patience with the question: babies were exposed or buried all the time, living and dead. Of course, it was more usually girls than boys who were robbed of their new lives, but that hardly mattered. Other women accepted it, and so should Jocasta. It was not regal, or reasonable, to make such an extravagant fuss about something which could not be helped or changed. Eventually, Jocasta's howls and screams had forced the truth from her: the child had never been buried. It had simply been disposed of, along with the rest of the refuse which was taken from the palace each day. There was no grave to visit. So her shrine – a miniature copy of the temple where the Oracle dwelt – was, perhaps, a peace-offering. Something Teresa proposed to give Jocasta somewhere to focus her prayers and attention.

And it had helped, at first. Designing it and building it took time, and that gave Jocasta something to think about. She could watch it grow larger, more finished with each day. Then, once it was built, she had to learn which offerings she should make, to which gods, in what order. If she could just get everything exactly right, Jocasta had thought, things might improve. Perhaps Teresa would suddenly confess to a mistake: the baby wasn't dead at all, but was being raised with a family nearby. A kind, loving family who would nurture her son until he arrived one day in the palace to reclaim his birthright. She would only find out the truth if she did everything exactly as the gods required.

But the day never came, no matter how hard she prayed, and no matter how carefully she made her offerings. She was never good enough to receive the truth she wanted to hear. Sometimes, Teresa would tell her that the Archer god was looking on her favourably, and that this was an appropriate time to embark on a new project (Teresa was always careful not to say 'pregnancy'). Jocasta refused even the suggestion with such screams and horror that no one tried to force her. In the months and years that followed her nightmare, she often felt close to losing her mind, but she retained enough of it to know she could not go through that whole horrifying process again. She could not.

Besides, she didn't want some other child, she wanted her child, the one she had already given birth to. She couldn't simply replace him with another baby. What would be the point? She would know from the start that it was an impostor. So instead of believing that the god – answering her prayers at the shrine with his cryptic messages from the Oracle – was guiding her towards something better, she felt that she was being punished and re-punished for wrongs she had never committed. Why did her child not arrive one day at the palace, having been alive all along? There were only two explanations, one of which she couldn't countenance. Which meant that the only possible reason was that she was somehow being found wanting by the same Oracle which had persuaded her husband that a son would kill him, and therefore couldn't be allowed to live. Was the Oracle punishing her? And if so, what for? But, of course, ignorance was no excuse. That was not how the Oracle judged things. She knew that, because (whatever its reasons) it had taken her child from her, without her ever being able to touch him.

'Thank you,' she said to Oedipus, as she placed the keys beneath her clothes. 'That's perfect.'

'Don't take it off,' he said. 'Even at night.'

She felt the metal burn against her skin as he spoke. 'I won't,' she said. 'Will you still be here when I get back from the funeral?' The crowds were gathering before the palace, and she knew she needed to leave.

'Of course,' he smiled. 'I'd come with you, if I didn't think it would cause a scandal.'

Jocasta felt a twinge of delight. 'You should come,' she said. 'The more mourners attend the dead king, the greater the respect we are showing him. No one could argue. And besides, I want you to.'

Oedipus shrugged, stood up, and offered her his arm. 'Madam,' he said. 'It would be my privilege.'

*

If any of Laius's friends thought it odd that his widow was now accompanied by a young man who none of them had ever seen before, they didn't dare ask any questions. Laius's guards, now Jocasta's guards, stood behind her, armed and quiet. Jocasta saw eyebrows rise, as one man looked at another, all asking the same unspoken question and receiving the same wordless reply. No one knew who he was or where he had come from. He didn't look quite like a Theban: his skin was paler, his build narrower, and his hair fairer than the majority of their citizens. Oedipus walked alongside her until they reached the burial mound, a short distance outside the city. He helped her over the uneven ground, where the path had been blistered by tree roots. And he stepped back, perfectly proper, when the moment of interment came. Jocasta stood for a moment with her head bowed, then scattered earth over the late king. The city seemed to let out a collective sigh: the king was properly buried. The gods would be satisfied that Thebes had conducted itself well.

And then she led the funeral procession back to the city gates. She continued to the marketplace outside the palace, which today had suspended business, in a gesture of mourning. Many Thebans had gathered there, preferring not to go outside the city walls, even for a funeral. Jocasta walked to the palace gates, then turned to face the crowd.

'Thebans,' she shouted. 'My husband is dead and I am now your queen.' A roar went up from the people. Jocasta could not quite judge if it was positive or negative: were they endorsing her position or calling it into question? 'I want to thank you for the support you have shown me in this difficult time,' she continued. 'My husband's funeral games will be held in the main courtyard in one hour. You are all invited to attend.' There was another shout, this one louder and more certain than the first. Funeral games were a worthy mark of respect.

Jocasta turned to Oedipus, who escorted her through the gates. 'That was well done,' he murmured.

'Thank you,' she replied. 'You have to give the people something, that's what Laius used to say whenever he held a party.'

'He had to be right about something,' said Oedipus.

Jocasta squeezed his arm. 'Shh,' she said. 'I can't be seen laughing. Not today.'

'Forgive me,' he said. 'Let me tell your housekeeper you've just invited three hundred people into the palace.'

Jocasta looked ahead of them, and shook her head. 'It's already done.' She pointed to a boy who was scuttling towards the kitchens as fast as his short, dirty legs would go. 'He's the kitchen boy and her little spy,' she said. 'She'll hate to open the wine jars again, but she won't complain. She can't. It's for the late king, after all. And Teresa was,' Jocasta paused as she searched for the right word, 'devoted to him.'

As the evening sky gave up its last trace of red, Jocasta thought that the games had been a great success: most people were drifting away now the wine had run low, and they were leaving without any doubt that she was now the regent of this city. She had felt Oedipus's eyes upon her as she spoke to one person after another. She had never spoken so many words in a single day. But, for the first time she could remember, she was not afraid of anything. She simply did what she needed to do: shook hands, squeezed elbows, patted shoulders, accepted condolences. Most people, it transpired, thought she had cut her hair in a moment of profound grief for her late husband. They were moved by her sacrifice, and she saw it made her queenly in their eyes.

After the games had finished, and the shadows were lengthening across the courtyard, she looked over the square to see her brother approaching – tall, with his dark hair receding slightly, though he was not yet old – accompanied by a small, pretty girl who reminded her of a fearful mouse. Her small hands clutched at a little leather purse, like a tiny creature's paws might curl round a nut. This must be the girl he had mentioned; Jocasta searched her memory for the name – Euly? Euny? She walked towards her brother, turning a smile on the girl.

'Creon,' she said. 'Thank you for coming. And how nice to meet you,' she added. The mouse-like girl must have tried to say something, but all Jocasta heard was a squeak.

'This is Eurydice,' said Creon, with an expression that Jocasta could not place for a moment, before realizing it was shyness.

So she took the arm of her brother's friend, and said, 'Tell me all about yourself. Let's go and find you some wine: I know exactly which servant has the best grapes, and you deserve something special. If my brother likes you, you must be wonderful.'

She only half-heard the girl demur and then go on to talk about how she and Creon had first met when he had admired the stole she was embroidering as she sat with friends in the afternoon sun – the stole she was wearing this very day – and asked how she could make such tiny, neat stitches. As she nodded and smiled at the girl's prattling, Jocasta continued to bestow a charm she had forgotten she ever possessed on every courtier of her husband's she met. Yet all the while, she found herself looking around for Oedipus, always making sure he hadn't left.

As the palace slaves encouraged the last guests out of the gate, she felt his eyes upon her. He was leaning against the courtyard wall, almost invisible in the darkening twilight. She turned towards him and he peeled himself away from the stone, straightening up and smiling at her.

'You did well,' he said. 'Wonderfully well.'

She couldn't imagine why she was so pleased to have his approval. She had not wanted anyone's approval but the Oracle's in as long as she could remember. 'Thank you,' she said. 'Maybe it will all be alright now.'

'It'll be much better than that,' he said. 'It'll be perfect. Do you think they realized you were considering them for a position?' He jerked his head at the last few stragglers, a group of men who had worked for her husband.

'Was I?' she asked.

'Of course. You've placated everyone for now. But you don't want them plotting against you in the future, do you? You've decided you'll have to marry one of them. He'll owe his position to you, so he'll be impossibly grateful and will likely shower you with all kinds of gifts.'

'I don't need gifts,' she snapped. 'I have the keys to the city treasury around my neck. Now my late husband isn't around to spend it all on wine and horses and foolish hunting trips, I'm hardly short of resources.'

'It would still be better to ally yourself with someone, though, don't you think? Otherwise they will all keep vying with one another for your attention. It's inevitable. And it's bound to cause problems sooner or later.'

Jocasta felt her shoulders droop at his words. She wanted to tell him he was wrong, but she knew he wasn't. The men were all very loyal and sympathetic to her today, but they hadn't intended to be. They had simply been outmanoeuvred by her. By her and by Oedipus, and his quick journey from the mountains. Once the dust had settled over her husband's grave, they would soon begin plotting again. But she had already spent seventeen years married to a man she didn't love, who did not love her. Surely she could spend a little while without the exhausting burden of a husband?

'I should issue a notice that I don't intend to remarry,' she said. She wondered how long she could get away with. 'For at least a year?'

'Good idea,' said Oedipus. 'That will give them something to aim for.'

'You aren't at all sympathetic,' she complained. 'You can see I don't want to marry another old man and it's not very kind of you to laugh about it.'

'But I can afford to laugh,' he said. 'Because I know you aren't really going to marry any of them.'

'You just said—'

'That you should remarry. Yes.'

'Well, there you are then.'

'I didn't say you should marry one of them.'

'You said they'd fight if I didn't. They'll destabilize the city.'

'They'd back off if they saw that none of them had a chance.'

'And how do I achieve that?'

'By marrying me,' he replied.

'That's the most ridiculous thing I've ever heard. How old are you?'

'Old enough. Come on, Basileia. I'm much more handsome than anyone else you know.' He preened at her and she laughed, in spite of her annoyance.

'What would your parents think? You came here to help your father's business, didn't you?'

'What better help than becoming a king? Everyone wants to do business with the father of a king.'

She heard the unconscious echo of her father's reasoning for marrying her off, all those years ago.

'Your mother will be expecting you home,' she said, trying to inject a tone of finality into her voice.

'I'll go back and tell her myself,' he said. 'The mountains are safer now, you know. A brave traveller killed a few of the Sphinx. On my way back through, I'll cull the rest.'

'You want to leave me?' she asked.

'Temporarily,' he answered. 'I'll be gone for half a month. Fourteen days. That's not long at all. And when I come back, I will have my parents' blessing, and my name will be sung from every corner of your city, because I will be the man who made the mountains safe again.'

'The same mountains which took their previous king from them,' she said. She had to admit, it would be easy to persuade ordinary Theban traders that Oedipus would be the perfect king. 'When did you start thinking about this?'

'About what?' he said, his face shining with false innocence.

'When did you start dreaming up this plan?'

He reached over and kissed her on the cheek. She knew she would feel the heat of his mouth for the next fourteen days.

'It hardly matters, does it? I've thought of it, and it's so brilliant even you can't find fault with it, and you are an extremely clever woman, though hardly anyone but me has realized it,' he said. 'I'll see you in half a month, Anassa.' And with that, he sauntered off into the city, as though he had all the time in the world.

13

The races had finished, and we had all moved across the square to the palaestra, built by the palace slaves in recent days. It was not a formal structure, just a neat sand square with sides as long as the track was wide, enclosed by a simple wooden colonnade for the spectators to watch from the shade. There was a small area at the back of the ground for the wrestlers to change their clothes and rub white chalk onto their hands and feet, in readiness for the bouts. My brother Polyn was an excellent wrestler: he possessed the short, stocky build that made him virtually impossible to knock off balance. And he was wily too, which made him all but unbeatable (although Ani once asked him if his run of victories might have any connection to the fact that most of the aristoi would not wish to dishonour the past and future king by knocking him on his back. He didn't speak to her for days).

An old man had just drawn a wide-toothed rake through the sand in neat lines, the semicircles where he turned back on himself still visible at the edges of the arena, so we knew the boys could fight safely. Although the raking had occurred while we were all over by the racetrack, so I didn't know whether sharp objects had been left in the sand but had now been removed, or whether it had only been the running track that was sabotaged. I whispered this to Ani as we took our places in the stands, but she shrugged as though it didn't matter.

I wished that Sophon were present: he no longer attended the coronations. He said the first five had delighted him sufficiently for one lifetime. Ceremonies and public festivals didn't interest him. He preferred to stay in his study, protected from the brightest glare of the sun, reading his most recently acquired manuscripts. Yesterday, he received two new treatises on farming and the proper way to maintain olive groves. He has never owned an olive grove, but he said he enjoys imagining how he would tend to the trees he doesn't have.

'Which one will you read first?' I asked him that morning.

'Which one do you think, Isy?' Sophon replied. He had always done that: answered a question with another one. He says it makes me measure my thinking. I say it makes every conversation take twice as long as it needs to, but I don't mind very much.

'I think you should read this one,' I told him, holding up one of the papyri. 'It seems to be full of advice on how to keep your barn in good repair.'

His rheumy eyes brightened at the thought, though he has never owned a barn either.

'Very good advice, Isy. We would all do well to think about such things. You may read it as soon as I have finished with it.'

'Thank you,' I said. 'I'd rather read about fishing, though.'

'Fishing?' He leaned forward to make sure he had

heard me correctly. 'You want to go down to the lake and fish?'

My siblings and I used to do this when we were small: my father would take us. He loved Lake Hylica. He had grown up by the sea in Corinth, and it was the one thing he missed in Thebes, more than a hundred stades from the water. I barely remember going there with him, only flashes of silver scales and slippery white bellies, leaping and gasping on a rock by the side of the water. After he died, my siblings and I would go together each year in the first warm days of the spring. Creon never allowed us to go in the summer: he said it was not safe then, because of the Reckoning.

'I haven't been to the water since before,' I said. Sophon knew before what. First I had been injured, then I had been healing, then I had been forbidden to leave the palace, and then the ceremonial days had begun. I was desperate to get away from the city for a day, to leave behind the sand and dust and the harsh sun. I needed to walk through the grass and watch the grasshoppers leaping across my path. I wanted to see the turquoise-tipped kingfishers which nested by the water, and the frogs which would leap out of the water onto the shore, ten at a time, if you arrived at the right moment. The trees by the lake offered a broken shade even in the hottest part of the day. Most of all, I wanted to feel water on my skin.

'I think you prefer swimming like a fish to catching them.' Sophon could hear my thoughts.

'The day after the coronation,' I said. 'I'll go then. Eteo will be free to come with me once the ceremony is completed.'

'Yes,' Sophon agreed. 'I would guess that the day after he ceases to be the king is the longest day of your brother's year.'

The coronation falls almost two full moons after midsummer, but I didn't bother correcting him.

Even though Sophon would doubtless have responded to my questions about the metal traps concealed on the running track with more questions of his own, I would have preferred that to Ani's indifference. She seemed not to have realized how badly Eteo might have been hurt, and how likely it was that he had been the intended target. Only my uncle, ordering the slaves to examine the sand themselves, shared my concern. Ani would have felt differently if it had been Haem who almost had his foot sliced open, I thought. But since our cousin was a wrestler, like Polyn, she showed almost no interest in the foot-races.

Wrestling bouts were enormously popular in Thebes. Sixteen boys would fight one another in the first round, the pairs chosen by lot. The eight winners would go on to fight one another, again chosen by lot. This would continue until there was one winner, who could wear the olive-wreath crown for the day, and the title of victor for the whole year. Polyn had a pile of these crowns – the leaves dried and curled so you could barely tell which plant they came from – stacked on top of one another in his quarters. But he would always fight for another.

The referee (one of the older palace guards, who had probably trained every boy in the competition at some point) produced an earthenware jar, into which each boy dropped a small wooden block which he had previously engraved with a rough symbol or picture. The referee shook the jar once all sixteen blocks were inside it, smiling as the spectators cheered the rhythmic sound. He reached into the mouth and pulled out the first two blocks.

Like the runners before them, the boys had already covered themselves in oil and red dust, and now they took their places in the centre of the palaestra. They stood a few feet apart: wrestlers cannot be close enough to touch one another before they begin. The referee reminded them of the rules – no gouging, no kicking, no biting – before announcing the start of the bout. The boys grappled with one another but it took no time at all before the taller of the two had been tripped onto his back three times: an automatic defeat.

Polyn's bout was next, but he did not need to go as far as knocking over his opponent three times. He pushed the boy off balance then took his legs out from beneath him. Once the boy lay winded on the ground, Polyn leapt onto his back and grabbed him round the throat. The boy tapped the ground twice in quick succession: he conceded, and my brother had his three points.

I tried to stifle a yawn. It was hot and the day had already been long. But the pairings were well matched: all but the first two took time to play out. Gamblers were watching intently, trying to assess which boys were likely to be a safe bet in the next round. There was a tempting smell of onions coming from the other side of the market-place: someone had begun frying herb pastries by the running track. I turned to see if the stall-holder had a tray he would be bringing over to the spectators soon, but a sudden shout drew my attention back to the palaestra. The first quarter-final was being contested, and the boy who had just been declared the winner had done so by grabbing the wrist of his fellow combatant and forcing back his fingers, until he cried out in pain. There was a lot of hissing from the audience, who believed this to be cheating. The referee shrugged and allowed it. But the boy facing us was nursing his hand in pain: one of the fingers was sticking up at a horrible angle, clearly snapped. As his taller opponent advanced on him, the boy backed off and conceded defeat.

There was something about the naked fear in the boy's eyes, and the way the taller boy moved, which made me want to join in with the booing of the crowd. But the victor swaggered off the sand, to be punched affectionately on the arm by my brother Polyn. They were friends then, he and the cheat. My brother won his quarter-final without such tactics, and began preparing for his next opponent: re-chalking his hands and feet so he wouldn't lose his grip. The pastries smelled so good, I could feel my stomach growling. My sister elbowed me when I turned to look again at the food-seller. We were supposed to be paying attention to the games, no matter how long they went on for, or how much of a foregone conclusion they seemed to be.

Polyn and his tall friend were the finalists, and the audience cheered enthusiastically. Many of the men watching would have bet on my brother as the winner: the real surprise was that they could find anyone to wager on a different outcome. But the taller boy was talented, and perhaps he would put up a more vigorous contest than

Polyn's earlier opponents. I leaned down to ask my sister how much longer they would be.

'It's all about your stomach, Isy. Why didn't you eat this morning? You know how long these days are,' she snapped. She was right. I did know that the coronation days were long. I'd just forgotten in all the noise and fuss.

Polyn was now facing us, and his friend reached forward to begin the final bout. They wrangled for a few moments before Polyn made a grab at his opponent's leg, trying to draw him off balance. But his rival was not going to fall for anything so obvious. He skipped back out of Polyn's reach and wrenched Polyn's outstretched arm as he went. It was just enough to pull my brother forward onto his knees. But he was up again in an instant: no danger of hitting the sand with his back, and losing a crucial point. They approached each other again, and this time my brother needed to defend himself against an attack at his ankles. If you could take out an ankle, the wrestler almost always hit the ground square on. It was the easiest way to win a point. But Polyn transferred his weight to the other leg, bent forward, and head-butted the boy back. The crowd cheered.

The taller boy was losing patience now, and he circled Polyn, looking for another opportunity. He hadn't noticed how far from the centre of the ground they now were, so when Polyn ran at him and shoved him with all his might, the boy stepped back in surprise. This was a foolish tactic that would take my brother off balance and leave him vulnerable to an easy attack. The boy was already reaching forward to grab Polyn's foot and pull him over. But the referee stepped in and declared my brother the winner. The boy looked down in horror to see that his back foot had strayed outside the fighting square. It was an instant defeat.

Polyn raised his arms in victory, and his friend looked on with a weary amusement. He was the better fighter, but my brother was more cunning. Only when he turned to watch Polyn receive his olive-leaf crown did we finally see his face: the whole bout had been about showing off the king to his people, so it was always Polyn who held our attention and the prime place in the square.

'Good match,' said my brother, grabbing his rival by the arm and raising it for the applause of the crowd. Polyn was a far more gracious winner than he was loser. The tall boy nodded and smiled and took the applause of the crowd, his eyes finally taking in the spectators, where previously he had been focused only on his opponent. For the briefest moment – no longer than it takes to blink – his eyes met mine, before he turned to receive plaudits from the other side of the square.

It was all the time I needed. The man standing on the sand, next to my brother – his friend and competitor – was someone I would have recognized anywhere, as soon as I saw his eyes. I had seen them before, once in the courtyard of the palace, and many more times in my mind when I woke up with my heart racing, knowing I was in danger but unable to do anything to keep myself safe.

My brother's friend was the man who had embedded a knife in my side.

14

If there was one thing Jocasta knew how to do better than anyone, it was endure days of waiting. When Oedipus left, she found herself wishing he would return almost immediately. How clever of him, she thought, to have insinuated himself into her life so completely that after only a few days of knowing him, she missed him. And missed him in a dense physical way, as though she were nursing a profound and worsening injury.

He had been gone for little more than a day when she began to feel a faint, familiar echo of the panic which had so often overwhelmed her in the years after her child died. Her mind jumped from one unpalatable thought to another: what if he never came back? What if he was killed coming through the mountains? He had to travel through them twice, going to Corinth and coming back again. What were the chances that a man could travel through the mountains three times in less than a month, and not be killed? She couldn't begin to imagine the likelihood. Thoughts flitted around her mind like trapped birds. What if he had been lying to her? Perhaps he had no intention of coming back. Perhaps it had all been a strange, cruel joke. She wanted to believe him, but how could she, now he wasn't standing in front of her, allowing her to judge his intentions from his frank, open expression? What kind of person arrived in a city for the first time and told the queen that she would marry him? He was probably mad, she now saw. Though he hadn't seemed mad, when she was with him. He had seemed all sorts of things: impulsive, passionate, impetuous, quick-tempered, but not mad. Still, she reasoned that he must be mad: how else could she explain his behaviour? When she looked at things like this, it would almost be a blessing if he didn't return. A lucky escape, as her mother would once have said.

By the fourth day, Jocasta was beginning to make pacts with the gods. If she could make the perfect sacrifice of a pair of dappled kid goats, Oedipus would return. Then she reasoned that a paltry two goats was insufficient tribute to Apollo. So she painted the altars with the blood of white bull-calves, but still it was not enough.

On the tenth day, she calculated that he could have returned to his city and arrived back in Thebes easily by now. He had simply said half a month to allow himself the extra time at home. But he must have known she would be worrying: how could he be so cruel as to idle away time in the city where he had spent his whole life, when he knew she was here alone, waiting for him?

By the twelfth day, she knew he was dead. The journey might not have been possible in ten days, but it was more than possible in twelve. The only reason for his continuing absence must be his death. It was easier to imagine him dead than cruel. Sorrow descended and she wrapped it around herself.

On the fourteenth day, Oedipus returned exactly as he had promised. But even he – who travelled so quickly through dangerous territories, as if he were strolling along to the marketplace – couldn't keep up with the rumours which raced ahead of him: a man, this stranger, had killed the Sphinx. By the time he reached the palace gates, a small band of people clustered around him. Some of them were travellers he had picked up on the other side of the mountains. He had encouraged them to accompany him through the risky terrain, and had dazzled them with his strategy for dealing with the Sphinx, which amounted to little more (so he explained to Jocasta when they were finally alone) than moving through the mountains in total silence – without pack animals or anything which slowed them down or made any noise – and always being armed and ready to fight assailants who might appear from any direction, particularly from above. The Sphinx may have been fearsome once, but they had become – in Oedipus's opinion – lazy. Too many people made it easy for them by travelling in large groups, which left stragglers and scouts alone to be preyed upon. They announced their presence with noisy conversations or clattering hooves. Oedipus made none of those mistakes. When faced with a group who were determined not just to survive them but to attack them, the Sphinx were easily outclassed. They had already lost men on Oedipus's first trip through the mountains. And it wasn't long before he had masterminded a successful attack on the rest. Giddy with excitement and thrilled by the bloodlust, the travellers were soon telling everyone they found on the road to Thebes. They had killed the Sphinx, and it had all been the strategy of this one man, of Oedipus.

Even Jocasta, cut off from most city gossip in the palace, heard the news that the Sphinx were gone and their killer was coming to Thebes to be rewarded for his work. She knew it must be Oedipus, but she refused to believe it until she saw him. Unable to wait any longer, she walked out into the main square to receive him. When he entered through the palace gates, his clothes stained with the blood of the mountain men for a second time, she felt her breath become quick and shallow. If only all these people weren't here.

'Welcome to my city, sir,' she said, and the travellers and Thebans he had gathered along the way began to beat their hollowed hands together in applause. 'I hear we have to thank you for your remarkable bravery and cunning.'

'You don't have to thank me, your majesty.' He bowed low, smiling, enjoying the audience and the performance they allowed him to put on. 'It was the least I could do to impress the city of Thebes, as I knew I must.'

'Why would you need to impress our city?' asked Jocasta, above enthusiastic cheers from his supporters. These were not Laius's wealthy friends, Thebes's elite. They were ordinary men and women who had heard of the traveller's exploits, and come along to see what all the fuss was about. They didn't know the rules of palace etiquette, it seemed, so they cheered whenever they felt like it, rather than waiting to be invited. Oedipus's eyes glittered as they met hers. No one had ever enjoyed himself so much as he did in that moment. He paused until the noise had died down, determined he would be heard by everyone when he spoke. He had, she realized, no doubt that she would agree to anything he proposed.

'Because I intend to ask their Basileia for her hand in marriage,' he said.

Jocasta looked at him, far too young but handsome and – so far – a man of his word. She thought of the time she had spent in the palace alone, and she felt the treasury key nestled beneath her collarbones on the cord he had bought for her.

'She says yes,' she said, turning and walking back into the royal courtyard leaving Oedipus, a vision of confidence, to chase after her.

The news spread through Thebes faster than the Reckoning once had. People were asked to repeat it, because it didn't seem possible. The queen, widowed less than a month ago, was to remarry? A foreigner? He looked how old? It took very little time before the self-appointed Elders of the city – mostly the same men who had travelled back from the mountains with Laius's body, expecting to depose the queen with little difficulty – arrived at the palace in a sweaty, disconcerted mass. Amphion, a man who had always irritated Jocasta because of his superior manner and florid dress, had been chosen as their spokesman, or perhaps he had appointed himself. They couldn't have made a worse choice: the Secretary of the Treasury of Thebes bore a marked resemblance to her late father, and she loathed him.

Still, she couldn't ignore the frantic scrambling of her servants, racing across the cobbled courtyards to tell her that Amphion and his friends demanded an audience with the queen. She told them to take back the message that the queen was currently engaged in other business, but that she would receive them the following morning. It was time to teach these men that they did not own her and could not simply expect her to put everything aside to meet with them.

The following morning, they were standing waiting for her in the public square. They nestled together, gossiping like the old women who hung their faded laundry over the steep, narrow streets outside.

'Gentlemen,' she said, walking up behind them. She saw the shock in their faces: the small, pale girl they had laughed at with their king was not afraid of them. And she was no longer a girl.

'We've heard the most ridiculous story,' spluttered Amphion, and Jocasta wondered how a man could be so self-satisfied that he didn't feel the slightest embarrassment at the way saliva bubbled in front of his teeth when he spoke.

'I'm sure you've heard lots of ridiculous stories,' she replied. 'It's probably the company you keep.'

Amphion's face darkened. 'This particular story is one you must refute. Immediately.'

Jocasta smiled. 'I'm sure you can't mean to give the impression that you are walking into my home and giving me orders.'

'I–'

'And I'm sure when you began speaking, you meant to say something like, "Good morning, your highness",' she continued. 'Because to start barking orders at your queen, without so much as a greeting and a wish of good health, is – I think we can all agree – rude.' She looked round at the cluster of old men, some of them beginning to realize that Amphion's influence might be ebbing away. There was a subtle shifting of position, as the more pragmatic ones edged back, realizing they didn't want to ally themselves too closely with their spokesman after all.

'Forgive me, your majesty,' he said, sarcasm dripping from every consonant. 'I thought we had something urgent to discuss, and that we might dispense with niceties for now.'

'Dispense is an odd word to choose, isn't it?' she said. 'It makes it sound as though you normally speak to me with the respect and courtesy that I might expect, given my position. And yet, I can't remember ever hearing you speak to me by name, let alone by title. Though I'm sure you know both my name and my position. You see, I've overheard you speaking about me occasionally, and – I'm sure you won't mind me being honest, since I know it's a quality you prize – you didn't come across well at all.'

He flushed so red that she wondered if he might be about to collapse to the ground, clutching at his chest.

'I am trying to reassure the people of Thebes that their queen is not about to act in a foolish and hasty manner,' he said.

'I'm just not sure that's true,' she replied. 'I think you've come here to tell me that I should marry one of you, so you can be king of the city, instead of the man you think I intend to marry.'

Tiny beads of sweat had coalesced on his temples to create small rivulets which were now running down the sides of his face. 'Do you mean to tell us that you don't intend to marry some foreigner? Have we been misinformed?' He gestured around him to include the men who were sidling ever further away.

'It's hard to imagine how that could be even the smallest part of your business, isn't it?' Jocasta said.

'I am the Secretary of the Treasury,' he snarled.

'Were,' she said.

'What?'

'I said you were the Secretary of the Treasury. Now you're just a rude old man who used to be important, and then wasn't any more, because he couldn't keep his spittle-flecked mouth shut. Guards.' Jocasta gestured to her men, who approached Amphion. 'This gentleman would like you to escort him from the grounds,' she said. 'And any of his friends who would like to leave as well. Gentlemen?'

The Elders looked at the ground and shook their heads. She had a sudden memory of Creon and his school friends, aged four or five, caught stealing figs from a neighbour's tree. Guilt was a great deal more endearing in children. The guards removed Amphion with an easy efficiency.

'Did anyone else have a question?' Jocasta asked, looking from one awkward face to another.

'Only one, majesty,' said a grey-haired, pinched-face man who she thought was called Taron.

'Yes?' she said.

'When might we meet the new Basileus?' he asked. She smiled.

'Clever boy,' she said.

The people of Thebes viewed Oedipus as their champion. Jocasta had never noticed, during her years in the palace, that the city was split into two unequal halves. Laius and his men were not especially popular with ordinary citizens: he was absent too often, and the common perception of him was that he was uninterested in the city, and tended towards snobbishness. His advisers, meanwhile, were viewed less favourably still. It was not only Jocasta who had seen them as a cabal of old men with no common touch. She, on the other hand, had a romantic appeal. A beautiful girl, married to a king whose sexual proclivities were the source of constant gossip, speculation, and more than a few drinking songs. She had spent so much of her time in the palace after the death of her child that she was perceived as a tragic figure, trapped in a court filled with aloof, unpopular men. Ordinary Thebans were rooting for her to marry again, but someone younger and more like them. And Oedipus fulfilled both criteria.

His entry to the city as its saviour – even though most Thebans had never travelled through the mountains – was the real reason they loved him, of course. Everyone knew someone who knew someone who had been lost to the Sphinx. It was easy to turn a now-vanished threat into something more serious than it had been. People didn't ask how dangerous the men of the Sphinx really were or how much of an impediment to trade they had been. They just celebrated the fact that the Sphinx were gone, and they had this handsome visitor to thank. Finally someone had done what their own king had failed to do for many years. And were the rumours true, that he had proposed to the queen the moment he arrived at the palace? You couldn't deny that he had charm. Exactly what the queen needed, everyone agreed. Was he too young? Better that than another ossified old fool.

The wedding was arranged with a haste which shocked the Elders and delighted the commoners. Jocasta was a widow for less than two months. She married Oedipus at the start of spring, just as the earliest fruit trees were coming into blossom. Thebans saw the flowers as auspicious. But Jocasta refused to consider auspices any more. The only thing that worried her about the day of her gamos was the absence of Oedipus's parents. She couldn't decide whether she would like to meet them or not. With every day that passed, she wanted Oedipus more, and more than wanting him, she desired him. She longed to consume him whole, and have his youth and vigour shine out from her pores. She wanted to wrap herself around him like a cloak and never let go. And she wanted to know everything about his past: his city, his home, his family. But she couldn't leave Thebes without a ruler, while she travelled with him to Corinth to meet his family and visit his home. It would be unsafe for her, as well as deeply unpopular with her citizens. So all she could know about her new husband was what he brought with him to her city. In the evenings before their wedding she begged Oedipus to repeat stories, so she could learn the names of everyone important to him. Of course she must meet his parents.

But at the same time, she felt a twinge of relief when he said they wouldn't be able to come. His mother's health was poor: she was confined to a chair, and could only travel short distances by litter. She could never make the long journey across uneven terrain that would be necessary to see her son in his new home. And his father was always loath to leave his mother for a few hours, let alone a few days: they were, Oedipus assured her, inseparable. And of course she wanted to hear this too, to know that he was the son of a couple who were so devoted to one another.

The notion of his chair-bound mother brought her another, different kind of relief. In their absence, she could render them old, much older than her. It was the only question she never asked him: how old are your parents? Because what if the answer was one she couldn't bear to hear: oh, about the same age as you. And her imagination took her further still. What if he hadn't mentioned her age to them? She spent terrible moments imagining a scene where his aged mother looked around for someone young enough to be her son's betrothed, before her puzzled eye eventually lighted upon Jocasta. It was unthinkable.

'Tell me again,' she said, as he lay on her bed, the golden strands of his hair glowing in the candlelight. He propped himself up on one arm, and ran his hands over her skin. She reached out to touch him, but the sight of her hand – every knuckle bearing the marks of every time she had bent every finger – next to his flawless skin made her draw it back so she could look at him unspoiled.

'You've heard it all,' he grinned. 'Let me keep a bit of mystery, so you don't get bored of me as soon as we're married.'

'Is there anything you want to know about me?' she asked. Oedipus's finger was tracing a silvery mark on the right side of her stomach. Did he know what it was? Should she tell him? Again, she found herself split. She wanted to share the terrible story of her loss, and have him hold her while she wept one last time for her missing boy.

Because she was determined that with this new marriage, the one she had chosen, she would finally put aside the grief which had crushed her through the last seventeen years of her life. She wanted to begin again, and she would. But wouldn't that be easier if she didn't tell him the whole wretched saga of the past?

'Tell me what you did, when Laius abandoned you,' he asked, quietly.

Jocasta was surprised. The only thing that had ever mattered to her about her dead husband was his refusal to have a son. Everything else had blurred away over the years. She was not now sure she knew Laius's eye-colour, if she ever had.

'I was relieved,' she said. 'It meant he didn't want to have anything to do with me, and the feeling was mutual.'

'It's peculiar that he wanted to get married, isn't it? Keeping up appearances, I suppose.'

'I think so,' she said. 'It was what Thebes wanted for him. He just didn't want it for himself. He resisted it as long as he could.'

'So he married you and then moved to the lower slopes of the mountains to live as he actually wanted to?'

'Essentially, yes.'

'And what did you do? Did you have endless affairs?'

'You are so rude,' she said, swatting him with a cushion. 'No, I didn't. I took my position seriously.'

He began kissing her neck and she felt her stomach contract. What was the point of explaining Oran, the father of her lost child, after all this time? What was the point of even remembering him, when he was so long gone, and Oedipus was so entirely present?

15

The morning after the coronation, I tried to leave the palace, but there was no one available to accompany me. I asked my sister if she wanted to go down to the lake, but she made some excuse about a headache from sitting in the blistering sun the previous day. I tried to remind her of the dappled shade by the water, but she waved me away, a damp linen cloth on her forehead. It was more likely she had planned to meet Haem in some quiet corner of the palace and was waiting for me to leave so she could begin to get herself ready. There was no one else I could ask to come with me: Sophon would not welcome the suggestion that he clamber down the uneven, rock-strewn paths with his stick. And I could not ask Eteo, because I didn't know what to say to him yet. That was one of the reasons I needed to go down to the lake: I wanted to swim away from the palace, and find my thoughts somewhere in the water. The painted dolphins which decorated the sides of the fountain in the courtyard were taunting me, swimming happily in their blue shallows.

In the end, I told one of the slave women that she would have to accompany me, and though she sighed and said she might be missed by the housekeeper, I pleaded with her until she agreed. We walked together through the courtyards: the sight of men scurrying around the second courtyard to do Polyn's bidding would have amused me on another day – each man so intent on his own importance as he followed his route, like ants swarming around a nest – but today it made me feel more afraid. I had no way of knowing how many of these men, of the aristoi, were a danger to me. Or if the danger had ebbed, now that Polyn was ruler of Thebes once again. Sophon thought the attack had been organized to discredit Eteo. So was I safe now that Eteo was no longer king? The fear which had paralysed me at the coronation ceremony when I saw the priest's knife had ebbed away today: I wanted escape.

The slave woman and I hurried through to the doorway which led into the main courtyard, but there we found the gates were closed and barred. Looking through them, it appeared that the front gates – from the main courtyard into the market square – were locked too, although the traders would certainly be at work by now. There were no guards standing by the gate. Only when I hammered on them did one appear on the other side.

'Open the gates, please,' I said.

He shook his jowls to and fro. 'Not today.'

'What do you mean, not today?'

'By order of the king,' he said. 'The palace gates are to be kept locked.'

'Until when?' I asked. The sun was still low in the sky, and if they opened the gates again soon, I would still have time to walk down to the lake before it grew too hot. The guard shrugged and walked away. The maid looked at me, waiting to see what I would do now.

'You can go back to the housekeeper and tell her our

plans have changed,' I said. She began to walk away. 'Wait.'

She slowed and I caught her up. I preferred to walk with her across the second courtyard than go through it alone. Once on the other side of it, she disappeared into the kitchens, and I walked back along the colonnade into the family courtyard. The fountain was spluttering in the middle of the square, and I decided to go and sit beside it. I should find Sophon and ask him if he knew what was happening. Why would Polyn have closed the palace off from the city? Was he keeping the rest of Thebes out, or keeping us in?

I sat on the edge of the fountain and unlaced my sandals: I had spilled water on them yesterday and now the leather had hardened and was biting into my hot feet. I swung my feet into the pool, while I bent the leather straps to and fro in my hands, trying to soften them again. I could smell the honeysuckle and thyme from across the square: my father had planted both, hoping to attract wild bees to the garden. His plan had worked. One summer when I was small, they swarmed across the courtyard and built their hive in a dead tree just outside the palace walls. We had honeycomb that summer, dripping it onto hard brown bread and soft white sheep's cheese. My difficulty with these memories is that I can never quite be sure that I've caught the right one from the mass of them flying around inside my head. I tie these two events together – my father planting the shrubs and the bees producing the honey – but I don't know if I'm right to. I don't always remember things in the order in which they happened, I don't think. I remember individual moments: my father dusting the soil from his hands and picking me up so I could see the flowers on the honeysuckle and the bees nuzzling their way inside the petals. But did those two things happen on the same day? Surely he would have planted honeysuckle before it came into flower, or the blooms would have fallen when the plant was moved? As for the honey: I remember eating it – sweeter than anything I'd ever tasted before – but I don't know who drizzled it onto my small, fat fingers. Were my parents still alive then, or was it my uncle who offered me the treat?

I sat by the fountain for a while, trying to tie the memories together in the right order, until Eteo's door opened and he walked into the courtyard, running his hand through his ruffled hair. He had clearly woken late. I waved and he walked over to join me. He didn't need to remove his sandals, having bare feet already.

'What's going on?' he said. 'Why aren't you and Sophon busy composing some epic tale together, on the glory of my kingship?'

I shoved him. 'I wanted to go down to the lake,' I said. 'But the gates are locked. On Polyn's orders, according to the guard.' I had been worrying that I would find it difficult to talk to him today, but it turned out to be easy.

'Why?' asked my brother. I shook my head. 'You could sneak out the back way,' he said. Eteo and I are the only ones who know about the door on the way to the ice store. Well, that isn't entirely true. Plenty of other people must know where it is: the palace staff, for a start. But it had been locked for so long that no one else ever thought about it. A door that doesn't open for a long enough time becomes the same thing as a wall, Sophon once said. I'm sure it was this kind of remark that provoked my siblings to stay away from his lessons. Still, I knew what he meant. Eteo had been with me when I found the key, years ago, hiding in a dark recess between a wooden chest and the bottom of the colonnade wall, outside our rooms. It was only visible because I was lying on the floor at the time, watching a bright green lizard scuttle along the ground. Lizards are usually brown or a dull, dusty green. But this one shone like a jewel. I was hypnotized by its radiant colour; Eteo by how it had avoided being eaten by a sharp-eyed bird when it was so bright.

The light glinted off something behind the emerald lizard and I reached under the chest to see what it was. The lizard scurried away in alarm, but I had this strange, ornate key to remember it by.

Eteo and I had no reason to keep the key secret, but we did anyway, because we both loved secrets. We waited until the others were occupied elsewhere, and carried the key from door to door, hidden in a pocket, testing it furtively, until we had exhausted every lock in the palace. It must have taken us a month. Only then did I remember the door that was not a door, in the ice-house corridor. We waited for days until there were no servants around, and our uncle wasn't in his rooms, which were close to the entrance of that corridor. The key seemed to fit, but we couldn't turn it at first, because the lock had stiffened with age. Then Eteo took a small bottle of olive oil from the kitchens that night, and we dipped the key into it, feeding oil into the lock to loosen the mechanism.

After all that, when we finally opened the door, we found it opened out onto nothing, the height of a man or more above the ground, which cut away beneath the palace because of the hill. There were no stairs or even a trace that there once had been any steps outside. We meant to make a rope ladder, so we would have our own secret exit from the courtyard, but we must have been distracted by something and we soon forgot about it. Once the mystery of the key was solved, we weren't so concerned with using it. We just wanted to know what the key was for. Besides, we'd always been able to leave the palace before today.

'I could sneak out that way,' I said. 'But doesn't it seem odd that we should have to?'

'You didn't go to Polyn and ask him what was going on?'

'I couldn't.'

My brother turned to look at me. 'Why not?'

And the noise of the fountain covered the sound of me telling him that it was because I was afraid of our older brother, and afraid of the friends he had chosen.

*

It was now half a month at least since Polyn's coronation, and I was no closer to leaving the palace, not even for one day. Polyn was no longer spending the nights in the family courtyard, in the rooms he had as a child. I didn't know where he was sleeping: perhaps one of the storerooms in the royal courtyard had been converted into the king's quarters. I wanted to ask the servants if they knew, but I could not bear to lose face in front of them, to have them gossiping about the fact that I didn't know where my brother was. And I didn't. He had so often been absent that it took me a few days to notice that I hadn't seen him at all since the coronation games. But there it was: he had not been in the family courtyard since he took the crown.

Eteo had not left his rooms since discovering that he had sentenced an innocent boy to death. Although he had always known that the boy with the knife was an unwitting victim of the same conspiracy which nearly cost me my life, there turned out to be a difference between knowing something terrible might be true, and discovering it was definitely true. He could not forget the cries of the boy's mother as her son was marched from the palace grounds, sentenced to death by the king. By him. And until he emerged from his seclusion and returned to the fountain, I couldn't talk to him. There was nowhere else I would feel safe discussing something so dangerous. Nowhere else where I would be certain we couldn't be overheard.

Meanwhile my sister, who should have been talking to Polyn on our behalf, since they had always been closest – me and Eteo, her and Polyn – seemed entirely unconcerned by his absence, and wouldn't have even noticed unless I'd asked her about it. Unless Haem mentioned something to her, or someone else talked to her about Haem, she paid no attention at all.

And then there was the problem of the palace gates. It was just for one day, the day after the coronation, that the front gates were barred. After that, the main courtyard was opened again to the people of Thebes. But the inner gates – from the royal courtyard into the public one – remained locked, and only Polyn's advisers and friends seemed able to come and go as they pleased, the guards stepping smartly aside for them. I could see slivers of this from the family courtyard, because the gates from there into the second courtyard were now shut and barred as well. There wasn't even a guard. There was no need for one. The gates had been closed for days, so they had become, as Sophon would say, no different from a wall. I could not go to my tutor in his study either. I didn't know if he was still sitting there waiting for me or if he had given up and left the palace. Or even if he had been told to leave.

I tried asking my uncle about the locked gates, but I achieved little. I told him I wanted to visit Sophon and borrow a manuscript. He replied that I was surely too old for lessons now, and could already read and write, sing and compose and play the phorminx – the five-stringed lyre that the older generation of Thebans prized above all other instruments – better than any other girl in the city. Flattering as this was, it did nothing to help. I asked again about something to read, and he said I could tell him what I would like and he would send someone to fetch it from Sophon's room and bring it back with him at the end of the next day. He and Haem were still able to come and go between the courtyards, though I hadn't yet seen the gates open for them. I wondered if I should just sit beside the gates for one whole day, and then at least I would force whoever came and went to explain why I could not. But I sat there for a while, and no one tried to enter. They could just wait me out. I thought perhaps when Eteo came out of his room, we could share the duty, and then it wouldn't require such perseverance. When I asked my uncle why he could move around the palace but I could not, he said that the security of the royal family was of unsurpassed importance, so we needed to accept these new measures to keep us safe. He thought I would understand that, after everything that had happened. But I didn't feel safe; only trapped.

I tried to comb out this tangled state of affairs so I could compose verses for my history, verses which Polyn would not enjoy hearing me sing. But I could not successfully unravel it all. I had to work things out in my head before I could start trying to write anything down. I didn't have enough parchment to make mistakes, and I didn't know when I would be able to get more. Sophon would have expected me to use reasoning to understand my predicament, and I was trying. After much thought, this was what I believed to be true.

I could not accept that my oldest brother had wanted me to die. But equally, it was inconceivable that his friend had infiltrated the palace and attacked me without Polyn being, at the very least, aware of it. Sophon had suggested Polyn was part of a conspiracy intending to disrupt Eteo's kingship, and it was true that my brothers had become virtual strangers to one another. Or perhaps it was always thus. I couldn't remember them being friends even when they were very young. Eteo always had more in common with Haem than with Polyn. So I had two contradictory beliefs: that my brother was involved, and that he could not have been so heartless. I could not maintain them both. But without further evidence, I would not condemn my brother.

I didn't know what kind of evidence I was expecting to find next. Would Polyn announce that the wrong man had been condemned for the attack on me? That would have weakened Eteo's standing with the people of Thebes, certainly, but not by very much: the boy was not from one of the elite families, and anyway, he was dead now. Besides, it might well discredit Polyn, too. Ordinary Thebans spent far less time thinking about which of my brothers was king at any one time than they imagined, at least if Sophon's judgement on the matter was correct. Prince, king: he often observed that the distinction was far smaller from the outside than it was on the inside. Both were a world away from being a market-trader or a cobbler or a smith. So though I understood why Eteo needed time alone to contemplate what he had done, I believed he was being eaten up by a baseless fear: people would not find out that he had condemned an innocent man. Apart from everything else, if the boy was publicly exonerated, Polyn would need to find another scapegoat. He was hardly likely to lay the blame where it belonged, on his own friend.

The courtyard gates were not, I believed, kept closed to keep us safe. The only danger I had ever been in was at the hands of my brother's friend, the aristos with the knife. If he was back inside the palace now – as he probably was – it could only be at my brother's invitation. And it was not credible to think Polyn would invite someone dangerous into our home and then worry about the danger. He was the king: no one could come into the palace without his knowledge and approval. The only other possibility – which I had discounted – was that Polyn himself was being forced to accept things he didn't want to accept, just as I had been forced to accept that I was locked into the smallest courtyard of the palace. But who could force their will on the king? The idea was absurd.

So my conclusion was that I was a prisoner in this part of the palace, for whatever reason and for however long Polyn decided. When Eteo emerged – if he could put aside his guilt – he would help me to work out what to do next. The guards ignored me, and I could have hammered on the gates all day without provoking one of them to come over and speak to me. But they would not ignore the man who was king until recently and who would be king again once the four seasons had passed.

The problem with my theory was that I could think of only one plausible reason why Polyn would behave as he had. There was one explanation which encompassed all the information I had considered: Polyn had no intention of sharing the kingship any longer. He had replaced Eteo for good this time, and he would not give up the throne again.

It was impossible to conclude anything else.

16

Jocasta lay on a couch covered with fatly stuffed cushions in the middle of the courtyard, her eyes closed. She could pick out the voices of both her sons and her daughter, as they squawked at one another in the shade of the east colonnade. In a moment, the coos and squeals of delight would no doubt be transformed into howls of pain and rage, but for now, the children were playing together as she had always imagined they would, and she delighted in ignoring them. She had never managed to explain to Oedipus that so long as she could hear the children, she was happy.

Even when she had a crippling headache – which happened sometimes now her belly was so swollen she could almost hear the baby's voice murmuring into her ears – she liked to be able to listen to the children, to be able to hear each one separately from the others. It had been easy when there was just Polynices, who screamed at the top of his lungs every day for months. Then, when Eteocles arrived, she had been astonished to discover that there could be a smaller baby than Polynices. She could see that her older son had grown longer, and heavier, and finally taller, as he sat up looking at his surroundings as though he might one day approve of them but not yet. Still somehow, he remained a tiny baby in her mind until Eteocles was born, undeniably smaller. The same thing had happened when Antigone was born, but with the added delight that now she had a girl. Two sons and a daughter. She could hear the difference in every sound they made: Polynices did everything noisily, even breathing. Eteocles was quieter, but snored like a cat. Antigone raged at the slightest provocation, and could never keep still. Even when she was just a few months old, she watched her brothers with vast green eyes, determined to escape the cage of her crib and join them in their adventures. And the new baby, what would she be like? Jocasta stroked her hardening stomach to see if she could feel a kick. This one was nowhere near as restless as the other three had been. She – Jocasta knew it was a girl from the way everything tasted somehow metallic, though she could not explain this to Oedipus – lay still for hours at a time. Just as Jocasta began to worry, the baby would give her a reassuring shove. Hand touching hand, with only her own skin between them.

She could hear her husband kicking a soft leather ball to Polynices, as Eteocles demanded they let him play. Would he be the first to crack the tranquillity with a scream? No, Antigone as usual was suddenly wailing at some real or perceived injustice. Jocasta listened to Oedipus scoop her up and tell her she could play on his team: the two of them versus the boys. Everything was as it should be.

She lay half-dozing in the sun, trying to remember what she needed to do today. But she had little to fret about: her brother was in control of things. He had become increasingly helpful as her children arrived, taking on more responsibilities each year. Creon wanted to ease her burden, he had told her when she was pregnant with

Polyn. He always rushed to put a stool behind her, as if her legs could not possibly hold the weight of her and her unborn baby. She had thought then what a good father he would be, when he and Eurydice had a child; once they did, she saw she was right. He doted upon his little son, who now came to the palace so often with his papa.

Eurydice and Creon had moved into a neat little house, just down the hill from the market square, near the palace gates, three – or was it four? Jocasta struggled to remember – years earlier. The smell of rotting vegetables behind the grocery stalls had made Eurydice queasy when she was pregnant, and for a while she clearly felt that the move across the city had been a mistake. She stopped attending the palace with her husband and withdrew into her own household. But once Haemon was born, she saw the virtue of the location. Creon could walk to the palace in a matter of moments, and Eurydice could come and go as she pleased, with the baby. If she wanted more time to herself, she dropped him off with Jocasta's brood. One more child made no difference in the palace, where plentiful nursemaids were always on hand. Eurydice was never the sister that Jocasta had hoped she would be, but she made Creon happy, and their son was a delight.

Jocasta thought she should ask Creon if he and Eurydice were planning to have another baby. She had been sure they would have armfuls of them when she saw them with Haemon. But first months and now years had passed, and still there was no second child.

She heaved herself off the divan, shedding cushions in her wake, and waved across the square at Oedipus and the children.

'I won't be long,' she called. She walked into the middle courtyard, and wished she had stayed where she was. Lying in the sun was pleasant enough, but walking in it, even this short distance, left her over-heated and exhausted. She could feel the sweat form beneath the linen tunic that pressed against her back. She opened the door to the treasury room, and found Creon sitting in the ornate wooden chair that had been a gift to Jocasta from a visiting ambassador from Athens.

'You look comfortable,' she smiled.

He leapt to his feet. 'Forgive me, sister. I was just—'

'You don't need to apologize,' she said. 'I must sit down.' Jocasta dropped onto the nearest couch, which was covered in hard padding: was it animal hair? She wished again she had stayed in comfort on the divan, and summoned Creon to her. She dimly recalled that one of the other children had made her as tired as this, but she couldn't remember which one. 'This baby is determined that I spend nine months lying on my back,' she said, accepting a small metal cup of water which Creon brought over, concern in his pale blue eyes.

'Should I send for some ice?' he asked. 'I know you like it.'

'No, thank you. I do like it, but the baby doesn't. It must be too cold for her. It makes her kick.'

'Ah, that's a pity,' he said. 'How are you feeling otherwise?'

'Puzzled,' she replied. 'Why don't you and Eurydice have another child? And why haven't I ever asked you before now?' His face coloured. 'Don't blush,' she added, smiling. 'Only one of us should be bright red and sweating, and it can't be you, because I came into the room that way.'

He thought for a moment. 'I did want more children,' he admitted. 'I would have liked three or four. But Eury . . .' He lost the words, and she forced herself not to fill in the silence, uncomfortable though it was. She would never know the truth if she allowed herself to be tactful.

'Eury was so sick when she was pregnant, she said she couldn't face going through it all again. And I was worried for her. It can't be safe for a woman to be so sickly.'

'Was she that ill?' Jocasta felt a sharp twinge of guilt. She knew her sister-in-law had suffered from morning sickness at all hours, but she didn't realize it had been quite so debilitating.

'She was sick all the time,' he said. 'Every day. She grew so thin in the early weeks – don't you remember? She could barely eat a thing.'

'Of course,' Jocasta said. But she was lying. She already had Polynices by then, and was expecting Eteocles, who was only two months younger than Haemon. She had felt for her sister-in-law, but hadn't been paying her particular attention. She had simply assumed Eurydice was sick sometimes, in the same way as Jocasta and every other pregnant woman was.

'Eury didn't want another child enough to be that ill again. I felt guilty even for suggesting it, to be honest. As if I was asking her to put her own life at risk again.'

'Well, if she felt that strongly . . .' Jocasta said. 'You have Haemon, that's the important thing.'

'I know,' he said. 'I do know. But I would have liked a daughter, too. You know I would have.'

'I'm sorry,' she said. 'I wish I hadn't asked. It was rude of me.'

'No,' he replied. 'It's good to be able to say that out loud. I wouldn't say it at home, you know. Eury would think I was criticizing her. Or expressing some sort of dissatisfaction with Haem, who – of course – is the perfect son. She has given me an heir: it's all I could have asked for. But it's quite separate from him, you know? Wanting a daughter. You understand.'

'I think so,' she said. 'This one will be a girl, I'm sure of it. Will you promise to take care of her?'

'Are you planning on exposing her on the mountain-side?' he laughed. He was looking across the room at the strong-boxes which contained Jocasta's gold, and the new tapestry she had asked him to acquire for her – blood red, shot through with gold, and woven so carefully the Fates themselves could do no better – so he did not see the shudder run through his sister's body.

She swallowed and replied in a light voice. 'Of course not. Oedipus loves having daughters, you know that. He prefers Ani to either of the boys, even though she fusses all the time. I'm just worried this one might get overlooked. She's quieter than the others.'

Her brother turned to look at her. 'How quiet?' he asked.

'No,' Jocasta said. 'She moves. Just not as often as I'm used to. Antigone punched and kicked me every day – do you remember?'

He nodded. 'It was driving you mad. The gadfly, you called her, because she stung you so often.'

'She'll never be short of attention,' Jocasta agreed.

'Which is why you must always look out for this one. She'll be the baby of the family, so she'll need someone to make sure she isn't ignored. Say you promise.'

'Don't you want to ask Oedipus?'

'Why? He would think it was a good idea, just like I do. I know he would.'

Creon looked at her flushed face, framed by damp brown hair which was now flecked with grey.

'I promise,' he said. 'I won't let you ignore her, no matter how noisy all your other brats are.'

'Good,' she said. 'Now will you bring the tapestry over here so I can look at it? Is it as beautiful as we were promised?'

'It is,' he said.

By the time they had finished, Jocasta was relieved to accept her brother's arm as he walked her back to the rest of her family. 'Will you stay for dinner?' she asked, as she watched Haemon run the length of the courtyard before flinging himself into his father's arms. 'I could send someone to fetch Eurydice?'

Creon's biceps bulged as he swung his gleeful son around him in a circle. At the same time, the tension in every other part of his body seemed to disappear.

'You're getting too heavy to do that,' he said, as he hurled Haemon round one more time before placing him on the ground. 'When did you get so tall?'

'I don't know,' squealed the little boy.

'Was it this afternoon?' asked Creon.

'No,' Haemon said.

'This morning, then? It must have been this morning.'

'No,' the boy shrieked with delight, running to look in the water beneath the fountain, to check if his reflection had grown taller.

'I think we'd better go back,' Creon said to Jocasta. 'Eury will have planned dinner by now.'

Jocasta tutted. 'Of course. I should have thought of it sooner. Polyn! Eteo! Come over here!' The two boys ran over, but stopped carefully before they crashed into her. They had learned to do this when she was expecting Ani. 'Will you go and pick some herbs and flowers for your Aunt Eury? So she knows we miss her and long to see her for dinner tomorrow,' Jocasta said. 'While your uncle has iced water with me and Papa.'

The boys nodded and bustled off, filled with sudden seriousness.

'There's no need,' Creon said.

But his sister patted his arm, and walked back to her divan, which still lay in the afternoon sun. She turned the hot cushions over, so she could lie on something cool. Oedipus walked out of the shaded portico where he had been sitting, and waved to Creon, pointing at a plain wooden chair he was welcome to use.

'I cannot stay for much longer,' Creon told him, sitting down. 'My wife is expecting us home.'

'You can stay for a little while,' Oedipus yawned. 'They'll start scrapping before they've done as they were asked. It never takes long.'

'They're not that bad,' Jocasta said, just as Eteocles shoved his brother aside to reach the rosemary. 'They're just boys being boys.'

But Oedipus was right. The boys were at war again,

and were no longer picking herbs. A moment later, Polynices brought over a mangled bunch of thyme stems, bent and broken from being pulled by competing hands. Haemon came over to take a look at the sorry bouquet. 'I'll do it,' he said, and took himself off to look at the plants. One of the gardeners was working in the far corner of the courtyard, and seeing Haemon's intense concentration, hurried over to assist him.

'Why can't my sons behave like yours?' Oedipus groaned. 'Little monsters.'

Eteocles and then Polynices, seeing that things were progressing more successfully without them, scurried over to help rather than watch their cousin carry out the important task alone. 'You see?' Jocasta said. 'They're not so terrible.'

Conversation between the three parents dried up, as it so often did. Jocasta wished her brother and her husband would at least feign the friendliness they couldn't feel. Creon had never liked Oedipus, though he had never said a critical word about the king. But Jocasta remembered the expression on her brother's face, when she first introduced him to her husband. He had obviously been warned to expect someone young, but her brother's shock had been vivid and ill-concealed. He was used to being the youngest man in his sister's life: she was ten years older than him, after all. And then he met Oedipus, and had to readjust his role accordingly: he couldn't be the baby brother if her husband was six – or was it seven? – years younger than he was. And he was no longer the only man Jocasta relied on, once she had a real husband, a proper marriage. It was an abrupt awakening.

And Oedipus was a proprietorial man. It was this kind of thing Jocasta occasionally wondered if she might have noticed before they married, had things moved less quickly when they met. Oedipus was the opposite of Laius, never happy in the company of men. He preferred to be alone with her, and his possessiveness stretched backwards in time. He disliked the presence of anyone from her life before he arrived in it. Teresa had barely continued in her employ at the palace for a month after Laius died. Jocasta had felt sure that her housekeeper – a free woman – would prefer to leave. But upset though Teresa was about Laius, she seemed to want to keep her position. Still, she could not have made her dislike of Oedipus more overt, nor her delight when he left Thebes a few days after he had arrived with news of the king's death: Teresa's spies must have been slacking, Jocasta had thought, because the housekeeper had been more surprised than anyone when Oedipus returned a half-month later to ask the queen to marry him. Teresa's response had been furious, and Oedipus had ordered her out of the palace within the day. She had turned to Jocasta, expecting the queen to overrule this upstart and tell him that Teresa was not to be argued with. But Jocasta had done nothing of the kind. Rather, she had taken her husband's arm, and told Teresa that things were changing at the palace, so perhaps it was time for her to move on. Teresa had spent a day holed up in the kitchens, waiting for the queen to reconsider. But when a new housekeeper arrived – Oedipus had put out word that the position was vacant and dozens of Thebans hurried to offer their services – she had been obliged to pack her things and leave. Jocasta thought about her occasionally, and wondered where she'd gone that day. After all those years living in the palace, would she have had anywhere else to stay? But it didn't matter. Jocasta had made her choice, and that was Oedipus. After so much of her life had been decided for her, she was determined to stand by her decisions now she was finally allowed to make them for herself. And soon, Oedipus was asking why the courtyard didn't have flowers and suggesting they knock down Teresa's ugly little shrine and replace it with an almond tree. And a few years later, when the tree came into blossom for the first time, Jocasta had forgotten that the square had ever looked different from the flowering place it had become.

If Jocasta was honest with herself, she knew that even if Creon had offered a boundless welcome to her second husband when they first met, Oedipus would probably not have warmed to him. Oedipus had always loved her jealously. He was irritated when he had to share her attention with the children – much as he loved them – and he certainly didn't love her brother. He always found the older man both condescending and excessively protective. 'Where was all this concern when you had a husband who hated you?' he once asked. Jocasta shrugged and reminded him that Creon had been a child when she was married off, and had known little about her life in the years that followed. She couldn't blame him. But she also couldn't focus too much on Creon's comparative youth, because he was several years (she rounded the number down in her mind) older than Oedipus, who had defended her against her husband before he even met her.

Jocasta had long ago decided that the best course of

action was to refuse to allow that there was anything wrong between them. She had learned never to be too fond of Creon when Oedipus was there, as jealousy only made him more impatient. Her husband needed to be unrivalled in her affection, and he was. She had always hoped they would warm to one another one day and things would become easier. She had tried to enlist Eurydice as an ally – encouraging her brother to marry the girl as soon as he could – but even when it was just the four of them (Creon and Eurydice living so close by) it made no difference. Jocasta tended to elide the status difference from her thoughts, but the others never did. Creon prickled to hear Oedipus called 'king'. And Oedipus relished Creon's lack of official position, choosing to refer to his work as 'helping your sister'.

Jocasta heard the children come running over with the flowers and herbs, tied with a neat little plait of grasses. 'That's beautiful,' she said to the three of them. 'Will you take it carefully to your mama?' she asked Haemon. He nodded.

'Time to go,' Creon said, and raised himself from the chair. 'See you tomorrow,' he told his sister.

Perhaps the flowers would persuade Eurydice to visit, Jocasta thought, as she waved her brother a lazy goodbye. But she knew she was the only one who wanted the four of them to be friends. And that was never likely to be enough.

17

I don't think about my parents every day, but I miss them more than I remember them. Growing up without them has left me with an uneasy sense that I have been careless with something fragile and irreplaceable: a precious bottle of perfume, perhaps. I can't reach into the past and take better care of them. But the one consolation I have always had is my three siblings. There are traces of my parents in all of us. Ani looks very much like our mother, and always has: the bright, birdlike eyes, the thick, dark hair. She is small, like our mother was, and delicate. Even her hands could be our mother's: the neat, sharp nails that she digs into the soft flesh of a ripe fig. Polyn is a compact version of my father: he has the same quickness in his expression, as though he is waiting for you to catch up. But Eteo has my father's build, and his long, ranging gait is so evocative that sometimes if he catches me unawares, I lose myself for a moment, thinking it is Papa.

But not any more.

Finally, Eteo came out of his room. He had always had these dark periods, even when he was a small boy. There was no consoling him when he was angry or upset: you had to leave him be until he was ready to talk again. I knocked on the door and called his name, quietly, in case he was asleep. I had done this every day, but he had not replied. Then one day, he opened the door and came out, blinking into the bright sunshine of the square. His eye sockets were puffed up, swollen like blisters. I reached over to embrace him, but his arms squeezed me back emptily.

'Come to the fountain, Isy,' he said. I saw no value in telling him that, as far as I knew, we were unlikely to be overheard anywhere, as we were the only people in the courtyard. Ani was somewhere with Haem, I guessed: I didn't know where. The slaves had come in early this morning with toasted barley grains and sour goat curds but they were long gone now.

'Where is everyone?' Eteo asked, looking around.

'It's been like this for days,' I told him. 'I've asked our uncle when they will open the gates again, and he shrugs and says we're safer like this.'

'Safer?' My brother raised a weary eyebrow. 'We'd be safer wrestling a mountain lion than in this place. I'm sorry, Isy, I abandoned you. I had to think about things.'

'You're here now.'

We sat by the fountain and I reached out to dip my hand in the water. 'What happens when you try to leave?' he asked.

'No one comes to open the gates.'

'What if you shout and hammer on them?' he asked, smiling tiredly.

'Not even then,' I said.

'But the slaves have been coming in and out?' he asked, jerking his head at the food which remained on a table under the colonnade, a fine linen cloth draped over it to keep the flies away.

'Less frequently than before. But yes.'

'Through the gates?'

'I suppose so.'

'When do they come?'

'Before I'm awake. They come back each night to take the plates and dishes away and refill them.'

'So we're stuck here,' he said. I nodded. 'Where's Ani?' he asked. I shrugged.

'With Haem, I think,' I replied. 'I don't know. I haven't seen her for days. They plan to announce their betrothal soon, I am sure of it.'

'You've just been here on your own?' he asked.

'Since the coronation,' I said. 'Ani is here sometimes, but she's always with him, so I can't talk to her.'

'You don't trust Haem.' Eteo nodded slowly. 'Or Ani?'

'I don't know who to trust except you,' I said.

'Then you're lucky I'm here,' he smiled. 'The slave boy has brought food into my room every morning. I couldn't face seeing any of them: Polyn and Creon and the others. Not once you'd told me about Lynceus. It didn't occur to me that you were out here on your own. Forgive me.'

'Lynceus? Is that his name?'

'Polyn's friend? Yes.'

'Polyn can't face seeing you either,' I said. 'He hasn't come back here at all.'

'I don't think he's ashamed of what he's done, Isy. Are you still thinking the best of him now, even when you have so much evidence against him?'

'I don't have any choice. The only alternative is to think the worst of him. And how does that help me?'

Eteo shook his head. 'Be realistic.'

'I am being realistic,' I said. 'What would you have me believe? That my brother agreed to have me killed, and it is just good luck and the skill of an old man that means I am alive today? Is that truly what you think?'

'I didn't mean to upset you,' he said. 'I'm sorry. Let's not talk about him any more.'

He stood up, and walked over to the table. He picked up two figs and threw one over to me. His aim was off and I had lean right back to catch it. I almost fell on my back, but my balance just held and I righted myself again. Finally I saw my brother smile properly. The weight of things seemed to shift from his brow bones and his face opened up, like an unfurling leaf.

*

I should have guessed he was planning something. It is how Eteo has always been: whenever he is upset about something, he withdraws from the world until he has thought things through. Only then does he act. There was no reason for him to behave differently now.

He was more determined to leave the courtyard than I was, which was hardly surprising. I couldn't go outside the palace, or even into its public areas, without an escort. If one of the slaves or one of my relatives didn't accompany me, no one would let me out as far as the main courtyard. So even if I had made an almighty racket hammering on the gates, I could only have reached the second courtyard, and that was where Polyn's friends, Lynceus included, would be. Eteo had no such restrictions on his movements, of course, so he had a great deal more to gain.

One of the odd things about my brother is that people

forget how quick he is. They watch him each year at the races, sprinting at full pelt, and they know he is fast. But because he is tall and has a lazy, sinuous way of walking, they don't remember that when he's away from the racetrack. Perhaps, too, they had forgotten that he wouldn't stay in his rooms forever, although that would obviously have been more convenient for them.

The next day, long before it was light, a slave came in carrying fresh fruit and cheese. He did not need a torch, because the moon was large and full that night, and the clouds covered it only intermittently. Besides, his arms were full with the dishes he was carrying. He had done this every night for days, he was not expecting anything unusual to happen. So he wasn't looking in the darker recesses of the colonnade, where Eteo was hiding, waiting.

I heard nothing, which can only be what my brother intended. The slave was not found until the next evening, tied up on Eteo's floor. He had been carrying in the new dishes, he explained (though by then no one cared), when a hand had clapped itself around his mouth and a blade bit at his throat. He did not resist, though he claimed he did not know it was the royal prince who was accosting him until he was bundled into his room. Eteo must have picked up yesterday's used dishes and taken them with him, to keep anyone from guessing that something was amiss. The guards weren't manning the gate very attentively, that much was clear: Eteo was a hand taller than the slave he had imprisoned, and more muscular. He left the crocks outside the kitchens and if anyone thought this was strange, they said nothing. The kitchen boy took them (no doubt complaining to himself that his fellow slave had slacked off) and washed them, as he always did. No one knew where Eteo was until after it was light. He must have hidden somewhere: my guess is that he went into one of the state rooms, which were rarely used, unless ambassadors were visiting from another city. The night-watch would not have checked those rooms more than once at the start of the evening, if they even bothered to do that: they would not have seen the point. It scarcely needs mentioning that every man on the night patrol is dead now, clubbed to death by the royal bodyguards.

Eteo was cleverer than me, so he had already worked out that Polyn was living in the old king's rooms in the second courtyard. No one has used them for as long as we have been alive, but apparently the old king (the one before my father) slept there. Eteo could have crept in to speak to Polyn before it grew light, but he did not. Instead he waited until the king rose and washed and ate and walked through to the treasury to begin the day with his advisers. Eteo then crossed the courtyard to the state rooms on the west side of the courtyard. No one stopped him. The guards would perhaps not have known that he was supposed to be locked in the family courtyard with me. He had been so quiet for days, perhaps they had forgotten he was there. They either did not see or did not question the fact that he was carrying a sword. It was hardly an unusual thing, to see a prince with a ceremonial weapon. But just because the hilt of Eteo's sword was studded with polished agate gems did not make the blade any less sharp.

He opened the door of the treasury, and walked inside, letting it close behind him. Polyn must have been shocked to see him, but perhaps he was not. He must have been expecting this, or something like it, sooner or later. It would have been unlike him to underestimate Eteo: the two of them have been squabbling since Eteo was born. My uncle was also in the room, as were two slaves, from whom I heard all this. I bribed them with honey-cakes so they would tell me, though they had sworn to my uncle to keep their silence.

'Resign the kingship,' Eteo said. He didn't shout.

'What can you mean, brother?' Polyn asked. 'Your turn is next year. You must be patient.'

'You are responsible for what happened to Isy. It was your man who stabbed her. How could you do such an appalling thing? The gods themselves must have stolen your senses, and they will surely punish you for such an impious crime.'

Guilt settled on Polyn's face for a moment, before flying away again like a weary bird. 'I don't know what you mean,' he replied. 'You were king when our sister was attacked. She was your responsibility.'

'She still is,' Eteo replied. 'And she is yours, too. We both swore to protect our sisters long ago. Father would have been ashamed of you. I am ashamed of you. To set a grown man to attack a girl, and your own sister. I tried to believe anything else before I could accept that you were capable of such behaviour.'

'How dare you?' Polyn leapt to his feet.

'I told you to resign,' Eteo said. 'I will banish you from the palace, and the city. You will leave Thebes before nightfall. You can beg Isy's pardon before you leave. I wouldn't give it to you, but she is soft-hearted and wants to think well of you, so she might. But you deserve nothing from her, or from anyone.'

'Get out,' Polyn whispered. 'I will not tell you again. I will call the guards and have you locked up in the caves beneath the palace. You think I fear the scandal? I don't.'

'Polyn, Eteo, calm down,' said my uncle. He said nothing else.

'I don't think you fear any scandal,' said Eteo. 'What kind of man could agree to an attack on his own sister? You filthy coward.'

Polyn reached for his own sword, but he wasn't wearing it. Why would he be, when he was sitting in the treasury with my uncle and his slaves? He stepped backwards, groping behind him for an ornamental weapon: a valuable silver knife which was usually used by the priests during their sacrifices. The blade was sharp, but the metal was soft, designed for killing a helpless victim, rather than for combat. He jabbed at Eteo, and drew blood from the arm my brother raised to ward off the blow. He cannot have believed that Polyn would really attack him. It is this which I think reveals the truth: Eteo took a sword with him – I don't deny it – but he did not intend to use it. He was trained to fight; he knew he could not defend himself against a knife with his bare arm. It was the behaviour of a brother, who believes his sibling is feinting, and will not really hurt him. He put up his arm, not his sword.

Eteo saw his own blood dripping from his slashed forearm onto the stone floor. And only then did he shake his head like a wounded boar, and raise his sword in anger. Polyn swiped at him again, and this time Eteo parried the attack with his sword. The tip of Polyn's knife shattered with the force of Eteo's defence. Polyn cursed as he looked at the blade: it was shorter, jagged now from the damage, but still sharp. He made one final attempt on Eteo, stepping in and stabbing at his neck. There was no mistaking his intent. Even a short blade will kill a man if it pierces him in the neck. He took such a large step that it confused Eteo, who was preparing to parry the knife again, expecting a blow to be aimed at his torso.

Eteo's sword – so beautifully kept, as the armourer had taught him when he was still a child – cut right into Polyn's chest. My oldest brother fell to his knees, dropping the knife as he went. Eteo must have been horrified by what he had done, because he dropped his sword too, and reached out to catch Polyn, who slumped forward into his brother's arms.

It cannot have been Polyn who shouted for the guards, because he would not have had the strength, as he lay, his head on Eteo's shoulder, his blood pouring out over them both. And it cannot have been Eteo, who would have called for a doctor, for Sophon, but not for the guards. So it must have been my uncle who shouted with a tone of such urgency that the guards ran from all over the courtyard – most with their heads still half-filled with sleep – and pushed the treasury door open, almost falling over one another in their haste to obey Creon's summons. They saw my brothers tangled on their knees and looked at my uncle for instructions.

'The king is dying,' he said. 'Here is his assassin.'

Thebes does not have many laws. But the guards knew what they must do. They picked Eteo up by his shoulders and dragged him outside into the courtyard. They pulled back his hair to expose his neck, and slit his throat like a bull.

Ani and Haem had run into the courtyard from wherever they had been hiding. The shout and the sudden stampede of feet had pierced even their solitude. And so it was the sound of my sister screaming which drew me to the gates to see what on earth had happened. Only when I put my weight against them did I find they were now open, as Eteo must have left them when he slipped through, earlier in the morning. I ran into the royal courtyard, my eyes on Ani, frantic because I thought she was hurt.

I stood in confusion, because she seemed uninjured, and Haem was beside her, also safe and well. Finally I turned my head to follow her gaze, and saw the guards bringing Polyn out of the treasury on a litter they had fashioned from one of their cloaks. My brother's clothes were blackened with blood and he lay limp and lifeless on the stretcher. I looked back at Ani, hoping she would find a way to tell me I was mistaken. But her eyes were not on me, they were on the guard I had almost run into, who was brandishing a knife with a rusty blade in his left hand.

Only then did I realize that the blade was not rusty, and that the lake of blood pooling beneath my feet belonged to Eteo. Only then did I see that I had lost both my brothers. Everything had gone in a few beats of my heart. Everything but my sister.

18

Jocasta would never know what had been the first sign of the new Reckoning. No one did. The first Reckoning had ravaged Thebes many years earlier, a few summers before Jocasta was born. Her parents had survived it because her father was away trading in other cities and, because they were young and yet to have children, her mother had accompanied him. Thebes had closed its gates, and all admittance to the city was prohibited for a month or more. When they returned, only a day or so after the gates were finally reopened, they were startled to see that things were worse than the rumours had warned. The disease had been merciless, and more than one in eight of their fellow citizens were dead.

Some areas of the city had suffered greater devastation than others: the lower district, in the centre of the town, had a higher death toll than anywhere else, but no one knew why. Jocasta's parents lived high up on the hill on the far side of the city, but they had still lost seemingly numberless neighbours and relatives. People learned not to ask, if someone didn't appear at the market for a few days, or if their shoes went uncollected from the cobbler. The answer was always the same. Whole families had died, because those who tended the sick were more likely to fall ill themselves. If one child developed the early symptoms, their parents knew they too would have little chance of survival. Their only hope was to throw the sick child out onto the streets, and hope that they had acted in time. The child would die wherever it was, so parents tried to save themselves and their other offspring. Hopelessness was one of many symptoms of a disease which began with a headache and so often ended, seven or eight days later, in death. There was no way of knowing who would survive and who would die. Healthy young people were culled as efficiently as in a war, while their ancient parents – so frail before the Reckoning came – somehow withstood the ravages of the plague.

The sickness afflicted different people in different ways: all had a raging thirst and an unceasing sensation of burning from within. The inner heat was so terrible that people fled the city, clambering over its walls to throw themselves into the lake. But they felt no cooler, no matter how long they lay in the shallows and no matter how much water they drank. And when they tried to return to their homes, the gates were still barred and they could not enter. So they lay dying outside the city walls, their groans a wretched hymn for those guarding the gates.

Despite the intense internal heat, the sufferers' skin was not hot to the touch at first. The disease moved downwards starting with a cruel, vice-like headache. Most patients would then begin bleeding in the mouth, from the gums and the ulcerated tongue. Then the chest would tighten and an awful hacking cough would develop. By then, many of the sick would be overcome by the desperate state of their plight. They could no longer raise themselves to eat. Only those who were nursed – and hydrated – had any chance of survival. Those who lived in smaller houses, which grew unbearably hot in the summer months, had no hope at all. The disease descended to the digestive system, and the death toll at this stage was highest of all: the weakness caused by vomiting and diarrhoea was impossible to fight.

Those who survived suffered further indignities: the disease penetrated their extremities, and often they lost all feeling in one or more fingers or toes. Many could no longer practise the trade they had worked in all their lives, unable to work the leather or cloth which they had previously cut without needing to look. And even a minor cut, now painless and so unnoticed, could quickly became fatal. Pain was a warning, and the warning had been taken away. Some lost sight in one or both eyes; some lost hearing; others lost even their memories and could not recognize their friends or remember their own names.

In the months after the Reckoning, Thebes lost something of itself. Its people had always prided themselves on their steadiness, their ability to take everything which befell them in their stride. But they no longer felt this way. Too many had died and too many rules had been broken. The dead had not been properly buried while the Reckoning ravaged the city. No one could leave Thebes and inter their loved ones in graves outside the walls, as they used to. So people built funeral pyres and burned the dead instead. Some were too weak or weary to build a pyre, so they simply threw their dead on one already burning. Some used ropes to drop the bodies of the dead or terminally sick over the city walls. But everyone noticed that the vultures and dogs did not eat the corpses of the plague-dead. Even when the ribs of a dog were poking through his mangy fur, he would go hungry before he would chew on the polluted flesh.

The city had a proud history of welcoming strangers and traders from all over Hellas. The rules of xenia – where a traveller could expect food and lodging from strangers which he would one day reciprocate – had always been sacrosanct. But those too had gone. The gates were kept locked during the summer months for many years afterwards. Only those who could afford to bribe the guards could get into the city during the hottest part of the year. And the bribe needed to be a handsome one: the penalty for allowing someone from the Outlying into Thebes when the gates were closed was death. Each spring, Thebes would look nervously at its omens and wonder if this would be the year the Reckoning returned. Parents frightened their children, telling them stories of the terrors that presaged their birth.

Gradually, the fear subsided. But this was largely because those who had lived through the Reckoning were dying, not from the disease but from simple old age. By the time the disease struck Thebes for a second time, it was fifty years after the first blight. Only those who had been children the first time were still alive. And people had long since forgotten the symptoms, lost beneath layers of exaggeration and rumour. So Jocasta did not know, could not have known, that when the first of her citizens began to complain of a vicious spiking pain in the head and an unquenchable thirst, Thebes was at the beginning of something far worse than the usual summer sickness.

It was the summer of Isy's fourth birthday, and it was

Sophon who came to the palace asking for Jocasta. He was tutoring Polynices and Eteocles in their letters and geometry, having long since retired from treating the sick. He was sixty years old and his hands were too shaky, his eyes too weak for dealing with people who were frightened by whatever ailed them. But no doctor could really retire, especially not him. People still turned up at his door, begging for advice on one ailment or another. The past week had seen the numbers increase at an alarming rate: parents worrying about their children, children fearful for their ailing parents. On this day, he told the boys that he needed to see their mother before they could recite the verses they had learned for him. The slaves took one look at his dishevelled appearance, and took him straight into the second courtyard to speak to the queen.

'There's something wrong,' he said, as he hastened through the doorway into the treasury. Jocasta turned in surprise to greet her old friend. She was sitting with Oedipus and Creon, discussing the provisions the city would need to import during the coming winter. They had expectations of a good harvest: the grapes and olives were ripening on the hills outside the city. As usual, they would need to import grain. Jocasta looked well, perhaps a little tired, Sophon noticed. Motherhood suited her. Her greying hair betrayed her years, of course, but it was a clean, metallic grey, and her face lifted as she smiled at him.

'What's the matter?' she asked. 'Are the boys arguing in your class? I know they can be a nuisance.'

'The problem is not in your household,' he said. 'It's outside. In the city.'

Oedipus swept round behind him and pulled up a light wooden chair. 'Sit,' he said. 'Get your breath back.'

The old man sat down heavily, banging his elbows on the carved flowers which covered the arms of the chair. He sat for a moment, looking at the stone floor. 'My queen,' he said when he raised his eyes again. 'Too many people are falling ill. It reminds me of before.'

'Of before?' she asked. But she knew what he meant.

'Of the Reckoning,' he said. 'The headaches, the fever. Those who fell ill first are now developing the cough, four days in. It's the same as before.'

'You were alive during the Reckoning?' Oedipus asked. 'But that was a lifetime ago.'

Sophon eyed him. 'That's hardly an accurate system of measurement,' he replied irritably. 'It is more than your lifetime, than any of your lifetimes.' He looked from husband to wife to brother, and his tone softened. 'But somewhat less than mine. I was a child when it took the city the first time.'

'How did you avoid catching it?' Oedipus said.

'I didn't.' The old man's shoulders heaved. 'I caught it, but I recovered. So did my father. My mother died of it, as did my sister.'

'And you recognize the symptoms again now?' Jocasta asked.

'I'll know for sure in three days,' Sophon replied. 'When they start to die.'

'What can we do?' Creon asked. 'How did they stop it before?'

'They didn't stop it,' Sophon said. 'No one could. It

consumed the lower city. It devastated us. And there was nothing we could do to contain it or prevent it. Everyone fell sick, no one was safe. Eventually, people either recovered or died. Those who recovered didn't catch it again.'

'We can't let that happen now,' Oedipus snapped. 'There must be something we can do. In Corinth,' he paused, thinking about the stories he had been told as a child, 'they said it came from the water.'

Sophon nodded. 'The same belief arose here. It was nonsense, of course. People who lived near the wells died because sick people congregated near the wells. The disease makes you thirsty.' His eyes were cloudy as he remembered drinking everything he could find, and still feeling his furred tongue and cracked throat, desperate for water. He saw again his father offering him the last cup of water in the house, though his own lips were split and bleeding.

'Does water cure them?' Jocasta asked.

The old man shrugged. 'Many of them will die even if they can get enough to drink. All of them will die if they can't. Or if they refuse to.'

'Why would they refuse?' asked Creon.

'Fear,' Oedipus said, before Sophon could reply. 'They will avoid the wells if they believe the water is tainted. People aren't rational when they're afraid.'

'They closed the city,' Jocasta said, snatching at the memory she didn't know she possessed. But she remembered her parents talking about it: their grand adventures in the Outlying, while Thebes was bolted shut.

'The disease must have come in from somewhere,' Sophon agreed. 'A traveller, a tradesman, someone brought it in with him, this time just as before. But shutting the gates can't help you now. The disease is already here.'

'It might prevent more travellers bringing it in,' said Creon. 'You should close the gates.'

Jocasta looked across to her husband, her eyebrows raised. He nodded.

'The gates will be closed in the morning,' she said. 'Only one announcement beforehand. If Thebans are away, they will have to manage until we reopen the city. Foreigners in the city will be able to leave if they wish.'

'They might be no safer out there,' Oedipus said.

'That's not my concern,' his wife replied. 'I am only queen of my own citizens. How do we persuade the people that the water is safe?'

Sophon sighed. 'I'm not sure you can,' he said.

'We can make an official pronouncement,' Creon suggested. 'Telling the citizens that the water supply has been checked and is harmless.'

'What would you think if someone said that to you?' Oedipus asked.

'I'd think they had something to hide,' Jocasta said. 'But what else can we do?'

The four of them sat in silence for a moment, until it was broken by Oedipus.

'Put guards around the wells,' he said. 'Order them out there now. Two guards on each well from sunrise to sunset.'

'The heat of the day is when people will need water the most,' Sophon protested.

'They will store water to use during the day,' Oedipus replied. 'If the guards are seen there all day, drinking the water as they please but preventing ordinary citizens from doing the same, Thebans will be furious. They'll wait till the guards leave, fill every vessel they have, and carry it back to their homes.'

'That's clever,' the old man smiled.

'It's infantile,' said Creon. 'Thebans will believe their queen is deliberately withholding water from them.' He turned to his sister, his hands spread in supplication. 'They will never forgive you. They'll blame you even if they survive,' he said. 'Follow this advice, and they will hate you. You can't win.'

'I don't want to win,' she replied. 'I just don't want them to die. Alive and hating me is better than dead.' She addressed the old man again. 'Is there anything else we could do?'

Sophon nodded slowly. 'The Reckoning was fast,' he said. 'Impossibly fast. It went through the city like a blaze. People were dead or recovered in a matter of days. If they recovered, they didn't catch it again. Those people must help us nurse the sick: first the old, who survived it last time. And perhaps, once they have recovered this time, the young. And it is not just nursing we will need help with. Bodies must be buried or burned, as soon as they are dead.' He ignored the horror which spasmed across Creon's face. 'The stench of this disease is nothing compared to the smell of the dead, piling up behind the closed doors of houses. The Reckoning wasn't the only thing that killed people the last time. Corpses are dangerous, and they carry their own diseases. We need somewhere outside the city walls. A lime pit. Do you understand?'

'So we need to have men ready to dispose of the dead,'

Jocasta said. 'That shouldn't be too difficult. My guards can organize that.' She thought for a moment. 'There are a few older ones. And those without children, after them. Their commander will arrange it.'

'They should cover their faces,' Sophon said. 'With scarves. It makes it easier to breathe if you can't smell the dead.'

'Very well,' she said. 'What else?'

'Nothing that will help,' the old man sighed.

'What else?' she asked again, reaching over to her friend and patting his arm so he understood that she needed to know everything, even if it would frighten her.

Sophon thought for a moment, and spoke again. 'Even if they have water to drink, and somewhere cool to sleep, even if this heat breaks and the disease breaks with it, and even if we can get rid of the bodies before they contaminate anything else, it might not be enough to save everyone who could have survived. Because people stop trying when they've lost too much. It's not something you can prevent. I survived because my father survived. I had him to live for and he had me. So although my mother was gone . . .' He paused to wipe away a tear which had sprung from his eye, pushing his hand into his face as though he wanted to punish it for its weakness. 'I had someone to feed me and look after me. And my father had someone to look after. He couldn't just lie down on the ground and weep for everything he had lost, though I'm sure he wanted to. And that's the one danger you can't guard against. The more people die, the more people have lost their reason to live. Do you understand?'

Jocasta nodded. Of course she did.

19

Everything happened so fast, but also too slowly. Someone – one of the guards, I suppose – reached around me from behind. His hands were covered in wiry hair, and the knuckles were swollen and calloused. He held me in a strange, clumsy embrace, and lifted me away from Eteo. I could hear Ani sobbing on the other side of the square, and Haem murmuring words of comfort. I looked up to see she had turned into his chest, her back heaving, one small hand clenched on his tunic. I stood alone as people walked around me: the guards carrying Polyn on a litter, reverently, because he was the king; the ones who walked past Eteo without noticing his precious body, as though he were a pile of refuse; my uncle, walking out from the shaded colonnade in front of the treasury and into the morning sun, which illuminated what would have been better left in darkness. I saw Creon's mouth move as he spoke to one of the guards, but too quietly for me to hear. There was a rushing sound in my ears, as though I had dived underwater. Everything else was muffled and distant.

Slaves rushed into the square from all sides, and stood waiting to be given orders: my uncle directed them calmly to remove Eteo from the courtyard stones. He didn't use my brother's name. He said 'this' and gestured. I stepped forward to help them, because it was my duty – mine and Ani's, as their sisters and closest kin – to prepare both my brothers for burial. But the slaves bustled past me, as if I were no more than one of the statues which stand in the four corners of the square. Both brothers would need to be washed and wrapped in white cloths. And we would need to place some small piece of gold – a ring or a thin chain – into each one's hands or around his neck. Thebans believe the ferryman will not take someone across the river of the dead without some payment for his trouble.

But even as I was thinking about all this, a part of my mind wanted to shout out that it was all ridiculous. How could my brother be buried, when it was impossible that he was dead? He was alive a moment ago; he could not now be something else. I was looking around the square, expecting Sophon to arrive and explain that he could revive Eteo, stitch him back together as he had done me, shaking his head and tutting about how we got ourselves into such scrapes. But he didn't come.

The slaves carried Eteo away before I could touch him. It was only later I realized they were taking him the wrong way: out towards the main courtyard, when he needed to be carried to the family square, so we could lay him out and wash him. I knew something was wrong at the time, but it seemed so minor, after everything else.

My uncle finally noticed me and my sister, and directed a slave girl over to each of us. She told me that I must go to the family courtyard, and wash my brother's blood from my feet, from where I had blundered into the square, too late to save him. Only then did I look down and see she was right: my feet were covered in Eteo's sticky black-red blood. I wanted to clean myself of such a terrible pollution, but simultaneously, I wanted to kneel down and rub my hands in the blood: to run my fingers through it and paint it over my face.

But as I felt my knees collapse beneath me, the guard who had lifted me back from Eteo a moment and a lifetime ago stepped forward and caught me. He glanced over at my uncle, and swung me up into his arms, as though I were a child. He carried me away from the scene of my brother's death towards the family square.

Not just the scene of one brother's death, the scene of my both my brothers' deaths. The loss of Eteo was so enormous, I could barely see around it to Polyn. I could not take in what had happened: my whole family gone except Ani. I heard the words of the slave girl, as the guard put me down carefully on a bench by the water pump in the corner of our courtyard, but I couldn't think how to do what she was saying. Soon, more slaves approached me, all carrying water and cloths. One undid my sandals and slipped them off, before wiping my ankles and feet with her cloth. She rinsed it out into a small wooden bucket, and I watched the water darken with Eteo's blood.

'Where's Ani?' I said to her, as she finished, folding her cloth in half and placing it on the edge of the bucket. My sister was still with Haem, I supposed, and I needed her. When she finally came through the gates, I stood and ran to her, forgetting I was barefoot until I was standing on the sharp stones beneath the colonnade. She held out her arms and, clinging to one another, we stumbled away from the courtyard to be alone together with our grief. We sat on one of the couches in her room – a puffy, cushioned thing which our mother used to lie on when she was tired. Ani's face was streaked with tears: her hair was sticking to the salt left on her cheeks. She reached over and squeezed my hand.

'Did you know what he was planning to do?' she asked.

'Of course not,' I told her. Though at that time, I did not know precisely what Eteo had done, only what my uncle said he had done, and I knew better than to believe everything people said in the palace. 'I knew he was angry with Polyn. I knew he wanted to get out of the courtyard. You'd know this too, if you hadn't disappeared.'

She blushed, knowing the accusation was fair. 'I'm sorry, Isy. I didn't think about him.'

'Or me.' I wasn't in the mood to make her feel better about how she had behaved.

'No,' she agreed, fresh tears springing from her eyes. 'I just wanted to be with Haem. He was planning to announce our betrothal today.'

I stared at her. 'He might have to wait until our brothers are in the ground.'

'I know. I'm sure he will. I didn't mean to suggest that . . .' She paused. 'I'm sorry, Isy. I know you've always admired him.'

Now it was my turn to redden. I had tried so hard to avoid letting them see that I cared for our cousin at least as much as she did. I had always known he would choose her. It would have been unthinkable for him to do anything else: quite aside from her beauty, she was the elder sister. I could not be married before she was.

'It doesn't matter,' I told her.

'It does,' she said, gulping. 'Who will want to marry you now, Isy? After what our brothers have done? I know I've told you before that you would be hard to marry off, but I thought there was at least a chance. You know how people have gossiped about our family since . . .' She refused to say the words. She always had, ever since she and I had watched our mother be carried through this courtyard on a litter. 'This will just confirm that what people say about us is true,' she said. 'That our family is cursed, has always been cursed. For two brothers to kill one another . . .'

'Cursed? What does that even mean?' I asked. 'Polyn and Eteo have never been close. Sharing the kingship was the only way to keep their dislike of one another in check. And then Polyn changed his mind about sharing Thebes with Eteo, as he has done with everything else since I can remember. The only curse is that Polyn should have been born an only child.'

She looked startled. 'Are you saying this is all Polyn's fault?'

'Ani – open your eyes. Or at the very least, use them to look at something other than your intended. Polyn is the one who tried to throw everything into chaos. Polyn is the one who tried to turn the people against Eteo. Polyn is the one whose friend attacked me.'

'You can't mean what you're saying.'

'I saw the man again, Ani. I saw him at the coronation games. I recognized him straightaway.'

'But you said the man who stabbed you had his face covered.'

'His eyes weren't covered.' Ani opened her mouth but

she did not argue. She knew that I would not have made a mistake about something like this.

'And that's why Eteo . . . ?'

'Of course. What did you think?'

'I thought he was seizing the throne, Isy.'

'But he's your brother. You know what sort of a man he is. Eteo isn't at all ambitious.'

'I know,' she said. 'But you must see what it looked like. Eteo attacked Polyn.'

'I don't believe that.'

Ani looked at me for a moment, and pushed her hair back, shifting the strand which had stuck itself to her face. 'It doesn't matter what you believe, Isy. It matters what everyone else believes, and they will all think Eteo was the aggressor.'

I knew she was right. 'We need to tell people that they're wrong,' I said.

She patted my arm. 'We will. We can do all this once I am crowned queen.'

I was so startled by her words that I could find nothing to say. How long after she saw our brothers dead did she decide she should succeed them?

*

I was in my own room now. There was a basket of raw, greasy wool which had been in the corner for so long it had acquired a thin coating of dust. I hated spinning, and always had. It was the appropriate task for women in the royal household, my uncle once said, when I asked him why I should work wool badly when we had a palace full of slaves who were skilled at spinning and weaving some of the finest cloth in Hellas. Creon knew I was happier in lessons, or playing the lyre, and he did not press the point.

But today, I needed to do something with my hands, or I would lie on the ground and scream my brothers' names until my throat was raw. I could not play the phorminx: there were not yet words or music for what had happened. There would be elegies to come. But not yet.

I sat on the floor next to the basket, pressing my back against the wall. I took a handful of wool and began to turn it over, picking out the burrs and seeds which had caught in it. I piled them up on the wooden stool, and began twisting the wool to make a thick, lumpy thread. It unravelled itself so quickly: how did the slave women keep theirs from returning to a puffy cloud of fibres? I pulled on the thread with my other hand, tightening it to keep it straight. Ani was right, of course: she would be queen now. No one would expect us to share the throne, as our brothers had. She would be queen, Haem would be king, and Thebes would be unchanged for most of its citizens. But the palace would be changed, and I would be changed.

Where would I go, when Ani and Haem had this courtyard for their own family? Would I stay in my rooms, as her unmarried sister? Ani was right about my chances of marriage now, but she always had been. I had spoken about it with Eteo many times, and he had always promised that I could live in his court, no matter how many children he produced. They'll need their wise aunt, he used to say, and I felt a wrench through my gut at the loss of my brother and his future. I tried to concentrate on protocol, so I could staunch my tears and catch my breath. The appropriate match for me was a prince from another city. But to be the sister of two murdered brothers was a curse in itself. People would believe the cruel tales about the gods persecuting the children of my parents: and who would want to ally themselves with someone who came from such a wretched house, of which stories could never be told without sadness?

I felt the grease spreading across my hands as I carried on twisting the wool, and saw the dirt was discolouring my nails. Eteo couldn't have known that Polyn would fight. He could not. He must have believed that our oldest brother would stand aside when presented with the truth: that his siblings knew what he had done. But had Eteo been foolish? If Polyn was so shameless that he could enlist a friend to attack me, he was hardly likely to be shamed when he was found out. Eteo should have foreseen this, and then he would still be here with me now, watching me and marvelling at how I could ruin a whole sheep's worth of wool in a matter of moments. My brother had made a simple error: he had assumed that Polyn would behave as he himself would have behaved. But Eteo was never like Polyn, could never have been so devious. So how could he think Polyn would behave like him?

I dropped the thread and watched it unfurl back to its unwound state. Why was the courtyard so quiet? The slaves should have brought Polyn and Eteo in to their rooms by now, so we could wash them and wrap them with the other women of the household. Where were they?

We should have known what was coming. Especially me; trying so hard to find the story that made sense of our home and our family, imagining myself a historian, an astute chronicler of events. I fell so far short of what I imagined myself to be. I was no historian, no poet; merely a fool, failing to understand every single thing that happened until it was too late. The humiliation of realizing this was terrible. Who was I, if I wasn't the clever, observant creature I had always imagined myself? I was no one. I was the stupidest of us all. Because I was watching so closely, and still I was tricked, like a gullible fool trying to spot which cup the ball is under: so confident in his prediction, so risible in his confidence.

In the time that I had been sitting with my spindle and my worthless woollen yarn, thinking only of my future, the palace had changed irrevocably. The neat destiny my sister had spied for herself was not to be hers after all. She was the heir in line to the throne, but the throne was no longer vacant. At the precise moment that I was wondering why the slave women had not summoned me to wash my brothers' corpses, I heard a distant, tinny peal.

I knew immediately what it was: a herald's horn, sounded for an official pronouncement in the main square. I stood up and ran to my door. They were announcing the death of the king. Ani's door swung open too, and her eyes met mine. She frowned, and reached out her hand. We scurried along the side of the family square, and then through the second courtyard, both of us trying not to look at the bloodstains which still covered the ground. The guards should probably have prevented us from crossing to the gates into the main square, but they were nowhere in sight. It was much later when I discovered they had all been marched out of the palace and executed, the standard punishment for failing to prevent the death of a king.

The final squawk of the horn had barely died down before my uncle stepped forward on a podium and reached out his hands to quieten the small but excited crowd which had gathered. Rumours about my brothers must have been racing across the city from the moment Eteo walked into the treasury this morning, and the murmuring was growing louder. My uncle stood waiting for them to realize that he would not speak until they were quiet. Eventually, their curiosity overwhelmed their desire to deliver gossip dressed as fact.

'Men of Thebes,' Creon said. 'The king is dead. Slain by his brother, cut down by bitter rivalry.'

The murmuring began again, more intensely than before.

'I stand before you a bereaved uncle,' Creon continued. 'Not one but both my nephews died today, each by the sword of the other.' I felt Ani's hand squeeze mine. She wanted me to keep silent, even as we heard him lie. 'It is a dark day for Thebes,' my uncle said. 'And it must also be a new beginning. It was never my desire to inherit the mantle of power from my sister; you all know me and you know this to be true. I was content to be the adviser of kings, I have never sought kingship for myself.'

The crowd of strangers nodded, flattered by the suggestion that they were party to decisions made in the royal household, when they simply happened to be in the market square as the news erupted.

'But I can shirk my responsibility no longer,' he said. 'Today I accept the role I now acknowledge I was destined to perform.' A priest in a hastily tied robe stepped up behind him with the bright gold crown which had last been placed on Polyn's head. My uncle bowed slightly, and accepted it over his own balding pate. The crowd cheered: one king was much the same as another to them.

So my sister did not become queen. And I realized at last – too late – that Polyn had been the victim of a conspiracy, just as much as Eteo.

20

Jocasta looked up at the sky. How had the sun moved so quickly? Sophon and Creon were somewhere in the city, carrying out her orders. She had asked them both to return to the palace before nightfall. Before the gates were closed for the duration of the Reckoning. Sophon had said nothing, only squeezed her arm as he left, smiling. She knew he would not be back until the sickness had passed through the city. The stubborn old man would be treating everyone he could, relying on his immunity to the disease, disregarding his age and increasing frailty. But her brother would return, bringing his family with him. If she could just keep them all safe, it would be something to cling to, while her city was battered by the vicious storm.

When the two men left this morning, Oedipus had wandered back to the family courtyard alone. When she returned there herself, she found him working in the garden, even though the midday sun was punishing. His grey tunic was wet, and his hair had furrows running through it, where he had pushed it back from his face with damp hands. He looked so beautiful that she paused to admire him. Her husband was twenty-seven years old, and to her eyes, he looked the same as when he arrived ten years ago. His eyes still glittered with flecks of gold, his unmarked skin still shone like ripe apricots. His muscles had retained every defined curve. Unable to avoid the comparison, she looked down at her own body and wished for the thousandth time that carrying each of her children had not left its traces on her. She had aged so much more than her husband, though ten years was a larger proportion of his life than of hers.

Every morning Jocasta woke up wishing that time might flow backwards at night, just for her, so she could stay where she was, a summer or two past forty until he caught up with her. She never complained of the backache she had when Ismene wanted to be picked up and carried. She never mentioned the soreness she felt in her hips and knees when she bent down to pick up a discarded wooden toy. She knew Oedipus would sympathize, would offer to rub her aching muscles, but she couldn't bear for him to think of her as old enough to have painful joints. She knew what scorn she had felt for Laius, who always had some niggling injury. So she ignored the discomfort, in the hope that it would disappear. But it never did: it simply moved to a different sinew or bone, to torment her anew.

'You have slaves to do the gardening for you,' she smiled, as she walked over to him. The children were too hot even to quarrel, and were drowsing under the colonnade.

He looked up from the plants he was cutting back.

'They're dying back a bit from the heat, but don't worry. The roots are healthy.'

'I'm glad,' she said.

'I'll go and talk to the night-watchmen after we've

eaten,' he said. 'They need to know what's going on, so they can drum up some extra men.'

'People aren't going to storm the gates,' she protested. But she knew there was no point.

'It's best that we're prepared,' he told her. 'My parents told terrible stories about the last time. They used to frighten me with them when I was a child, tell me to hurry up to bed because the rats were coming. That's what they called the plague orphans, in Corinth.'

'We don't need to close the palace because your parents terrified you with bedtime stories,' she said.

'Your doctor told you to close the palace,' he reminded her. 'What's your brother doing?'

'He's organizing men to guard the wells and prepare to bury the dead,' she said. 'He'll be back here before it gets dark.'

'Are you sure they should stay here?' Oedipus asked. 'Eurydice, Haemon: they're definitely not ill?'

'Would it matter if they were?' she said.

'Yes,' he replied. 'Of course it would. My darling, I don't want to see you go through the pain of losing your brother or your sister-in-law or your nephew. But you must know,' he took her shoulders and shook her gently, so she raised her eyes to meet his, 'I would see them all die before my eyes, rather than let them anywhere near you or the children. You know that.'

And she nodded, wondering how he could make a declaration of love sound so much like a threat.

Jocasta had tried everything to distract Oedipus from the setting sun, but as she looked across at him from the divan where she was pretending to sleep, she saw him glance up in irritation: he was finding it hard to see as the evening drew in.

She stood up and walked behind him, reached around her husband, draping her hands on his chest. 'Have you finished with your plants for today?' she asked.

'I'm just thinking about all the things we need to do,' he said.

'There's nothing to do.' She feigned a languidness she didn't feel, but she had done all she could for her city. At dawn tomorrow, criers would walk though the streets announcing that Thebes would close her gates, for as long as was necessary. Any travellers needed to leave immediately, or they would be locked in regardless. When the weather broke, she would consider allowing the gates to be opened for people to leave, although there would be no admittance to the city for two months, at least. The plague had come in from the Outlying; she could not take further risks.

'What do you mean, there's nothing to do?' Oedipus tugged her wrists, pulling her hands away from him. 'I want to be sure the children are safe. How long do you think the illness takes to show itself? We need a quarantine period for anyone who left the palace today or yesterday. They can't come near you or me or the children until they have proved themselves healthy.'

'That's a good idea,' Jocasta murmured into his ear, knowing this was her best chance of diverting his attention from the sinking sun. She felt him squirm a little from the tickling sensation of her breath in his ear, and gently kissed the lobe. He took a deep breath, but then moved away, saying, 'That'll have to wait, my queen.'

'No,' she said, as he turned to face her. 'Nothing has to wait.'

'The gates need to be closed,' he said, gently unhooking her fingers from his arms. 'I'm going to order the men to do it now.'

'They know when to shut the gates.' She tried to laugh. 'They do it every night.'

'But tonight is different, lover. Tonight they need to be locked and barred. No one in, no one out. They need to understand that there are to be no exceptions.'

Jocasta loathed arguing with her husband. They hardly ever raised voices against each other. He was impetuous and could be quick-tempered, but she rarely allowed things to escalate into a full-scale disagreement.

'I'm not sure Creon's back yet,' she said. 'They need to wait for him.'

Oedipus reached down and cupped her chin in his hand. He had beautiful hands with long, slender fingers like a musician. He rarely played the lyre these days, but she loved to watch him when he did. He shook his head gently. 'They can't. We need to lock up, whether your brother is here or not.'

'He's only away because he's doing the job I asked him to do,' she cried. 'You can't punish him for that.'

'He should have sent Eurydice and Haemon up here before he left,' Oedipus said. 'I wonder why he didn't.'

'Because he thought he'd be back in time,' she said. 'Please.'

'Are you really begging me to allow your brother into

our home?' he asked, wrenching his hand away from her face so quickly that she felt her head lurch on her neck, and winced from the pain. 'When he's been all over the city today? Do you think that's wise? When he might bring in the plague and infect you, or me, or our children?'

'He's my only brother,' she said, tears falling from her eyes. Oedipus had never planned to wait for Creon, she realized. She hated crying in front of her husband; she knew it made her look old. She turned her face away from him.

'He should have come back sooner,' Oedipus said, and stalked off to the front of the palace. Jocasta listened to the pebbles crunch beneath his anger, until he was too far away for her to hear. She sat on the edge of the divan and heard the distant grate of iron on stone. The gates were closed. Then a loud thud, which took her a moment to place. It was the sound of the thick bars of black pine – rarely used – sliding home across the inside of the gates. She strained to hear the sound of Haemon, squealing with excitement because he and his parents were spending the night at the palace and he had just found out. But the sound didn't come. They hadn't arrived in time. She felt a stabbing pain in her left temple, and knew it would soon be followed by a similar pain on the other side. She walked over to the fountain and dipped her hands in the water, then drew small circles around her throbbing brow. Sometimes the coolness eased the pain, but not tonight.

*

A month later, they reopened the palace gates. The plague had danced through the city this time. It did not annihilate everything it touched, and was – according to those who remembered its first incarnation – less ruinous this time. Many Thebans had boarded up their windows and stayed inside for the duration – darting outside to collect water in the darkest portion of the night – and most of them had survived.

Of those who were infected, many more lived than died. This Reckoning was more predictable than before: it picked off the very young, the very old, the sickly and the weak. But it did not cull the healthy with the same careless vigour it had shown before. Once again, it fed on the lower reaches of the city. But it was not catastrophic, only terrible, so the city did not descend into anarchy, as Jocasta had feared might happen, with their queen locked behind the palace gates. There was anger that the water supply was guarded for the duration of the sickness, but none of the guards was lynched, as had looked likely at one point. The citizens did not like their queen withdrawing from her city when it was in crisis, but most were honest enough to admit that they would have done the same themselves, if they had been able.

Jocasta sent her criers through the city, proclaiming the end of the Reckoning and asking her citizens to continue their vigilance against the symptoms of the disease in future. On the day the palace and city gates were reopened, she hoped her brother would appear, but he did not. She knew he must be angry with her. She had asked the guards – discreetly, when Oedipus was busy elsewhere, playing with the children in the garden, as the heat had finally broken – whether her brother had arrived at the palace on the night the gates were closed. They had arrived much too late, she had discovered. Long after sunset: Creon and Eurydice, the latter carrying Haemon on one hip, his legs swinging as they walked. Creon held a torch in the thickening night, to light their way across the uneven stones and old vegetables left rotting in the market square.

Creon had carried out every task Jocasta had entrusted to him. He had travelled across the city, speaking to her men directly. He had warned Eurydice that she would need to pack their essentials while he was away, but when he returned he found she had ignored him, saying she preferred to stay in her own home, no matter what was coming.

A bitter argument had followed and he had hurled clothes and valuables into two large cloth bags as quickly as he could. But Eurydice refused to leave the house. What about looters, she asked. What if people broke into their home and moved themselves in? How could they prove it was theirs? Eurydice was more afraid of losing her home than her life, Creon told her. But by the time he dragged her and Haemon from the house, darkness had fallen. They walked in silence the short distance up the hill to the palace. Even Haemon – usually so talkative – was quiet. He knew his parents were angry with one another, and was fearful of making things worse. When the family reached the palace gates, the guards, who had known him for more than ten years, refused him entry. The gates were barred, one of them shouted from inside the courtyard. No exceptions.

Creon was unlike his brother-in-law in almost every regard, not least in the way they each expressed anger.

While Oedipus radiated his annoyance, conveying to anyone who could see him that he was displeased, Creon was contained. He did not attempt to reason with the men, but simply turned around to take his family home. Only his closest friends could have deduced his feelings.

'Where are we going? Why aren't we going in?' asked Haem.

'I told you. I said they didn't want us there,' Eurydice hissed. 'Everyone can see it besides you: your sister doesn't care a jot for anyone but herself and her husband.'

Creon was too weary to argue with his wife. He walked back to his house, and unbolted the doors. He used his torch to light a smoky candle, then extinguished the larger flame with a handful of sand.

'I'll get food and more water tomorrow,' he said. He took his son's hand, and half-carried him to bed, the candlelight flickering on the walls.

His wife sat alone in the darkness until he returned.

'We were too late,' he said. 'That's all.'

'We're their family,' she said. 'That should be all.'

He nodded. 'I thought they would let us in. We should have left earlier. If Jocasta had been there . . .'

'If Jocasta wasn't there, it was because she didn't want to be,' Eurydice snapped. 'She knew you were coming back tonight. She hides behind Oedipus, you know that. She won't criticize him or disagree with him, even when it means throwing us to the wolves.'

Creon smiled. 'I'm not sure we should add wolves to the list of things we need to protect ourselves against,' he said. But Eurydice wouldn't take the cue and ally herself with her husband against the world.

'You always take her side,' she said. 'Always. She uses you, and then she ignores you when it suits her. You're the only person who can't see it.'

Creon turned away from his wife and went to bed. The next morning, he rose to find she had not come to bed herself. When he walked into their living space, he was surprised to find it empty. He looked around for a sign from his wife, something to indicate where she might have gone.

Eurydice had been taught her letters by her father long ago, but she rarely used them. So it was several moments before Creon noticed the wax tablet on the table. It belonged to Haemon, who used it in his lessons at the palace. Sophon must have let him bring it home to practise scratching onto the wax without pushing through and damaging the wood beneath. It was a challenge for a childish hand. Even when he saw the tablet, he didn't notice the writing at first, assuming the ill-formed letters must be Haemon's. Only when he had looked everywhere else and found no hint of Eurydice's whereabouts did he look at the tablet more closely.

'I have a headache and the thirst,' she had written. 'Look after him.'

21

On the day of Polyn's coronation, I had thought the only thing I wanted was to feel safe again in the palace. In my home. But I was mistaken. We had never been safer, my sister and I. No one could now enter the palace without prior consent from my uncle. None of the aristoi – Polyn and Eteo's friends – had been allowed in since the day my brothers died. They had been replaced by their fathers: Creon preferred older men for his advisers and colleagues. But we were now prisoners in what used to be our home. Every door and gate had been locked. I hadn't seen anyone but my sister and the servants for days.

I finally persuaded my uncle over dinner the night after they died that I should be allowed to see Sophon. I told him my lyre had fallen out of tune, and I had broken one of the strings retuning it. He told me I should be weaving, behaving as though he had always been king, as though nothing terrible had occurred only a day earlier. Ani produced a sample of the cloth I had made: a rich, red wool, woven into a lumpy, scratchy, ill-shaped piece of fabric, and he decided it would be foolish to waste such expensive materials on me. I could keep trying to spin my own threads, but what I produced would not sell on the cheapest market stall. It was – Creon sighed – an embarrassment to the royal household to have produced women so unskilled in fine work. But he didn't say what anyone else would have: who will want to marry you with such a lack of the wifely skills? He had no need.

'I need my lyre or I cannot sing at the wake,' I told him. Thebans understand that paying our duty to the dead is more important than anything which happens while someone is alive. The announcement of deaths in the royal household meant that the city was in mourning, and would remain so for five days, until the burial was held. There would be fires and feasting, sacrifices and music played that night, as a sign that we had paid the dead their dues and were then allowed to re-enter the world of the living. Until the burial, Ani and I were in a liminal state: tainted by the dead, unable to fit in to normal life.

My uncle nodded his head in weary assent, and told me he would send Sophon into the family courtyard the next morning. 'You must use your time to compose a song for your brother,' he said. I thought I must have misheard the final word.

'I will,' I told him. 'I am already trying to think of the best way to twine their two stories together.' We were sitting around a small table, and Haem was reaching out to take a piece of flatbread, still warm with griddle-marks stamped across it, like a brand. Creon was holding a bowl of chickpeas in one hand, and scooping them onto his plate with a spoon.

'The song will be only for Polynices,' Creon said, and Haem froze just for a moment. Creon turned his head slightly to look at his son – who was sitting opposite Ani, rather than next to her, as usual – and Haem flickered back into life, picking up the bread he had been reaching towards.

'I could write a song for each of them,' I said, as though I were agreeing with Creon's suggestion. Sitting next to Ani, who had dropped her head, allowing her hair to hide her face, I could hear her shallow breathing.

'Just for Polynices,' he repeated. 'Eteocles will not receive a wake. He was an enemy of the city.'

'Don't be absurd,' Ani said, looking up at last. She had forgotten that arguing with Creon is never the best way to change his mind. You have to persuade him to do things differently, over time. Contradicting him only drives him to occupy his previous position more immovably. I saw Haem's eyes flash a warning, but too late. Creon turned his gaze from me to my sister.

'You will apologize for speaking in such a way to the king,' he said. 'You are no doubt distressed by the loss of your brother.' Ani has never been able to resist provocation.

'Two brothers,' she said. 'We have lost two brothers.'

'And you will mourn one,' he told her. 'Polynices was the king of this city, and Eteocles tried to overthrow him. It was treason. Thebes does not don her mourning garb for traitors.' The last word was almost spat onto the table, as he slammed the earthenware bowl down. I jumped, even though I was watching him do it.

'We can have a private, family funeral for Eteo,' I said quickly. 'I will compose a song for Polyn's wake. Ani and I will bury Eteo together, away from the rest of the city, if it pleases you.' My sister looked at me as though I were an imbecile.

'We must bury both of them together. In death as in life,' she said. 'You know that.'

'They were not close,' I reminded her. 'The burial is what matters. Everything else is just . . .' I ran out of words. I did not wish to be disrespectful of Theban traditions, or insult my uncle. But Ani should have known what I was saying was true. If Eteo didn't receive a fine white linen shroud woven by the best craftswomen in the city, it didn't matter. We were both shrouded in grief. That would suffice. He just needed to be buried, to be safe beneath the earth, so his shade could pass into Hades, and rest easy.

'You can't mean what you're saying,' she said. 'They must both be interred in the family grave. Eteo was not some peasant farmer, to be buried in the earth by his sisters. He was king of the city. He must be paid all due respect, not just for his death but for his life.'

'Niece,' said Creon, 'I can only imagine you are sick with grief. You will do me the courtesy of silence, or I will lock you in your room for a month until you are cured. Then you will miss Polynices' funeral, which I know cannot be what you want.'

'Why don't you say something?' Ani cried at Haem, who had been examining his plate during this whole conversation, his reddened ears the only hint he could hear them.

There was a pause. Haem did not look up, but only said, 'My father is right. Traitors and heroes are not the same. They cannot be treated as though they were.'

I wondered if these were his own thoughts, or those of his father. Ani could not have been more appalled if he had reached across the table and slapped her.

'So no one will stand up for Eteo,' she said, pushing back her chair.

'Ani,' I said. I wanted to take her to her room and tell her to stop this, before she pushed Creon into doing or saying something more dreadful. If he confined us both to our rooms, neither of us would be there to mourn our brothers at their funerals, a disgrace too terrible to contemplate. We needed to be patient, and work on my uncle over the next few days. Haem had agreed with his father, that was a valuable beginning to our bargaining: our views did not even taint our cousin, so surely we could be left to bury our brother. I was exasperated with Ani. On top of our grief she had added further difficulty.

'Sit down,' Creon said, without looking at her. She stood, uncertain whether she would make her point better by continuing to argue or by storming off to her room. A moment later, she decided on the latter. The slam of oak on oak as the door smacked into its frame echoed around the courtyard.

My uncle stood up. 'Very well,' he said to me. 'Your sister is incapable of civility or common sense. She would see the city celebrate a man bent on its destruction, it seems.' I bit my cheek, knowing I could not reply without worsening matters. But it was too late for that. 'So I shall make my point quite clear,' Creon said. 'Polynices will be buried as our traditions and family duty requires. He was – as Haem says – a hero. Eteocles will not receive a state funeral, as I have explained. As your sister seems unable to comprehend why, I shall explain things to her in a language she understands. The traitor will not receive a burial of any kind.'

With those words, he stalked out of the courtyard. Haem leapt up and followed him, casting a guilty glance at me as he went. And the next morning, you could have heard my sister's scream all the way up in the mountains, among the black pine trees.

*

She was shaking when I burst into her room. There were old curtains on the windows of the sleeping quarters on this side of the palace, because it faced east and without them it would have grown too hot in the mornings. I rarely used mine: I liked to see the sun at the start of each day, as it crested the mountains outside, and I have never minded the warmth. But Ani was a light sleeper and always drew hers at night. So when she had woken, she pulled back the curtain as usual, and looking out onto the hillside behind the palace, she had seen what no one should ever have to see. I gasped when I saw it myself, horror pushing all the air out of me. I put my hands on her shoulder and turned her around. I held her face against my chest and closed my own eyes, so I couldn't see either. When the slave girls ran in shortly after me, they screamed and drew the curtains closed again, and left without speaking, one clutching at the hand of the other.

I took Ani into the courtyard, and beckoned one of the servants over to us.

'Prepare a room on the west side of the courtyard for my sister,' I said. 'She'll sleep there tonight. And send someone with some wine for her now.'

The maid returned moments later with wine, water, honey and herbs from the kitchens. I used the honey to counter the bitter taste of the herbs, and gave the drink to Ani, holding it for her between sips. She drank it slowly, and gradually the shaking stopped. I took her to the newly prepared room – which was plain and dull but comfortable enough – and watched over her until the wine and herbs soothed her to sleep. Then I walked across to her room on my own, and pulled the curtain back. Terrible as it was, I could not do my poor brother the disrespect of refusing to see him.

At first glance, it looked almost like he was sitting against the rock, his head lolling as though he were dozing in the warm morning sunshine. But of course he was not. He had been propped up, his head rested against the rock for support, its second mouth gaping, black. One of his legs was turned at an impossible angle, and his sandal was only half on his foot. It must have been loosened when he was dragged outside. I tried to tell myself that he was just asleep, but he looked further from sleep than anyone I had ever seen.

I felt the sobs shudder through my body, now I was alone. Ani's grief had been so loud, I couldn't hear my own. So I let it consume me for a while, sitting on the floor of her room, looking out at the ruins of the person I loved most in all the world. I cried myself past thinking, past words. But after I had shed every tear, I knew what I needed to do. I had to bury him, of course.

I could not leave him to rot outside the palace, pecked at by birds and mauled by stray dogs. That my uncle could even consider allowing such a thing was horrifying. He knew his duty to the dead, as did we all. But there was nothing to be gained from speaking to him: Ani's outburst last night had seen to that. Creon would bear any disapproval from his subjects rather than change his mind. The one thing he had never been able to tolerate was any hint of weakness in himself. So having forbidden a burial for Eteo, he would not reconsider. But I had to find a way to put my brother beneath the ground. I could not leave him, casting about on the banks of the River Lethe, watching as his brother crossed into Hades, and he was left behind. The dread king and queen of the Underworld would never forgive such a slight.

I tried to think what I could do now. I remembered that my uncle had given me permission to speak to my tutor today, and decided I should do what I had asked to do. I stood up and drew the curtain across Ani's window again, begging my brother's forgiveness for leaving him, for turning away from him. I went back to my room to put on my sandals (a new pair had been placed in my room; the bloodstained ones had never been returned). I changed into a long, formal tunic and picked up a dark red shawl to cover my shoulders. I plaited my hair into a neat braid, and pinned it up behind my ears. My uncle would no longer permit us to walk around the palace dressed like children, I was sure. He used to chide me before, when Eteo was king, for not taking due care of my appearance. And since I wanted to go into the second courtyard to find Sophon, I knew my best chance was to behave as he wanted me to. After everything he'd done to become king of my city, it would be foolish to imagine that he didn't intend to use that power in every aspect of his rule, however petty.

It took me an age to persuade the guard that I had the

king's consent to leave the courtyard, but eventually – after checking with my uncle's advisers that I was truly allowed to walk through to a room I used to visit every day – he unlocked the gate and allowed me out. I skirted around the south then west side of the square, trying not to look at the faint pink discoloration which still marked the stones beneath Eteo when he died. I knocked on Sophon's door, and opened it carefully.

My tutor seemed to have aged years in the days since I last saw him. He stood slowly from his chair, supporting his weight on the sticks he had propped against his legs.

'Jocasta,' he said, and tears sprang from his eyes.

'You can't have forgotten me so quickly,' I said. But I wasn't sure he even noticed that he had called me by my mother's name. He opened his arms and I ran into them and embraced him. 'I don't know what to do,' I told him. And he patted my hair, as I had stroked Ani's earlier.

'You must not antagonize your uncle further,' he said, when he released me and sat back on his hard chair. 'And that goes twice over for your sister. She misjudges her situation. How can she not understand?'

'I'll make her understand,' I told him. 'She doesn't realize it was Creon who orchestrated all this: Polyn and Eteo at war with one another. She doesn't think like that.'

'No,' he nodded. 'Your sister has always been so open. She thinks everybody is the same as her.'

'Creon has forbidden us to bury Eteo,' I said. I let the words sink into the crags of his face. 'Is there anything you can do to persuade him he's mistaken?'

Sophon shook his head slowly. 'I doubt it. Your uncle is a difficult man, Isy. I have worked with him for many years, and I would never regard him as a friend. He is closed off from other people. He loves Haemon. And you, of course.'

I thought I must be hearing things. 'Me?'

'Creon was devoted to your mother for many years. He never liked your father. But it took something terrible for him to give up on your mother.'

'Do you mean Aunt Eury?'

'I do. But even though that soured his relationship with your parents, he kept coming here every day, after the Reckoning. Partly because he always wanted to be where the power was.' He swung a shaky arm around the room. 'And partly because he liked to see you. He used to tell you stories when you were very little. Perhaps you don't remember.'

I did not.

'Your uncle longed for a girl of his own, and you were the daughter he could not have. Your father was thrilled when Ani was born: how could he not be? Everyone told him how much she looked like your mother. Your father's great regret was that he had come into your mother's life so late. He always wished he could have met her when she was young. So Ani was enchanting for him: he felt he could finally see what Jocasta looked like before he knew her.'

'Ani was my father's favourite,' I said. People had told me so many times that it scarcely hurt any more, like pressing an old bruise.

'No,' Sophon said. 'No, she wasn't his favourite. He loved you all. If he had a favourite, it was your mother. He adored her from the day they met to the day she died.

But he always wanted children. He would never have been satisfied without you. But your uncle was devoted to you.'

'If that were true, he would let me bury my brother,' I said, angry.

'Go to Polyn's funeral tomorrow. Do everything he asks. Perhaps you'll be able to persuade him as the days wear on,' Sophon said. I began to cry again, thinking of poor Eteo being bitten and pecked while I could do nothing to put his body out of reach of scavengers. 'But if you're asking me for my opinion, it is this: your uncle is unlikely to change his mind. Still, the priests will tell him that he is committing a terrible wrong, against your brother and against the gods. They cannot pretend otherwise: they would fear to be struck by lightning for their perjury. All is not yet lost.'

I knew he was right. I wiped the tears from my face with the edges of my shawl before I stepped outside Sophon's study again. My uncle might be persuaded. I would have to pin my hopes to that.

22

The heat of the summer was fading but the memory of the dead burned ever brighter. Once people had stopped fearing for their own lives, they started to ask questions. No one doubted that the Reckoning had come back to claim another generation. But why? And why now? No one wanted to articulate their darkest fear: if the disease had been gone for fifty years, and returned, perhaps it could never be outrun. Thebans wondered if they had made a mistake all those years ago, when they unlocked their gates after closing the city against the first plague to ravage their world.

Whose idea had it been to open the city gates again? People argued for days about it. Some said it was the fault of Laius, the late king. But where was the satisfaction in blaming a man long dead? Others thought the order to unbar the gates had come from the queen. But the most popular view was that it must have been Oedipus's idea. The queen's husband came from the Outlying, didn't he? So of course he would want to open up the city to others like him. But it couldn't have been his idea, someone argued. The gates must have been open before he arrived in the city, or how did he himself get in? This was dismissed as sophistry by most. Besides, even if the gates had been open for the odd foreigner to enter the city, Oedipus had encouraged Thebes to look beyond her walls. He had championed trade with his own city, Corinth, and the opening of further routes both north and south. He had changed Thebes from fortress to market. And now look where they were: placing offerings on the graves of their dead children.

Jocasta was partially aware that the mood of the city had turned against her. She had never thought very much about her popularity because she had never needed to. Laius hadn't been a popular king, and he had lived and died exactly as he would have wished. Well, perhaps he had not died exactly as he had wished. But close enough. Still, as the days grew shorter, Jocasta felt the city turning cold.

She indulged in brief self-pity: she had done everything right, and followed the advice of her friends and experts. But because they had used subterfuge to persuade the citizens that the water supply was safe, she could not now claim credit for having lied to them. And she had closed the palace gates, which had perhaps contributed to her citizens' sense that she had cut herself off from them in their moment of crisis. But she had four children, and Sophon had warned her that the young were especially at risk. Surely people would understand that? Thebans would know – the women would know – that she had to keep her children safe. But a tiny voice in her ear told her that a woman who had buried her own infant in baked-dry ground sprinkled with lye would have little sympathy left over for a woman with four healthy children running about the palace grounds. She had locked down the city to prevent further contamination coming in from outside.

But how could people measure what hadn't happened? If the gates had remained open, many more cases of plague would have devastated her city, she was sure. But there was no way to prove it. People only counted the deaths there were against how many fewer they wished there had been.

Jocasta wished, more than anything, that she could talk things over with her brother. But the distance between them could not be traversed. Creon had come back to the palace a few days after the gates were reopened, and begun working on the tasks he had been forced to abandon during the plague. He had never reproached his sister for allowing the gates to be barred against him, never asked her how she could have abandoned him and his family, never shouted at the unfairness, never wept over the loss of his wife. He continued to offer advice when she sought it. But he never discussed anything personal, and he left promptly each afternoon. He no longer brought Haem to play with his cousins, but kept the boy at home. Jocasta had tried to apologize for their enforced separation, tried to express her sorrow for what had happened to Eurydice (though Oedipus was quick to remind her that her sister-in-law had already been carrying the sickness when he had closed the palace, and that she – and the whole family – were lucky the plague-riddled woman had remained outside). Jocasta could not find the words to bring Creon back to her. She wanted to touch his arm and beg his forgiveness, but after the contagion, the city had lost the habit of touch and so, she found, had she.

—

One morning, when the leaves were beginning to drop onto the ground and scratch her feet as she walked through the courtyards, Sophon arrived, asking to speak to her. She could see he was upset. He looked to have aged ten years since the start of the summer. Purplish-brown shadows were painted beneath his eyes, and his expression was oddly sympathetic. She stood up and wrapped her hands around his.

'Thank you for coming,' she said. 'What a terrible summer.'

'You did everything you could,' he told her, the words she had been longing to hear from someone. 'You are alive, your children are alive. You did well.'

Tears sprang from her eyes, and she wiped them away with her fingers. 'Do you honestly believe that?' she asked. 'I feel as though everyone hates me, and I don't know why. I thought I'd done everything right.'

She took him across the square to the padded chairs by the fountain, which were piled high with cushions. Jocasta waved away a servant who sprang up to arrange them comfortably for the old man. She picked up a pillow in each hand, and propped them behind Sophon's back as he settled himself onto the seat.

'You're going to tell me something horrible. I can tell.' She took the seat next to his, leaning forward, her hands gripping a cushion so hard her knuckles were white.

'How?' he asked.

'I've known you for over half my life,' she said. 'Longer than I've known anyone but my brother, and he . . .' She couldn't finish the sentence. Sophon took a moment to phrase his reply.

'I don't agree with your diagnosis that everyone hates you,' he said. 'But I must tell you the truth: the Thebans I speak to every day are not happy. They think you should have done more to help them. I always ask: what should the queen have done? Most of these people don't know I am your friend. So they are not trying to spare my feelings. I ask them because I want to know what they say, what they believe. And none of them has an answer. They all say the same thing: they just feel that you didn't do enough to help your people in their darkest hour.'

'Should I have been by your side?' she asked. 'The queen, mopping brows and checking fevers? Would that have saved lives? Even one life?'

'Of course not,' he replied. 'Your place was here. But the rumours that are swirling around the city . . . You would hate them.'

'What rumours?' she snapped. 'I suppose they all think we spent the summer eating and drinking and laughing in the palace, while they faced death alone.' She coloured, as she realized that this description was not entirely inaccurate. Oedipus and the children had spent a blissful summer, much of it in this garden. If her brother and his family had been with them, Jocasta might have enjoyed it too. But she could not weep for every Theban lost to disease or anything else. She was the queen: she could not allow herself to be consumed by pity or sorrow.

Perhaps people thought she should have sealed the city years ago, when Laius died. But the Reckoning had been gone for decades by then: how could she have known that it would one day return? Besides, Thebes had more pressing needs, for food and trade. The city was self-sufficient for some months of the year, but it would never be able to feed its population without importing some foodstuffs. Besides, Jocasta had always thought her city had a tendency towards self-importance. It needed the Outlying, however much its citizens preferred to imagine it did not.

'I don't want to upset you,' Sophon said. 'But you should know. You need to combat the gossip-mongers, and you can't do that if you don't know what they're saying. Has no one said anything to you? Your brother?'

She shook her head. 'Creon has not spoken much since the gates reopened,' she said. 'His wife died. He grieves for her. You must tell me. What are people saying?'

The old man looked at the ground for a moment.

'They say that the plague is your doing,' he said, the words spilling quickly from his mouth.

'My doing? How on earth could that be?' She laughed at the ludicrousness of it all. 'Have I poisoned the water supply? Who could possibly believe such nonsense?'

His rheumy eyes met hers for a moment, before she looked away. 'They don't think you are causing it on purpose,' he replied. 'But they nonetheless think you are the cause of it. They believe the city is being punished by the gods.'

She let out a snort of annoyance. 'I sometimes believe the city is being punished by the gods,' she said. 'Or why would stupid, small-minded people survive, when so many innocent children have died? You can't be serious.'

'I wish it was a joke,' he said. He reached out and touched her hand. There was worse to come. 'People believe you are committing a terrible crime against what is right and decent. You and Oedipus. They think that you have both affronted the gods, and that the plague is the consequence of your behaviour.'

'How have we affronted the gods?' she asked. 'Because Oedipus knocked down that ugly shrine and replaced it with a garden? Because I no longer prostrate myself before an unseeing oracular god, day after day, for no purpose? Since when did Thebes become a hive of religious devotion? I didn't see many of them going into the temples when I was a child.'

'You would now,' Sophon told her. 'People have become increasingly,' he paused, to think of the appropriate word, 'superstitious over the past few years.'

'Because they're afraid,' she said. 'I understand that.'

'You won't understand everything they're saying,' he said. 'Maybe you should send for Oedipus.' She was about to refuse, then realized the old man was trying to protect her. So she stood up and walked over to her quarters, returning a few moments later with her husband.

'What's this about?' Oedipus asked, as he perched on the edge of the fountain, facing them both. 'Jocasta said there's something you think we need to know.'

'Please believe that I would very much rather not be telling you any of this,' Sophon said. 'But in my experience, rumours don't disappear merely because their object doesn't know about them. Gossip is spreading and it can't be stopped by me. People say you have angered the gods with your marriage. With your children.' He exhaled, and his shoulders slumped forward.

'How?' Oedipus scoffed. 'That's ridiculous.'

'They're saying you can't be married,' Sophon said,

looking up to meet two appalled faces. 'They're saying you're mother and son.'

Oedipus gave a hard bark of laughter. 'That's the stupidest, most unpleasant thing I've ever heard. You can't be telling me that anyone is taking this seriously?'

Sophon nodded. 'I'm afraid so.'

'They know I came to the city ten years ago, for the first time?' Oedipus asked. 'And that Jocasta had her first child nine years ago?'

The glance between Sophon and Jocasta took less time than a beat of her heart, but it gave her away, just the same.

Oedipus didn't speak to her for three days. He left any room she entered, using the constant presence of their sons and daughters to keep conversation trivial. Even at night, he stood by her as they put the children to bed, but as soon as they were outside, he ignored her. He slept in another room, and locked the door. She placed her hand on his arm, and he flung it away, as though she were unclean. On the third night, she gave in and, even though her pride loathed doing it where the servants could see her, she fell to her knees before him and begged his forgiveness.

'How could you keep something like that a secret?' he asked. 'How?'

She reached out and took his hands in hers. 'I'm so sorry,' she said. 'It was all so long ago.'

'It wasn't always long ago,' he replied.

'It was,' she protested. 'When I met you, it had been sixteen, no, seventeen years earlier. I had already spent half my life trying to forget what had happened. I wasn't trying to keep a secret. Everyone knew. Everyone here, I mean, and I so much wished they didn't. I think one of the things I liked most about you, when we met, was that I didn't have to live with you knowing something awful had happened to me. You weren't sorry for me, like everyone else had been.'

His face softened slightly, though it could just have been the twilight playing on his skin. He gripped her by the wrists and pulled her up onto her feet. There was something undignified about a middle-aged woman on her knees.

'You could have told me,' he chided her. 'Not then, but later.'

'I know,' she said. 'I wanted to, often. But then I fell pregnant so quickly, and we were having our first child. We were embarking on a family together. I didn't want you to think I'd been there before.'

'But you had,' he said, and turned away from her.

'I swear to you I had not. Nothing was the same as before. I was on my own then. I had no one to take care of me. Except Sophon, and I only met him because I nearly fainted in front of him. It was all so awful. Everything was awful.' She began to weep as the long-hidden memories flooded through her. 'And then the baby was dead anyway. So I went through it all for nothing. I never even saw him.'

'What?' He turned back to face her, and wiped her tears away with his thumbs, though they were instantly replaced. 'What do you mean?'

'She took him away,' Jocasta sobbed. 'The cord was

wrapped around his neck. She said it would be worse if I held him, so she took him away. And,' she gulped the words, 'I've spent the rest of my life thinking about him. I imagined him growing up, getting bigger, learning to say my name, walking, running. I used to sit in here, on my own, so I could think about him in peace. Do you know what I mean? I just sat here, imagining him.'

'Do you still think about him now?'

She nodded, guilty. 'Sometimes. But when I try to find him in my mind, now I see Polyn instead. Or sometimes Eteo.'

'Do they look like you imagined he would?' Oedipus asked.

'I don't know,' she whispered.

'I wish you had told me,' he said. 'You've been hiding part of yourself from me.'

'I never wanted to spoil things,' she said. 'I was always frightened you'd guess. That you'd see the stretch marks on my skin and work it out.'

He shook his head. 'I didn't have anyone to compare you to. You know that.' He sat down beside her. 'What are we going to do now?'

'About these horrible rumours? I don't know. I can't prove the baby died.'

'Wasn't Sophon here? He is a witness, he can confirm you're telling the truth.'

'No,' she said. 'He wasn't here on that day. He wanted to be, but something happened. He was dragged off to the other side of the city for some reason, I think. I can't remember why. There was just me and Teresa.'

'Who?'

'She was the housekeeper. When you first arrived here.'

'Oh, her. She's probably dead by now, isn't she?'

'I don't know,' Jocasta admitted. 'Yes, she must be. She would be ancient.'

Oedipus nodded, and squeezed her hand. 'It will all be alright,' he said. 'Even if we can't find her, I will send a message home. My father will explain to everyone that I was born in Corinth. He'll swear to it, and so will dozens of people who knew me when I was a boy. I promise.'

'Will you send a message to him today?' she asked.

'Of course,' he said. 'I'm not entirely sure how to begin such a letter, but I'm sure I'll think of something.' He smiled at her, and she tried to smile back, but another sob broke through instead.

23

On the day of Polyn's funeral, I awoke early. The ceremony had to be carried out before dawn. Using a torch, I hunted around for my clothes, catching a glimpse of myself in the polished obsidian mirror Ani had given me for my last birthday, which seemed to have been a thousand years ago. I only half-recognized the girl looking back at me. Without Eteo, I felt like some of me was missing; I expected to see a scar or a missing eye or ear. Something that hurt so badly should be visible. I couldn't help thinking that the mirror might as well show nothing, if it couldn't show the truth. So I dropped it, expecting it to smash into a thousand tiny pieces. But it split neatly in two, and I was left with two worthless mirrors, where before I had only one.

The funeral procession would begin from the main courtyard of the palace, where Polyn had lain in state for several days. We had washed his body and covered it in oil and wrapped him in a white linen shroud. With every action we performed, I thought of the terrible lack of these same rituals for Eteo, who still lay outside the palace, mourned in secret, unburied. My sister and I had performed the prothesis for Polyn: chanting at his bier, tearing our hair, rending our garments, pummelling our breasts and hollering our grief to the skies for all to hear. The ritual informed the dead – wherever they were – of how they were missed by the living. But as the hours passed, I had begun to think that the ritual was for us, the living, to give expression to every corner of our grief. I had wailed for my brothers equally, and somehow they both knew it.

Ani and I would be allowed to participate in the ekphora, accompanying our brother's body to his final resting place: the tomb which already held our parents. Somehow, I had to think of a way to persuade my uncle that Eteo should also be laid to rest, even if he was not buried with the rest of our family. As Sophon had said, Creon was a superstitious man: I thought perhaps I could persuade him that my mother's shade could not be at peace while her younger son was prevented from joining her in the Underworld. But Sophon would scowl if he heard me saying such things: he thought that religion was nothing more than superstition, and it was beneath those who had studied to believe in what he considered to be stories for children. Our gods are conveniently like us, he would say, and why should they be? No answer I offered to this question ever satisfied him, until I gave in and said it must be because we invented them. We create gods that resemble us because that is all we know. They are not like us, therefore, but rather of us. Sophon believed that if horses could speak to one another, they would create gods which looked like horses. And perhaps he was right. But none of that would help me to persuade my uncle that Eteo could not be left outside the palace to rot.

I dressed in a plain linen tunic which I had not previously worn. The tunic I had for the prothesis was too badly torn to wear for the funeral procession, which was the formal, public display of grief. I would rather grieve in private, like other people. But that was not permitted for members of a ruling household. Over the simple tunic, I wore a dark grey linen robe. The hem had a stark, angular pattern woven into it, up and down, like mountains and valleys. I would wear my hair loose, rather than in its usual plait. And my feet were bare, as was proper for the ekphora. When you place a body in the ground, you should be touching the ground yourself.

I crossed the courtyard to find my sister before it became any lighter outside. If Creon had noticed that she was sleeping on the other side of the square, he had said nothing. But we were both trying to be discreet about it, in the hopes that he wouldn't find out. The slaves were surely keeping quiet to protect her. She hurried back with me to my room, and finished her preparations there. When the maid opened the door and told us our uncle awaited us, we covered our heads with dark linen shawls and followed her outside.

The main courtyard was crowded with people, even though it was still early in the morning. Thebes last buried a king and queen more than ten years ago. People would not let such a solemn a day go past without sharing in our grief. Ani and I walked with our eyes on the ground, as was appropriate, escorted by the maid until we reached the palace guards, and then by them until we reached Polyn's bier. There was a rustling from the crowd, as they bowed their heads. A priest stepped forward, his head covered and his manner supercilious. He offered up his prayers to the gods with the certainty of one who believed that the gods were lucky to have him.

The procession would now carry Polyn from the courtyard to the cemetery. Ani should have been the chief mourner, because she was closest to Polyn, both in age and in blood. But as she moved to take her place at the front of the litter, my uncle raised a hand, and the guards moved closer together, holding her back. Creon turned to face the crowd, including us in his speech almost incidentally, because we happened to be nearby.

'I shall accompany my nephew, hero and defender of Thebes, to his tomb,' he said. 'It is appropriate that one king should be attended by another.' The word he used to describe himself was Basileus: a ruler over his people. Before today, I had always heard my uncle called Anax, lord: a respectful title and one that conveyed his superior status to virtually anyone who spoke to him. But it had not been enough for his vaunting ambition and desire for power. I wondered if other people were as shocked as I was, but all I could hear was the crowd murmuring in agreement. Creon was their king now.

Ani was so quick that I heard her voice before I felt her move to the side of the guards, who had been distracted by Creon's speech, and place herself in front of them.

'I wish to speak,' she said. Her voice rang out like harsh music, and people instinctively turned to look at her, as they always had.

My uncle remained impassive, but Haem's expression spoke for both of them. Whatever she said, Ani would be lucky to finish this speech with her life. The crowd muttered in surprise, but their approval was audible. Even my uncle would not interrupt his grieving niece before a crowd of citizens, who were shifting their positions, all trying to catch sight of her. Though she was wearing the same dreary grey as everyone else, she shone as she spoke.

'People of Thebes, I thank you for coming here to pay tribute to my dead brothers.' Shock rippled across the square. Was she going to defend a traitor? 'Your presence is a great comfort to me and my sister in this darkest time in our lives. You know that we were orphaned when we were just seven and five years old. Since then, we saw our brothers as both parents and siblings: the only family we had.' I tore my eyes away from her to look at Creon. His guards were doing the same thing, casting questioning looks at him, hoping to find out what they should do, as my sister casually disregarded our uncle, eliding him from our family as she spoke. 'We cherished them and loved them equally. It was a day of unbearable cruelty which robbed us of the two of them. Today, Polynices lies before you as a hero. My brother Eteocles does not. His corpse has been dumped on the hillside behind the palace.' There were shouts from the crowd, but I couldn't make out the words or the intent. Were they angry with Ani for defending Eteo? Or were they angry with Creon for his brutal treatment of the dead? I couldn't be sure. 'Yes,' she continued. 'His body lies outside the palace on the hill, and it has done so for three nights.' Someone near the front of the crowd yelled 'Shame!' and more shouts followed.

'So I say this,' she continued. 'As we take Polynices – my brother, our king – to the cemetery, to the tomb of my family, I beg you to collect the body of my brother Eteocles – equally a brother, equally our king – and bring him too. I know you have been told that he was a traitor. But he was my brother, and I loved him. My sister Ismene loved him better than anyone. And so,' she paused to be sure she had absolute silence, 'so did Polynices. They argued – what brothers would not? – but they loved one another, all the same. Neither of them will rest easily if they are separated in burial. They were together in life and together in death. Let them be together again now, and forever. Please, Thebes, I beg you: do not let my family's tomb be desecrated by withholding what we owe.'

There was no doubting the mood of the crowd. Whatever they had been told about Eteo, they now stood in agreement with Ani. The sins of the living should be punished in life, but not after death. The limits laid down by the gods were quite clear. My uncle acted with decisive swiftness. He barked at the guards and several of them surrounded my sister. Four of them shielded her from the view of the crowd, while one pinned her arms to her sides, and another clamped his huge hand over her nose and mouth. She struggled frantically, but with no effect. I stepped forward to help her, but my uncle had foreseen this, and as he walked past me waving his hands calmly to quell the discontented crowd, he leaned in to my ear and said, 'Try to help her and I will kill her.' I knew he wasn't lying, so I stood powerless, watching my sister fight for air, then fall unconscious. When her body fell limp against the guard who was holding her arms, he bent down and swung her up into his arms.

'As you see,' my uncle said, his voice loud enough to command silence, though he did not shout, 'as you see, my niece is not well. Her words are pretty enough. Aren't they?' He gazed out at a crowd who had suddenly become aware of the number of armed men around them. You could see men's eyes flicker, as they remembered that they had left their sticks or knives at home to attend a funeral. They were not equipped for an uprising on a dark, bereaved day. Creon nodded, agreeing with their imagined response, and continued. 'Who could argue with the notion that brothers should be united in death? What man could be so audacious? I tell you, Thebes, I will argue. I say that no niceties should be observed when we speak about a man who turns on his city and on his own brother. None at all. Not because I choose to disrespect the dead. Not because I believe the gods of the Underworld will be pleased, if I rob them of their prize. But because I am the king of this city, and these are the choices I must make. Eteocles was a traitor. A traitor and a murderer. If he had not been, we would still have Polynices on the throne. I would not have been required to undertake the responsibility of kingship, so late in my life. It was against my choice, but I would not – will not – see Thebes descend into civil war. I will not see her undermined from within or from without. This is a city which has suffered enough. More than enough.'

The mood of the square was palpably changing again. Men who had cheered Ani were now clinging to the words of my uncle, seemingly unconcerned that they were supporting a diametrically opposite position to the one they had held moments earlier.

'But I, I have not suffered enough,' Creon said. 'You remember how I lost my wife in the Reckoning eleven years ago. And when Thebes lost her queen and king the following summer, I also lost my sister, and my brother-in-law. And now, this year, I have lost two nephews. But still I stand here before you, ready to face your anger, when I tell you that we shall not allow those who turn on their city to be treated in the same way as those who defend it. Because if I allow it for my nephew, a boy I loved,' his voice cracked so convincingly I almost believed him myself, 'and who I watched grow up alongside my own son, then I allow it for anyone. For everyone. And I will not see our city – my home – destabilized like this. Hear me now, and do not mistake me: anyone who betrays his city, who betrays you,' he pointed at the crowd – first one group, then another – including them all in his promise, 'that traitor – even if he is my own blood – will rot outside the city walls, unmourned, unwept and unburied. Thebes will stand, and the traitors will fall. Do you hear me?'

The crowd roared their approval. My uncle continued in a whisper, forcing people to quieten one another and lean in to hear him. 'So although I wish I could bury my nephew – and I do, Thebans, wish that very much – I will not endanger our city and I will not endanger you by giving way to my baser instincts. My hot-headed niece will spend a few days in the caves beneath the palace while she considers her behaviour here today. Guards: take her away, and give her bread and water, enough for three days. She will make her formal apology to the city Elders before she leaves her cell, I promise you that.'

It was a masterclass in rhetoric. As my sister's insensate body was carried out of the square, I turned to my uncle and begged.

'Let me go with her. Let me reason with her.'

He smiled without showing his teeth. 'There never has

been any reasoning with your sister, Ismene. She may look like her mother, but she has always had the disposition of her father. And if she isn't more careful – a great deal more careful – she will end up exactly like him.'

With these words, he signalled to the men who attended Polyn's bier. I recognized none of them: the aristoi might be somewhere in the courtyard, but they were not carrying my brother to his grave, as would have been appropriate. And neither was I. 'Come with me,' said my cousin, who had appeared beside me as Ani was carried away. 'Come back inside, before he turns on you as well.'

'I should be with Polyn,' I said.

Haem leaned so close to me that I could feel his breath on my skin. 'This is your only chance to bury Eteo,' he said.

24

Jocasta had never been able to understand how time moved so much more quickly as the years progressed. Looking back at her earliest years in the palace, she remembered the leaden weight of time, crushing her beneath its crawling pace, the hours which stretched into days, the days which expanded to fill months. But once the children were born, whole seasons seemed to pass before she had even noticed they had begun. The apples fell from the small tree in the shady northern corner of the courtyard, and she would dimly wonder when the pink-edged white flowers had bloomed and how she had managed to miss them. As she tried to cling to days that slipped through her grasp, she sometimes wished for the terrible days of the past, which dragged themselves out in front of her like a waterless desert she was forced to cross before she might sleep and repeat the whole tortuous process again the next day.

And this year, she would have given a great deal to be able to postpone summer forever. If she could only stop time at the start of spring, when the days were beginning to grow warmer, but the real heat was still months away. Thebes had limped from a devastated autumn into an unusually cold winter, but no one complained as the sharp north wind whistled through the gaps around windows and doors. Instead, people wrapped up in layers of clothes and shared blankets during the long winter nights. They congratulated one another on tolerating the cold so hardily. Everyone knew the Reckoning thrived in the heat. It had only ever visited the city in the summer, like a malevolent migrating bird. In the winter, it curled up, disappeared, shed its power like an old skin. Everyone was brave when their predator was gone. And, people whispered excitedly as they huddled around stoves and tightened their woollen robes around their thickest tunics, if it was cold enough for long enough, perhaps the disease would be wiped out altogether.

The hope that the plague might be exterminated by the snow – which was still falling three months after the shortest day of the year – was one which even Jocasta fell prey to. But when she asked Sophon for his medical opinion, he shook his head. He did not believe the plague was gone; it was more likely that it was only biding its time, waiting to unfurl its wings in the warm summer days. So Jocasta watched the trees change, from black to white as the blossom covered their canopies; from white to crimson, as the new buds were revealed, tightly wrapped against the branches; and from crimson to green, as the leaves unfolded and the fruit began to grow. And with each arriving day, the weight of foreboding which she carried around with her increased.

Gradually, the rains eased off, and the days grew hotter, more cloudless. By the time the long grasses swaying on the hillside behind the palace had yellowed in the dry heat, the diagnosis was undeniable: the Reckoning had returned. Word spread through the city more quickly than the plague itself, and once again, people stood in the streets in the heat of the sun, and prayed to the gods that their children would be overlooked again this time. They hastened to the temples and begged Apollo, the Archer, to shoot his arrows elsewhere, at other cities, other districts, other families. They poured wine and sacrificed kid-goats and new-born calves in the hope that this bloodshed might be enough to sate the Archer's greed. And then some withdrew, locked their doors and hoped that the strategy which had saved them last year would work a second time. Others were more angry than afraid because they knew no preventative measures could save them, not while the city harboured a king and queen who lived in a lawless, godless union. There was no point praying that the Reckoning would brush past your home and leave your family untouched. The city's only hope lay in purging itself of the pollution it contained. Only then would the god cease his punishment.

Jocasta did not want to shut the palace gates again this year, if there was any way she could avoid it. She placated Oedipus by closing off the family courtyard first, and keeping the children and their nurse safe behind locked doors. She and Oedipus moved around the palace as usual, but visitors were never permitted to approach too closely. They didn't approach each other too closely either. Eventually, though, Jocasta had no choice. A messenger from Sophon told her that the disease was more powerful this year: although he did not consider it to be more contagious, it was killing a larger proportion of those it infected. She wavered then about shutting the gates, but allowed herself a little more time to make the decision.

In the end, it wasn't because of the plague that they had to shut the palace gates. It was because of the crowd.

It must have begun to form at night, because the gates were always closed at dusk. But one morning, the guards went to open up the main courtyard, yawning as they went because everyone struggled to sleep when the nights were so short and so hot. They found a small crowd pressed up against the gates, who began jeering and booing as soon as they caught sight of the men inside. Irritated by this rudeness, the guards responded with obstinacy, and left the gates locked. By the time Jocasta awoke, the watch commander had sent a message with one of the slave boys to say he was waiting to speak to her in the royal courtyard.

'Highness,' said the watch commander, bowing low. 'There is a crowd of people outside, and they are angry. I have said that the gates must be left closed until I countermand the order.'

'Do you know why the crowd is so angry?' she asked. His expression told her too much. 'Why today, in particular?' she clarified. He thought for a moment.

'No,' he said. 'But if you want my advice?' He paused to check that she did, and she nodded. 'Don't open the gates,' he said. 'They're troublemakers.'

'Is that your professional opinion?' she asked him, trying to smile.

'Yes,' he replied.

'And what do you think they'll do if they can't come in and petition their queen?' she asked.

'Give up,' he said. 'And go home. Some of them are drunk, madam, and that makes men behave in foolish ways. One idiot says they should march up to the palace and air their grievances, as though they couldn't do that during daylight hours. They arrive in the night like criminals, hammering on the gates as though they had any right to enter. They're nothing more than a noisy rabble, desperate to cause a nuisance. Give them the satisfaction and it'll only mean they resort to such behaviour more quickly next time.'

Jocasta nodded. 'Very well,' she said. 'I'll be guided by you. Leave the gates closed today and we'll open them again tomorrow.'

But when the guards looked out from their gatehouse the next morning, the crowd had doubled.

Jocasta did not want to disregard the advice of the watch commander. But, at the same time, she had lived for years feeling besieged in her own home. She refused to do so again. When she asked Oedipus for his opinion, he seemed unconcerned. Leave things till tomorrow, he yawned. We're all safe inside. So she took the advice of her guards, and left the palace closed for another day.

But on the third morning, the crowd had thickened again, and she decided she must speak to them, to find out what they wanted and why they wouldn't leave. She no longer agreed with the watch commander, that they would go home when they were bored. She found Oedipus idling in the courtyard, and asked him if he would come with her.

'Why? Do you think they want to see me?' he asked, his eyes half-closed against the sun.

'I don't know what they want,' she said, and the anxiety in her voice forced him to look up.

'You're afraid,' he said. She nodded. 'Afraid of people outside the gates?' he asked. She nodded again.

'The watch commander says there must be a hundred of them,' she said. 'More even.'

'You have the palace guards on your side,' he reminded her.

'Please,' she said, and reached out her hand to him.

Oedipus stood up and walked across the square hand-in-hand with his wife. 'I don't know what you think I'll be able to say that you can't,' he said, as they crossed into the second courtyard. Jocasta stopped when they reached the colonnade which connected it to the main square. She looked at Oedipus to be sure that he had heard it too: a buzzing sound from the front of the palace, indicative of far more than a hundred people. She nodded to the guards who walked out ahead of her. There was a slew of abusive shouts from outside the gates, but the guards did not react. They had always been so loyal to her, Jocasta thought, and she could feel tears prickling her eyes. She breathed through her mouth, hoping to control herself. She reached for her husband's hand, and he squeezed hers. But she didn't know if he was taking comfort or offering it. 'Wait for me here,' she said. 'I should talk to them alone, I think.'

'Are you sure?' he said. She nodded, and walked through the archway and into the public square.

The wall of sound was deafening. Jeering, baying, screaming at her. She couldn't even make out the words, almost any of them. She heard one high-pitched voice, screaming 'Whore', which carried over the melee. Jocasta walked slowly, calmly to a point in front of the locked gates, which people were thumping and kicking as they shouted. The gates barely moved in their sockets, and she took comfort in that. Her home was solid, even in the face of all these people. She did not speak, but simply stood waiting for them to stop. How had her city turned against her so entirely? Was this why Laius was so keen to travel? Did he know that Thebes turned on you, in the end? For the first time in her life, she wished she could ask her first husband a question. Gradually, the crowd subsided to a low malevolence.

'Thebans,' Jocasta said, refusing to shout. There was a sudden cacophony of hushing, as those who couldn't quite hear tried to silence those who were too far away to hear at all. 'You are gathered outside my gates and you are angry. I know the Reckoning has returned to our city. Perhaps you think I don't care. But I assure you, I am doing all I can.'

'Liar,' screamed someone, and it was repeated with approval. Jocasta felt the colour suffusing her cheeks.

'You may shout if you wish,' she said. 'But it will not change the facts. Doctors are working across the city: I have arranged it.'

'Lies,' shrieked another voice, but this one was quickly hushed.

'You may ask them,' Jocasta continued. 'They will tell you that I have paid them in advance to see any patient who needs their help. They will treat you and your loved ones, expecting no payment from you. Ask them. They have no reason to lie.' There was a shuffling among the crowd.

'Where has it come from then?' shouted one woman.

Jocasta looked across at her: a small, shabbily dressed girl with matted brown hair straggling to her shoulders and a baby balanced on one hip. The girl wore a brown tunic with its many holes patched in a pale grey fabric, clumsily made stitching holding each repair in place. The majority of this crowd wasn't vicious, Jocasta decided. Just scared. And she knew what it meant to be scared.

'I don't know,' she admitted, looking directly at the girl who had asked her the question. 'The doctors don't know either. But if you go back to your homes, and try to stay indoors for a few days, that will help to control the spread of it. Thebes will be rid of it more quickly if you heed my advice.'

'Is that why you've shut your gates?' sneered a man wearing a battered straw hat to protect him against the sun.

'Yes,' she said. 'It isn't safe for large numbers of people to congregate at the moment. That's why I'm asking you to go home. The disease thrives in conditions like this: hot weather, lots of people crowded together. I have closed the gates to try and keep us all safe.' The sneering man spat on the ground and Jocasta stiffened. 'The disease may well travel through bodily fluids,' she added, and had the spiteful satisfaction of seeing the people standing closest to him shudder away. 'I will order my gates to be reopened when it's safe again,' she said.

'It will never be safe,' a woman screamed. 'We're being punished.' The crowd surged forward and smashed into the gates again. Jocasta watched one man's head crack into an iron strut, and an angry red weal flowered on his forehead. Those at the front were in danger of being crushed.

'Punished?' she asked. 'For what?'

'For you,' someone yelled. 'For your relationship with him.'

Jocasta had almost forgotten Oedipus was listening in the shadows, though the crowd couldn't know he was there. 'Oedipus is my husband,' she said. 'Why would you think that deserves punishment?'

'He's your son,' came a voice from the middle of the crowd and across almost eleven years. Jocasta couldn't place it: was it her mother? It couldn't be: her mother had died years earlier. She looked hard at the direction the voice had come from, but she recognized no one in the sea of sun-browned faces and spittle-flecked teeth. 'My sons are in the palace,' she said. 'They are just ten and eight years old. Your accusation is a vicious slander.'

'Not those sons,' replied the voice. 'Your first son. You know the one I mean.'

'Who is that?' Jocasta said. 'I can't see you.'

The crowd separated to reveal an ancient woman whose spine had curved so completely that she was bent almost double. She leaned on a wooden stick disfigured by teeth-marks, as though she had been attacked many times by dogs. She wore ragged clothes so filthy that they could have been any colour before they were covered in grease and dirt. Her face was like a walnut, dark and wrinkled.

'Your first son,' the old woman repeated. Jocasta shook her head, trying to shake off the sensation that she was watching a conjuring trick. The voice of someone she knew, coming from a face she had never seen. The woman had almost no teeth, Jocasta noticed, just a few blackened stumps. A dirty stole covered the woman's head, and a few thin strands of white hair protruded from beneath it. 'You remember,' the woman said.

Jocasta felt the world shift, as though she had lost her footing and was falling sideways towards the ground. But she remained on her feet.

'You,' she said. 'My first child was stillborn. You would know that. You were there.'

Teresa's face split into a toxic smile. 'He wasn't still-born,' she said. 'I just told you that, because I couldn't let you keep him. I couldn't keep my sons, so why should you be any different?'

'What?' Jocasta said. 'What are you saying to me?' The crowd was split between those who could hear her conversation with Teresa and those who had begun to peel away, persuaded by Jocasta's advice to go home. But a few people were moving closer, keen to hear what the old woman knew.

'King Laius revered the gods,' Teresa said. How she relished her audience, this once-powerful old woman who had become invisible. Her voice was growing louder, clearer with each syllable. 'He attended the Oracle, and consulted with the priests. They told him that he would one day be killed by his own son.'

'Oracles do not always speak the truth,' Jocasta said, her voice cracking on the final word. 'They're just words, interpreted by people like you, to say what you want them to say. They predict nothing, guarantee nothing. Laius died from a fall, after being injured by one of the Sphinx: he wasn't murdered by anyone.'

'You didn't always feel that way, my dear,' said Teresa, her blackened bottom tooth catching her top lip.

Jocasta felt the shame shroud her in heat. 'No,' she said. 'I used to believe every word that came to me from the Oracle, when I was lonely and afraid. Now I know better, because no poisonous old woman is trying to distort everything which happens for her own cruel purposes. Now I understand that Oracles give messages we aren't supposed to understand: the gods do not offer their wisdom in predictions, like soothsayers or magicians. I believed you to be long dead, but here you are, still trying to upset me by making up lies about my dead child. I would have thought that was beneath even you.'

She nodded to the guards, who had been standing by the main gates, in case Jocasta needed them.

The watch commander nodded back. They would arrest the old woman immediately. He murmured to his colleagues, and twenty men soon stood ready.

'They're not lies, not now,' Teresa said. 'Everything I'm saying is true.'

The crowd looked between the two women, the queen and the crone, unsure who to believe.

'You have always lied to me. But my son died,' Jocasta said. 'Arrest her.'

The crowd retreated from the gates, not wanting to miss what happened next, but not wanting to be caught up in the arrests either. Thebes had always been a martial city under the old king. They had little choice: the first visit from the Reckoning had made Hellas a lawless country for many years. But under the queen, the city had lost some of its hardness. She had kept the guards from exercising too much power. Nonetheless, when faced with a troop of heavily armed men, the citizens were nervous and they began to dissipate.

Teresa shrieked as the men carried her off, spears pointed outwards so no one could interfere with their progress.

'Horrible lying old witch,' Jocasta said, to no one. And she walked towards the gates to watch Teresa disappear from view. Only a few people remained outside now, including the shabby girl who had spoken before, whose baby was now crawling on the ground behind her.

The girl looked at her in disgust. 'So you say. But what's your explanation for the plague, then? You tell us the beggar-woman's lying, but why are the gods punishing our city, if it's not because we harbour criminals in you and your husband-son? Why?'

Jocasta looked at the girl who was sweating in the heat, blotches on her neck and shoulders. She felt only pity. The child was not yet twenty, and afraid for her baby.

'I can't answer that,' she said. 'No one knows where the plague came from all those years ago, and no one knows now. It is not unique to our city. It is happening across Hellas.'

'It's easy for you to say that,' the girl replied. 'Safe in your palace, knowing you'll live to see your children grow up.' And with that, she spat at Jocasta, the saliva landing thick and warm on the queen's cheek, dribbling down onto her upper lip. It was so unexpected that Jocasta flinched as if she had been slapped. She raised her hand to her mouth and wiped away the phlegm with her sleeve. The watch commander raised a hand, but she shook her head and walked away from the gates, back into the palace. What would it achieve, arresting a frightened girl?

25

Haem and I hurried through the corridors and colonnades of the palace, without anyone asking where we were going or why. The guards who seemed to have nothing better to do than stop me moving around the palace when I was alone were blinded by the presence of my cousin. We walked into the family courtyard, and Haem stopped dead. I looked at him, annoyed.

'I give you permission to enter the women's quarters,' I said. 'Come on. I need your help.'

'I can't,' he said. 'I'm risking enough bringing you back here while my father is busy elsewhere . . .'

'Busy taking the role that my sister and I should be playing in our brother's funeral?' I asked. He nodded, but did not speak.

'You know he is wrong about Eteo,' I said. He nodded again.

'He would never forgive me if he thought I had gone against his decision,' Haem said helplessly. 'I'm all he has.'

I could not reply. Creon would still have had two nephews, if he had been able to bear being the second or third most powerful man in our city. He would have a niece standing by him now, if he had not demanded that his men lock her in the cells beneath the palace. He would have me if I weren't sneaking around behind his back to try and ensure my brother received some sort of burial, to appease his shade and placate the gods. I could feel little sympathy for Creon's isolation. And my cousin was weak, I could see that now. His mouth had no strength, his soft jaw revealed no determination. I wondered how I could ever have thought I loved him.

I wished that Ani could help me, but whatever was happening to my sister, I could do nothing to change it. I would have to deal with my family one member at a time. Polyn was being carried to his tomb as I scurried off to my room to find what I needed. Ani would have to wait. At least I could overturn the most terrible injustice, and lay Eteo to rest. I swung open my door, and a sweet, rotten stench filled my nostrils. I knew it was him. I took off my formal dress and left it on the bed, so I was wearing only my charcoal-coloured tunic. I dug a thick scarf from my wardrobe and wrapped it around my face, to try and ward off the smell. I wondered how long I would have, before the funeral party returned to the palace. I needed to be quick. I opened the door of a small cupboard next to my bed, and groped around for the key which Eteo and I had found, all those years ago. My fingers closed round its cold edges and I exhaled. The key was the first thing.

I ran into the courtyard and towards the south corner. An old, battered door stood closed, but not locked. It contained only gardening tools: a small spade, a fork, some rope and a few other things. I took the spade and the rope and ran on towards the ice store. There was no sign of my cousin anywhere: he had ensured he could not be tainted by what I was about to do. The servants were nowhere in sight either. I rounded the corner of the deserted corridor and stopped by the door which led nowhere, to thin air. It was the only route out of the palace where I could be reasonably sure I wouldn't be seen. As I jiggled the key into the ancient lock, I wondered if Haem knew I could get out here, or if he thought I would be trying to leave via the main gate. The key stuck for a moment, and I thought the lock must have rusted over. But eventually there was a snapping sound and the door swung open into my waiting hand. I was worried that the hinges would rasp in protest, but they were quiet.

The rope was thick and dry, but still I forced it into six fat, ill-tied knots. I passed the rope around the bars which covered the tiny window at the top of the door, and fed it through until both ends hung loose in my hands. I pulled on them as hard as I could, but the bars didn't move. I would have to hope they would hold. I threw the spade out onto the ground beneath me, and looked around for a loose stone. I found a broken piece of flagstone just along the corridor against the wall, and pushed it into the space next to the doorpost.

I dropped the spade down onto the ground, then I took one length of rope in each hand, and jumped. I felt a quick burn on my palms as they slid down before my hands juddered into the knots. I was not so far from the ground now. I dropped down the rest of the way, bending my legs as I landed. I stumbled forward and pitched onto my knees. One of my ankles turned over on the uneven ground. But I had made it outside. And as the rope had pulled the door almost closed behind me, the stone I had wedged into the doorframe held it slightly ajar. I would be able to get back inside, when I had done what I needed to do.

I didn't have time to stop and think about the space that opened out before me. I had been enclosed behind the palace walls for so long, I had forgotten what it was like to see the whole of things, not just squares through the windows. But while I had been thinking about how I would get myself outside – and finding everything I needed – I had been able to avoid thinking about what I was coming out here to do. I could not stand here admiring the mountains and the trees, because I needed to walk around the edge of the palace and up the hill a little. I needed to look at my brother's broken body, not askance through a window, but standing beside him. And then I had to find a way to cover him with earth, as quickly as I could, to protect him from scavengers. I had nothing left to give him but this.

I picked up my spade, and began to walk up the hill. The palace was so forbidding from the outside, with its high stone walls and tiny windows: it faced inwards, mostly lit from within, from the open squares which poured light into the rooms along their sides. As I turned the corner of the building, I looked up the hill and there he was. I felt a horrible wave of revulsion: the gods force us to see our own death when we look upon the dead. Except it was scarcely him now, scarcely even a person. I could feel the tears running down my cheeks, as a burning sickness filled my throat. It wasn't my brother. It didn't even resemble him. Only by repeating this in my head could I persuade my legs to keep climbing the hill. It wasn't him. Not my brother. Not the man I loved.

The smell of death – I tried to think of the proper words, to distract myself from what they truly described

– the stench of putrefaction was much stronger out here. But at least I had prepared myself for that, covering my face once more with the scarf I had brought, breathing through my mouth, trying to set my mind on the physical task ahead of me. Still I could not prevent myself from collapsing to my knees and retching onto the ground. A body should be wrapped. My brother should have been kept in linen. He should be under the earth.

I hadn't anticipated the noise. There was a humming sound, like a distant buzzing, angry crowd. But the crowd wasn't distant at all: they were flying around him, crawling over him, defiling him further, as though the insults, the injuries he had sustained had not been enough. They swarmed around his neck, feeding off the blood which had coagulated around the fatal wound. I drove my nails into my palms as I forced myself to see that his eyes were gone: two blackened sockets were all that remained from the sharp beak which had enucleated him, my brother, my poor blinded brother. I could see the birds, sitting on the hillside above me, waiting for me to be gone so they could get back to their vicious work. I wanted so much to run away, to turn and shoot back down the hill, the way I had come. But I knew I had to dig next to where he lay: I wouldn't be able to carry him on my own. I could look at him no longer. So I turned my back on the brother I loved, and I began to dig.

For a while, I thought it was hopeless. It was hard to guess how much time I had before Creon and the funeral party returned to the palace. And even harder to guess how long it would be before any of them noticed that I was missing. Creon had planned the celebrations of Polyn's life in the main square this afternoon; he would expect me to be there, certainly. But it was possible that his argument with Ani this morning had put him off the idea of a full wake. My shadow was shortening all the time, but I had scarcely shifted enough earth to cover my own hands. I didn't know what Creon would do if he caught me out here. But it scarcely mattered now. What worse could he do to me than this? I kept digging.

The ground was dry, and so hard I was worried it would break the edge of the shovel I was using. But gradually, I found myself standing next to a pile of earth, though every muscle in my arms was screaming for me to stop, and my back ached from bending over. The sun was almost directly overhead now, it must be close to midday. I knew I should run back to the palace, as Creon would be back shortly. But I could not. I had done too much to give up now. If he slammed me into prison with my sister, so be it. Part of my mind would not be quiet, reminding me that it wasn't my own safety I should worry about: it was Ani's. What if Creon decided to punish her, as a way of punishing me? But I silenced the question: this is what Ani wanted, as much as I did. She was in no position to perform the task herself, but she would never forgive me if I valued her comfort over that of my brother. And I would never forgive myself. My parents were dead: I could never have another sibling. I would see Eteo into his grave, into Hades, where he belonged.

I dug more soil, more and more, and finally I had made a hole which looked like it could contain him. I turned to face the boulder against which my brother was resting. No, not resting: that was what a man would do. And this was not a man, not my brother, not any more. It was just a thing, a thing I needed to place in the ground to appease the gods. I crushed every instinct which told me not to touch the dead, to shy away from the insects and the ruination. I walked around to his flank – not his, its – and knelt down. I begged my brother's forgiveness, closed my eyes, and pushed. His body slid away from me, and lurched towards the grave. I opened my eyes a little, to see how far he had moved. Then closed them again as I shoved him once more across the small patch of ground. Finally, I heard the thudding sound of him dropping down into his grave. I opened my eyes, and realized I was crying so hard I couldn't see anyway. My brother was in the last home he would ever have.

It didn't take much longer to cover him over and pile the earth on top. I left a gold ring on his blackened hand to pay Charon for the ferry. I muttered a short prayer to the gods, asking them to be sure that the earth would lie light above my brother. Then I found five large stones, each the size of two fists, and used them to mark the head of the grave. It was a poor memorial, but it was the best I could do. And it was enough.

I had been gone for too long, I knew. I ran back around the palace wall, and hid the spade in the grass beneath the door: no one would see it from outside the palace, and I couldn't carry it back up the ropes. My arms were so tired from digging that I wondered if I could climb at all. But I needed to get back inside and this was easily the quickest, safest route. I reached up and pulled on the two ropes, making sure they would still take my weight. I twisted one below the other, once and then once more, and spread my arms wide to tug the loose knot as high as it would go, so that the cords were bound together. Otherwise, when I rested my weight on one of the knots, the ropes might easily slip from my hands and slither free of the bars at the top.

I reached above my head and pulled myself up until my feet found the first knot. I gripped the ropes tightly, and moved my foot until I found the next one, a few hands above the first. I reached my left arm up and then used my right to heave myself up another foot. My shoulders were burning less than my biceps, but I held on and kept climbing. Once my feet were on the final knot, I could grab the stone floor beneath the door to take my weight, lean forward and push the door open. It groaned quietly and slid away from me. With one last wrench, I dragged myself onto the flagstones and lay panting on the ground. I was trying to listen out for servants or guards who might find me, but I could only hear my own breath. After several moments, I raised myself to my knees and then my feet. I kicked the stone away from the door jamb and reached into my pocket for a small knife which had once belonged to Eteo. I hacked through the ropes and let them drop to the ground, pushed the door shut and locked it with my key. I hurried back down the corridor and saw that the courtyard was quiet. I scuttled across to my room just in time for Haem to step out of the north colonnade and call out.

'There you are, Isy. Are you awake at last? My father is waiting for us in the main square. I sent word that we would be there as soon as we had each had time to wash and refresh ourselves.' He was walking towards me as he spoke, so by the time he had finished his sentence, he was close enough to mutter, 'You have grass stains on your legs and you need to get all that soil off your hands. As fast as you can. We don't have long. He doesn't know you've been outside. Is it done?'

I nodded. 'I'll be quick.'

And as I changed my clothes and scrubbed my knees and elbows clean and tried to force a comb through my sweaty hair, I wondered how long it would be before Creon discovered that Eteo was safe, under the earth. And what he would do when he found out.

26

As Jocasta turned from the gate and walked alone across the main square towards the second courtyard, she could feel Oedipus's eyes upon her from the shadows. She wished she could break free of the protocol which expected her to be regal at all times, so she could hitch up her skirts and run. Instead, she walked as fast as she could and didn't pause when she crossed the colonnade where her husband was waiting. She heard him hurry to catch up with her. He said her name and – lifting her hand – she cut him off.

'I don't want to talk about it until no one else can overhear.' She kept moving and he strode along beside her. They crossed the second courtyard without seeing a soul: the slaves somehow knew to keep themselves scarce. She crossed into the family courtyard, and found herself short of breath.

'Where are the children?' she asked, looking around the deserted square.

'In lessons or in the nursery, the same as every morning,' he replied. 'Let's go to our room.' He took her hand, but she wrenched it away from him.

'We could be overheard by slaves in the next room,' she said. 'I will not have our conversation repeated. I want somewhere private.' Oedipus looked around the courtyard, feeling foolish. Another room was hardly likely to appear.

'Let's sit by the fountain,' he said. 'No one can overhear us there. We'd see them coming from any direction, long before they could hear us.' He reached out and took her hand.

'Hiding in the middle of the square,' she said, trying to smile.

He led her to the fountain. 'Sit here,' he said, and left her perched on the edge of the stone wall which surrounded it. He picked up two heavy chairs, and lugged them over to her. He placed them next to each other, but facing in opposite directions, so they could talk while keeping an eye on everything around them. He dug a piece of cloth from his belt, and dipped it in the fountain water. He reached over and wiped her hot, red face, like she did for the children on days such as these. She sat perfectly still and – when he had finished – he threw the rag on the ground.

'Was it really her? Teresa?' he asked.

'Yes.'

'I didn't recognize her.'

'I didn't either,' she said. 'Even when I knew it was her. She was unrecognizable. It was horrible, like hearing a familiar voice coming out from behind a mask.'

'You do know she was lying to you?' Oedipus asked.

Jocasta felt a shudder rack through her body. 'I don't,' she said. 'I don't know what to believe. I thought she was telling the truth then, but she could easily have been lying to me: then or now. She's a horrible woman.'

'And she has a grudge against us. She blamed me for

Laius's death, and then I threw her out of the palace. She looks like she's been living on the street ever since, waiting for the chance to get her revenge. She can't hurt me directly, so she's hurting you instead. You must be able to see that. She was a vicious old witch then, and she still is now. Her face finally reflects her true character.'

'But why would she make this up now? Isn't it just more likely that she's telling the truth at last? I told you, I have always felt that he was alive. Always.'

Oedipus reached over and took her hand in both of his. 'Jocasta, if something happened to one of the children—'

'Don't say that,' she hissed, making the sign to ward off the evil eye.

'I have to. If something happened to one of our children, I would do what you did. I know I would. I would imagine them continuing to grow up. I'd never stop. I thought about it last summer, when the plague came. I thought if anything happened to any of them, I wouldn't believe it. They're realer than you or me. They occupy space more than we ever could. And how could all of that just disappear? It couldn't. So they wouldn't disappear for me: I would carry them around, I'd imagine them. But that wouldn't make my imagination reality, would it?'

She ignored him, and he squeezed her hand again. 'Would it?' he repeated.

'It's not the same,' she said.

'No, it's much worse for you. You carried that child, Jocasta. He was inside you for nine months.'

'I didn't want him at first,' she said dully. 'I didn't want a baby. They made me have one. They wanted a girl to be

Laius's heir. So they made me get pregnant. I wished and wished not to be, and the death was my reward and my punishment from the gods.'

He squeezed her hand so hard that she yelped, and he apologized, rubbing the bones he had crushed a moment earlier. 'I wish I could have come sooner,' he said. 'I wish it every day.'

'You were just a child,' she said. 'That's precisely the problem.'

'There is no problem,' he said. 'She's locked up now, and she can die in prison, for all anyone cares. Spiteful old hag. No one can believe that I could be your son. No one. The idea is ridiculous. It was ridiculous a year ago, and it is even more ridiculous now.'

'How is it ridiculous?' she asked. 'You were adopted. Your father said so. You don't think he was lying as well, do you?'

Oedipus rolled his eyes, impatient at Jocasta's need to repeat an argument they had conducted several times before. 'No, I don't think he was lying. And I also don't think that he was lying when he said I was adopted from a family on the next street over, who couldn't afford to feed a fifth child. Why would he make that up?'

'I don't know.'

'Well, that's the question, isn't it? Do we believe my father, who has no reason to lie to us, or an old woman who has every incentive to do so?'

'Your father lied to you through your whole childhood,' she said. 'Why didn't he tell you you were adopted before?'

'Because he didn't think there was any need, until I

sent a messenger to him and asked,' he said. 'Some people do keep secrets even when there is no reason to.' The barb in his tone was pronounced. 'And why is my father suddenly the villain in this story?'

'Because . . .' She ran out of words. 'I don't know. He isn't.'

'Jocasta, please just think for a moment about what Teresa is suggesting. Do you really believe she could have stolen your baby, taking advantage of the fact that he – unlike all other babies – didn't make a sound when he was born? That she could have hidden him somewhere? Where? In the palace?'

'She wouldn't have hidden him here,' Jocasta snapped. 'Don't be an idiot.'

'Very well.' Oedipus raised his hands in mock surrender. 'So she hid him outside the palace. She happened to know someone so well that she could just give them a baby, no questions asked, and they would take it. Why had you never seen her with this friend? And where were they when she left the palace a few years later?'

Jocasta blanched to hear him describe her purgatory as a few years, when it had felt so very much like forever to live through.

'I don't know. Maybe they died.'

'Maybe they died,' he agreed. 'Before or after they went on an eighty-mile trek across mountains infested with bandits and brigands, carrying a baby? For no discernible reason except to give him away to a family who happened to live on the street next to my parents? And that family accepted this unwanted child, but then changed their minds and gave him away to their neighbours?'

'Of course it doesn't sound true if you say it like that,' she said. 'Stop trying to make me feel stupid.'

'Then stop being stupid,' he said. 'It sounds impossible because it is impossible. You had a baby which died. My parents adopted an unwanted child hundreds of stades away from here. These two stories didn't connect until I met you. You know it.'

'No,' she screamed, leaping up from the chair. 'You know it. You know it because you always have to be so incredibly clever. You know it because you would never be taken in by a malevolent old woman who probably wouldn't hate me so much if you hadn't thrown her out of her home. You know it because you would rather admit to anything than that I might be right about something and you might be wrong. Even when it's something as terrible as this. And instead of trying to make things better, you're just sitting there, correcting me and belittling me and telling me I'm stupid. How dare you?'

'I'm sorry,' he said.

'You aren't. If you were sorry, you wouldn't be doing it in the first place. I have tried to be calm about this. I tried last year, when we sent a messenger to your father. And I kept trying when he sent his reply and made everything worse, not better. And instead of acknowledging that, and trying to help me, you just pretended everything was perfect, and that all my fears were irrational and idiotic. And now look. Now, it's come back again, like I knew it would. Like I said it would. And it's what people out there believe. That's why they hate me. It's why they hate us. So why don't you go out there and tell all of them that they're stupid to believe something which is undeniably technically possible? Go on. Go and tell them. Go and tell them they're all idiots because you know best. Treat the rest of the city like you treat me.'

'I am sorry,' he said again.

'No,' she said. 'Not this time. I'm going to our room. To my room. I don't want you in there tonight. I don't want to share a bed with you. I don't want to see you.'

'Where do you want me to sleep?' he asked.

'I don't care. Sleep in the children's room, sleep in the garden, sleep wherever you like. But don't come near me. I can't bear it.'

That night, Oedipus slept on a too-hard couch covered in too-soft pillows in an unused bedroom, waking often and wondering for just how long his wife was going to be so angry. She hardly ever lost her temper, not even with the children. As he rolled over uncomfortably, he wasn't sure he could remember ever hearing her shout like that before. It was understandable, he supposed. The face of that rancid old beggar-woman would revolt anybody. And she of all people knew how to upset his wife. She had practised doing it for years. But surely Jocasta would calm down by tomorrow. She couldn't stay angry with him, when none of it – none of it – was his fault.

But when the morning sunlight poured in through the windows and he woke in a sleepy haze, his wife did not appear beside the bed, to kiss him and apologize for her harsh words. He watched, embarrassed, from across the courtyard, as two slave women knocked on Jocasta's door and received no reply. Was she really punishing him like this, for all to see? He wanted to hammer on the door and demand she stop being such a brat. But how would it look, a husband pleading with his wife to be allowed into her room?

By the afternoon, he was worried. She had been in there for nearly a whole day. She must be hungry. Although, now he thought about it, he couldn't be certain that she hadn't left the room during the night, could he? Perhaps she'd sent someone to the kitchens to collect some bread and fruit, so she could spend the day sulking, making him feel guilty and look stupid. He refused to rise to the bait. No one else seemed worried, after all. The children had asked their nurse where their mother was, but she just told them Jocasta had a bad headache, as was often true.

As dusk fell, Creon wandered awkwardly into the family courtyard.

'Sorry to intrude,' he mumbled. 'I was just looking for Jocasta.'

'She's got a headache, I think,' Oedipus replied. 'She's been in her bedroom all day.'

'Her bedroom?' asked Creon, and Oedipus felt a surge of resentment against his wife, as his awkwardness was clearly visible to all.

'Yes,' he said. 'She went to bed early last night and she hasn't come out again yet.'

'Has anyone been in to check on her?' Creon asked.

'No.'

'Should we . . . ?' Creon gestured at the door.

'Should we what?' Oedipus blinked at his brother-in-law.

'Make sure she doesn't need anything,' Creon said.

'I'm sure she would have asked if she needed something. But don't let me stop you,' Oedipus said.

And Creon went over and knocked on the door. 'It's your brother,' he called.

Oedipus held his breath for a moment, his ears straining to hear a reply. But Creon knocked a second and then a third time, before he gave up.

'She must be asleep,' he said.

'I think so,' Oedipus replied. 'She does sleep very heavily, when she has these headaches. You know.'

'Well, tell her I'll see her tomorrow and I hope she'll be feeling better,' Creon said, and he turned, his shoulders slumped, and walked back the way he had come.

The following morning, there was still no sign of Jocasta. Oedipus had spent the night in the courtyard itself, curled uncomfortably on one of her divans. He was certain he would have woken if she had opened the door. So perhaps she wasn't punishing him. Perhaps she did have a terrible headache. In which case, he wouldn't lose face if he went to her room, even when she hadn't apologized, would he? He took a deep breath, and knocked on her door. Their door. Palace etiquette had been thrown aside when they married and decided to share a bedroom instead of maintaining separate quarters. But Oedipus had never wanted to spend a single night away from his wife, and he never had, until now.

There was still no reply. He turned the handle and pushed at the door, but it didn't move. She had locked him out. Locked him out of their bedroom. He could feel the anger rising. What if she was sick and needed help? She hadn't thought about that when she locked the door in a fit of petulance, he was quite sure.

Oedipus could no longer leave things as they were. The children were becoming fractious, no matter how much the nurse placated them. Antigone wouldn't stop grizzling, and even Ismene, who was normally so placid if Eteocles was there to amuse her, was frowning and refusing every spoonful of food. Exasperated by their behaviour, he hurled a small wooden stool at the flagstones, and watched the splinters jump across the floor. All four children began to cry, but still his wife did not appear.

'Very well,' he shouted. 'You obviously want your mother. Go off to your lessons and I'll bring her to you.'

He beckoned a slave over, and told him they would need to break through Jocasta's door. The boy, who couldn't have broken through a sheet of papyrus, nodded sceptically.

'Fetch Creon,' Oedipus sighed. 'He'll help.'

While he waited for his brother-in-law to arrive, he examined the door. It was made of thick oak panels and had only one lock, in the centre of the left-hand side. There were two bright bronze hinges on the right, and it was difficult to say whether the lock or the hinges would be the easiest thing to break. Or would the panels of the door split through?

Creon came hurrying behind the boy, then shooed him away.

'The child says you want my help to break down the door?' he asked, frowning.

'She's locked it from the inside.'

'And there isn't another key?'

'I don't think so,' Oedipus said. 'I've never known her lock the door before. Shall we test it?' He backed up, eyeing the hard wooden surface.

'I don't think we could just smash through it with our shoulders,' Creon said. 'It's solid oak, isn't it?'

'Do you have a better suggestion?' Oedipus asked. 'She might be lying on the floor; she could be unconscious.'

Creon whistled the boy to come back over, and sent him to fetch the guards. A few moments later, the watch commander appeared with four men. Oedipus explained the problem and the commander nodded. Two of his guards fetched axes, which he instructed them to put to use.

The noise was astonishing. The metal blades rasped on the old wood, and even after several blows the door was barely scratched.

'Forgive me,' said the commander to Creon and Oedipus. 'It's awkward. Keep going,' he added, to the guards.

'Once they've gone through the wood panel in one place, it'll be quite quick,' Creon said. The two guards stepped back and handed their axes to their comrades, who swung the metal with fresh arms. Finally a small crack of light appeared on the upper left quarter.

'Concentrate your efforts there,' Oedipus said, pointing. The watch commander raised his eyebrow a tiny distance. He jerked his head up, and the guards did as Oedipus had asked. A few deafening moments later, and a chunk of wood had broken through.

'Force it,' said the commander, before Oedipus could offer any more advice. The four soldiers shoved their combined weight against the door, and felt the panel give a little.

'Come on,' said Oedipus. 'Surely that's enough.'

The men pulled back and shoved themselves against the door again. Finally, there was a splintering sound, and the panel closest to the lock gave way. One of the guards reached through and groped around for the key. If Jocasta had taken it away from the door, they would need to smash more of the door around the lock to break in. But his face relaxed. He had the key in his hand, and he turned it, first the wrong way, and then correctly. The lock clicked open and the men stepped back. Oedipus nodded his thanks, and opened the door.

'Where are you, my darling?' he said. 'Did you lock the door and then realize you didn't feel– ?' He broke into a terrible howl.

Creon leapt forward. 'What is it?' he asked. And then, 'No.'

Jocasta was hanging from a hook in the ceiling. No one could remember what it had once been intended for. But now it held the queen, suspended by a rope. She wore a plain white gown which Oedipus couldn't recall ever seeing before. It looked like a child's nightgown, one she must have brought here all those years ago, and long since stopped wearing. Her face was puffed up and purple, her hair was matted to her skull. She must have tied the noose around her neck and then jumped from the bed.

'Get the doctor,' the watch commander said to his men. 'Go now.'

But it was much too late for that.

27

I followed my cousin out to the main square, where Polyn's wake was beginning. I had forgotten my five-stringed lyre, and had to run back to collect it. I hoped I would be able to play it well enough to mark the death of both of my brothers. The words I had composed were appropriately vague, but I would know – Eteo would know – they were for him as well as Polyn. I had not practised for several days; Thebans would consider it profoundly disrespectful for a sister to sit playing a phorminx while her brothers awaited burial. I knew what I wanted to sing, though: I had rehearsed it all in my mind. And the plangent tones of this instrument – which was old even when it was given to me – would be ideally suited to my song.

I wished Ani was there, hastening along beside me. Or rather, she would have been walking at her own pace, and Haem and I would have slowed down, to avoid leaving her behind.

'Have you seen my sister?' I asked him.

He shook his head. 'She's in the cells, in the caves beneath the main square,' he said. 'I'm sure of it. But I haven't spoken to my father about it. He issued the sentence this morning, he will not be in any mood to issue a reprieve this afternoon.'

It took me a moment to realize that he was speaking

literally. Ani had been taken to jail this morning, and then there had been Eteo, and then it was now. I felt as though Ani had been locked up a month ago. I wanted to step back from the gathering crowd and spend some time with my own thoughts, but of course I could do no such thing. The sun was dropping fast, and the servants were beginning to light the torches, even though they were not needed quite yet. Each one was placed in a bronze holder around the walls of the main square, so that it never grew fully dark. Creon was over by the altar, performing one last set of ritual offerings to the gods he believes in so devoutly. And yet, how could any priest pretend to him that his gods would tolerate the burial of one man and not another? It was nonsense. Either the dread lord of the Underworld expected his dues to be paid for the dead, or he did not. It could not be halfway between the two, and any priest who said otherwise was no more respectful of the gods than my uncle himself.

There was something not quite right in the courtyard. The servants were moving with their usual invisible efficiency, the priests were intoning, the musicians were playing, the crowd was gathering. But, something was wrong, as if the incense which burned over the altars had been tainted, or everyone in the courtyard had begun speaking a different language. I felt eyes upon me, too many of them. Of course people would stare – I have grown up as the child of a polluted union, I am used to the stares – but this was more than usual. Haem looked across at me, frowning. He felt it too.

'What is it?' I asked. He shook his head. But we both knew the answer, even before the watchman ran in through the main gates, and prostrated himself before my uncle, pressing his forehead against the stones as though that would be enough to save him.

'Forgive me, Basileus,' he said.

My uncle looked irritated at being disturbed from his piety, but not as much as I would have expected. Perhaps he had prayed enough. Or perhaps he realized the gods would not hear him today.

'What do you want?' he snarled.

'Forgive me,' the man said again. 'I don't know how it happened. Or when.'

Creon pressed his lips together, as though he wished he could spit the man out, like a piece of rancid pork fat. 'Tell me,' he said. 'Be assured that I will not ask again.'

The man sat back on his heels, his grey tunic stretching taut across his belly. 'I was not the only man on watch, king,' he said. 'But my comrades and I drew lots, and it fell to me to bring this news to you. Your nephew, the traitor, has been buried.'

Creon's face was unreadable, even to me who had known him for my entire life. The anger was plain in the creases around his mouth. But I saw a trace of something else there too. Was it possible that he was relieved?

'Continue,' he said.

The man looked frantically around him, expecting guards to appear on all sides, their spears pointed down at his ribs. His chest was heaving with the effort of running into the palace and scraping himself down on the ground.

'It happened sometime today, Basileus. This afternoon, perhaps. The traitor lay open to the air this morning: I saw a dog feeding off him myself.' If he thought this would ingratiate him with my uncle, he was mistaken. Revulsion flickered across Creon's face. I felt my own chest tighten. Even the knowledge that Eteo was finally safe did not undo the damage done before I could bury him.

'He was buried today, on your watch?' Creon asked.

'There were six of us on patrol, majesty.' The man stumbled over his words, so quick was he to explain that it was not his fault alone. 'Whoever did it, they slipped past us.'

'For how long,' Creon asked, luxuriating now in the man's evident fear, 'would you estimate you were in dereliction of your duties?'

'Basileus, it was not for long. I promise, not long at all. Only enough time to return to the guardhouse and find my fellow watchmen to take over from me.'

Creon nodded. 'I should have you all executed,' he said mildly. Perhaps he was remembering how few guards the palace now had, after he had ordered so many to be killed on the day Polyn and Eteo died. 'You expect me to believe that a whole troop of men found their way out to the back of the palace and buried a full-grown man in the time it took you to return to the guardhouse? How long were you asleep for?'

The courtyard had grown very quiet when the watchman ran in, but you could hear the news spreading around the square. The traitor had been buried; someone had buried the boy; both of the dead kings were now beneath the ground; someone had heeded the words of the princess; Creon's law had been broken; the gods' law had been obeyed.

The tension was extraordinary, like the strings on a lyre

that has been allowed to grow too warm near a fire. As the wood expands, the strings snap, one after another. As each one gives way, the remaining strings are pulled tauter still, trying to do the work of themselves and their brothers. Even my uncle, people were muttering, could not order that his own nephew be disinterred. It was bad enough that he had sought to disobey the gods by leaving the boy unburied. But to dig him out of the ground was unthinkable. Was Creon really about to demand that the watchman commit such a terrible crime?

'I swear,' said the man, stretching himself out on the ground, his belly pushed into the flagstones, spilling down into the gaps between them, 'I was not asleep. They must have been lightning-quick.'

I felt useless nerves filling my belly. I had not even considered that Creon would have ordered guards to watch over Eteo. But I had not seen anyone when I was outside, not even a shepherd in the distance. Outside the walls, where the palace almost hangs over the hill beneath us, it is usually quiet. Goats graze on the other hills, and olives grow on the lower slopes. But no goatherds or farmers use the land around the palace. I suppose the men charged with keeping watch over Eteo had simply assumed it was unnecessary. I had been – though I could barely think the word – lucky. I corrected myself: in this one regard, I had been lucky.

'She was right,' I heard a man say. 'The girl was right.'

Crowds are curious things: made up of individuals, but with a character entirely their own. As people realized what the man was saying, they remembered what my sister had demanded this morning. She had asked for Eteo to be buried, as was proper, and now he had been. Yet the girl was in prison, wasn't she? Beneath the palace square? Was she beneath their very feet as they stood waiting for the music to begin and the wine to be poured to honour the shade of my brother, Polyn? But then how had the other king been buried?

It never occurred to any of them to wonder if I might have had anything to do with it. I was still the youngest child, the one they could overlook. I felt Haem next to me, breathing shallowly. He too had realized how close I must have come to getting caught. Or was he waiting for the watchman to admit that he had taken a bribe to look the other way, from the young prince, the heir to his father's throne?

I would never know the truth, because I realized at that moment that it was not important, and in the chaos which followed, I did not ask him. What mattered was that the people of Thebes were beginning to appreciate that my sister had been wrongfully imprisoned. And if she could arrange, from a subterranean cell, for her brother to be buried, she was powerful in a way that the all-powerful king was not. She must be a favourite of the gods, for who else could have assisted her? This morning, the king had seemed to be a stern but patriotic leader. Now, he seemed to them to be an arrogant fool, alienating the gods by persecuting their favourite. And what could be more pathetic than a grown man afraid of a girl?

Suddenly, anger was rippling through the courtyard, like wind across the wheat crops which grew in the lowlands outside the city. They were shouting, stamping, whistling and clapping their hollowed hands together.

The guards, to whom Creon looked, stood back, impassive. They were new recruits, and they had no experience in this kind of situation. My uncle sought out one he knew, but though there were a few older men who I recognized – standing with their spears by their sides, seemingly blind and deaf – he did not see them, or if he did, he realized they would not obey him.

The crowd called my sister's name, 'Ani, Ani', punc tuated with the stamps of their feet. My sister must have felt the very walls of her cell shuddering from the noise and the dust which rose up as they smacked their sticks and boots into the ground.

'I'm going to fetch her,' I whispered to Haem, though no one could have heard me over the noise they were making. 'Before there's a riot.'

I was standing near to one of the older guards, and I grabbed his arm. 'Can you take me to Ani?' I said. 'Take me to my sister.'

The man looked around him as though he hadn't heard, or was uncertain what I might be asking. Then he dipped his head in a brisk nod, and walked away. I ran to keep up with him.

In the furthest corner of the square, behind the throne room and the temples, was a dingy forgotten corner with a battered ancient door – blackened over the years – in front of what I had always assumed (if I had ever given it any thought) was a storeroom, built into a recess in the outside walls. The white stone had turned grey with dirt and time. The guard reached to his belt and I thought he would produce a key, but instead he drew out a dagger by the hilt. It was this which he thumped against the door five times, before stowing it back at his waist. There was the sound of wood scraping on stone and something heavy shifting in its socket. The door swung open before us, and I could see that far from hiding a small cupboard, it opened onto a dimly lit flight of stairs. The guard who had opened the door from within raised his eyebrows at his comrade when he saw me, but he said nothing, and stepped aside.

The tunnels beneath the palace were dark and I was relieved when the guard pulled a torch from a wall-sconce and carried it ahead of us to light our path. The steps were smooth and worn beneath my feet, and the air was musty. Water dripped from the roof of the caves, and had left rust-brown deposits down the damp walls.

The sound of our feet – his boots, my sandals – echoed off the walls as we followed the twisting corridor through its many turns. I had no sense of which direction we were travelling in: without the sky to guide me, I was lost. But eventually, we came to a long straight stretch, where the man half-turned his head, and said, 'Not far, now.'

'Whereabouts are we?' I asked.

'You're going under the market square,' he said. 'The cells were built in the caves which open out onto the far side of the hill. Don't worry, Potnia, your sister isn't alone in the dark. Although the sun must be almost set by now.'

I was startled by the formal title: no one had called me 'Princess' in years. I was too young to warrant it until recently. But someone had used the honorific before, long ago. I couldn't remember who. My father, I supposed. I shivered, although I hadn't felt cold until just now.

As my companion had promised, the darkness grew slightly less complete when we reached the far end of this tunnel. Then he turned right, down a shorter corridor, and there were three small doors on the left-hand side, each one barred with a thick pine plank, and each one with a small grille in the top, through which the prisoner could be seen. But so little light was now spilling in from outside, it was virtually as dark as the tunnels we had come through.

'She's in the furthest one,' he said.

Even though I was desperate to see her, I hesitated before stepping forward. I had a sudden horrible vision of Ani lying dead in the cell, her tiny frame collapsed on the ground. I felt as though the walls and ceiling were rushing in to crush me, as though all the air had been taken from my lungs. I stumbled, and the guard put out his hand to support me. 'Steady,' he said.

'Forgive me.'

'Forgive you?' he laughed. 'You must be the only person in Thebes who would come down here voluntarily. And as it's getting dark, too. You're a brave girl. Now, give me a hand with the pine log, so your sister can get back where she belongs.'

He strode ahead, and I tried to shake the image of my dead sister from my mind, concentrating on following this stranger who thought I was brave.

'Here we go,' he said, as we slid the wooden bar from its housing. He allowed his end to drop to the ground and propped it against the door jamb. The door swung open of its own accord.

And there before my eyes my nightmare was made flesh. Next to a small, dirty cot, my sister swung from a rope she had fashioned from her own stole. I screamed, but the guard was quicker to act: he dropped his torch and ran forward and lifted her from the waist. Reaching into his belt, he pulled out the knife and slashed through the fabric noose. My sister slumped into his arms.

I reached down and picked up the torch from my feet. Its sputtering light flickered back into brightness. The guard turned and I saw Ani's face, reddish-purple next to the white rope around her neck. Then she coughed, and I almost dropped the torch again, in fear and relief.

'Ani!' I screamed. 'Are you alive?'

She did not reply, but the guard nodded. 'Her throat won't let her talk for a moment or two, Potnia. Lucky you came when you did.'

My sister opened her eyes and pointed upwards.

'I need to get her back to the main courtyard,' I said. 'Will you help me?'

The guard glanced at the ground. 'I'll carry her out of the caves for you. But I can't take her into the palace. I have three daughters. Your uncle—'

'I understand,' I said. There was no point arguing with him when we both knew the words he wasn't saying: my uncle didn't hesitate to punish guards with death. The man could not afford to take the risk.

I walked beside him, carrying the torch, while he carried my sister. When we finally found ourselves out on the hillside, he dipped Ani's feet to the ground and set her down. 'Can you stand?' he asked. She nodded uncertainly. But as he let go of her, she did not fall.

'Thank you,' I said to him. 'If it is ever within my power, you will receive a rich reward for the service you have done my family today.'

The guard smiled. 'Thank you, Potnia.' He took the torch from me, for it was still just light enough to see in the fading twilight. He retreated back into the caves, and I took my sister's arm, so she could lean on me. We began the darkening trudge up the hillside to the city walls.

'What were you thinking, sister?' I asked.

'I should have known it would be you who came,' she whispered. 'I was hoping it would be Haem.'

It took me a moment to understand her meaning.

'You wanted him to find you and cut you down?' My sister had always had a weakness for dramatic gestures, but this was excessive even for her. Her eyes glittered.

'I will be queen of Thebes, Isy. I am the rightful heir. The throne is mine. I knew Haem would have supported me if he'd rescued me from death by my own hand.'

I stopped dead. 'Are you serious?'

She pulled my arm, hurrying me along. 'Of course I am serious. Never more so. Our brothers are dead, I will be queen or I will be dead. I will not live like a child for the rest of my life.'

'But you nearly died. What if it had been Haem, and he hadn't been able to open the door in time? Or what if he hadn't had a knife to cut you down?'

'He's not an idiot,' she snapped. 'He would have done something when he saw me hanging there.' I shook my head. 'I have to separate him from his father,' she said. 'Or he is no use to me at all.'

'I thought you loved him,' I said, and she squeezed my arm.

'I do,' she replied. 'In a way.'

'Well, I'm sorry he didn't come,' I said. 'But he covered for me. I buried Eteo this afternoon.'

Ani nodded, though it made her wince. 'I knew you'd think of something,' she said.

We had reached the edge of the city and climbed a few steps into the deserted market square. I thought she would ask about Eteo, but she seemed happy to know no more than that he was properly interred.

'I thought our brothers were important to you,' I said.

'They were, Isy. But they're in the past and I am here now. They're both buried, you said?' I nodded. 'Then there's no more to discuss,' she continued, as we scurried across to the palace gates. She paused, then said, 'Isy, I overheard the oddest thing this afternoon, as I was waiting for you to come and get me.'

'What did you hear?'

'The guards walked past my cell to check on me several times,' she said. 'Two of them, making sure I was safely locked up. I don't know how they imagined I could escape.' Her thoughts had already returned to herself.

'And one of them said something . . . ?' I prompted her.

'They had both helped to carry Polyn to the tomb, to our family tomb,' she said. I nodded, as we continued to walk across the slippery cobbled stones. 'And they said when the tomb was opened for him to be placed inside . . .' She paused and looked up, to check I was hanging on her words.

'Yes,' I said.

'They said the tomb was empty. Don't you think that's strange?'

'I'm not sure strange is quite the right word for what I think,' I said. 'Empty?'

'Mother and Father must be buried somewhere else,' she said. 'But I can't think why, and I have been trying, all day.' I felt a sudden rush of love for her, the last of my family.

'I'll think about it, too,' I said. 'We'll make sense of it.'

'Well, that will have to be your responsibility now,' she said. 'I won't have time.' Annoyance rose up in my chest where the love had just been.

'Why not?' Sometimes, you cannot avoid giving Ani the pleasure of making you ask.

'Because when we walk into the palace,' my sister said, 'the people of Thebes will make me ruler of the city. I know they will. So that will be my life now.'

And as she spoke, we had arrived at the palace gates. We walked into the main courtyard and the crowd fell silent. But only for a moment, before they began shouting her name, and calling her Basileia, Anassa, queen.

28

When he saw Jocasta suspended from the ceiling, Oedipus snapped in two. One of the guards reached above him to cut through the rope which had taken her life, and her body fell into her husband's arms, as though he were carrying her across a threshold at the start of their life together. He held her for a moment, then laid her down on the bed, because she was heavier now than when she was alive. Creon stood back and allowed Oedipus to cling to his wife's body and weep.

By the time Sophon arrived, it was clear to everyone that there was nothing he could do. But the guards who had gone to fetch him hadn't delivered their message with any care for the fact that the man they sought was sitting in a room with the queen's four children. Come quickly, they had said. The queen needs you. Sophon had hurried out behind them, and the children followed him because their mother was the queen and if she needed their tutor, she might well need them. Besides, they hadn't seen her for two days, and if she wanted the doctor, she would want to see them and admire their songs and handwriting and stories. So they ran behind Sophon all the way to their mother's room. They could hear a man crying, which sounded terribly wrong, as men never cried. Especially not their father, though they had never known another man to be in their mother's rooms. But why would their father ever cry?

The grizzled watch commander had stepped outside the room to breathe some air untainted by the faint stench of death, and he noticed the children hurrying their way along the colonnade to see their mother. He muttered, 'Stop them', to the guard standing next to him, and pulled the bedroom door closed behind him. The guard stood for a moment, uncertain what he should do. His training had been in hand-to-hand combat: he had no idea what protocol required of him in this situation. But he had a son and a daughter the same age as Eteo and Ani, although his girl was the older one: tall with a grave expression that occasionally cracked into mirth when she found her little brother beguilingly funny.

'Come on,' he said, reaching out to Eteo, the child who had run most quickly through the courtyard. 'You're it.' He tapped Eteo's arm, and ran across the courtyard laughing like an imbecile. The watch commander was about to bellow at him, before noticing that his words had had the required effect: Eteo jabbed his brother and ran after the guard, squawking with delight at the unexpected game. Polyn patted Isy on the head and declared her it, and she raced after her siblings on her small, spindly legs. Picking on the youngest should have provided an easy victory, but Isy was nearly as tall as Ani already, and soon caught up with her sister.

The watch commander eased the door open a crack and peered inside.

'The children are outside,' he said. 'Just so you know.'

Oedipus was impervious to words. He knelt by the side

of the bed, his head resting on his wife's belly. Sophon leaned over the top of the bed, but there was no need to check for a pulse. Jocasta had been dead for many hours already. Creon stood apart from the others, his expression one of confusion rather than grief. He caught the watch commander's words, and frowned.

'Take the children to the kitchens,' he said. 'Tell the servants to look after them. Keep them out of the way until I come and get them myself. Do you understand?'

'Of course, sir,' said the watch commander. His hair and beard were grey: he was too old not to know that today would reveal who was in charge of Thebes now the queen was dead.

Sophon stood up, the bones in his back cracking as he straightened. He looked at Oedipus's shaking body and walked across the room to Creon.

'How did this happen?' he asked.

Creon shook his head. 'I don't know. She found those rumours very upsetting, about the missing baby. You know.'

Sophon looked puzzled. 'The baby was born dead. She knew that.'

'She didn't know it well enough, perhaps,' Creon replied.

'I am sure she did. There must have been something else, to force her to commit such violence against herself.'

'I don't think so.' Creon watched the old man realize he would not find his answers here.

'Oedipus.' Sophon spoke quietly, and Oedipus did not reply. The doctor shuffled over to the bed, and put his hand on Oedipus's shoulder.

'Oedipus, I need you to talk to me for a moment. Forgive me, but it cannot wait.'

Oedipus gulped himself quiet. He turned around, so he was sitting on the floor, facing the two men. 'What is it?' he asked.

'I need you to tell me what happened,' Sophon said.

Oedipus stumbled his way through a description of Jocasta's final act as queen: calming the crowds at the gate and sending them home. His voice cracked when he told Sophon about Teresa and her taunts. But Sophon merely nodded and encouraged him wordlessly, as though he were trying to calm a frightened dog. He listened right through to the end, when Oedipus described the young woman who spat at his wife, and surely pushed her over the edge into madness, and then argued with him once they were back inside.

'How else could she have done this to herself? To the children? To me?' he asked. 'Unless she was mad?'

Sophon didn't reply, but asked instead if Jocasta had felt unwell after the unpleasant exchange with the young woman.

'Unwell? I don't know what you mean,' Oedipus said. 'She was upset, so she came back here and locked herself in her room. She might have had a headache. You know how often she was prey to them, especially after an experience like that.'

'She didn't talk to anyone else before she came in here? Stop to play with the children, or anything?'

'No, of course not. If she'd taken time to play with them, she'd still be alive. I'm sure of it.'

'I doubt it,' said Sophon.

'I don't know what you mean.' Oedipus was becoming angry.

'You think she had plague.' Creon realized the point of the old man's questions. 'You think the woman who spat on her gave her the plague.'

Sophon nodded. 'I do,' he said. 'I have known Jocasta for almost thirty years. She didn't kill herself because she thought she was involved in an incestuous relationship with her own child. The very idea is preposterous. She hated that people were suggesting it, and I'm sure she was angry and upset. But that wouldn't be enough to make her take her own life. People kill themselves when they believe it's the best option they have. They're rarely correct, of course. But if they're suffering terrible pain, or they know – without any doubt – that they will soon be suffering, it isn't an incomprehensible choice.'

'People survive the plague,' Oedipus said. 'She would have given herself that chance.'

'I think she believed she would die,' Sophon replied.

'It's that old hag's fault,' said Oedipus. 'She will be executed before the end of the day. I'll do it myself with my bare hands.'

'Will that help matters?' asked Creon.

'Why would you say that?' Oedipus asked, dragging himself to his feet. 'Was this your idea? Were you in it together, you and Teresa?'

'I understand that you have lost your wife,' Creon replied. 'I ask you to remember that I have lost my sister.'

'Lost her? You couldn't wait to be rid of her, could you?

You've spent years weaselling your way into this palace. She never did anything without you in the end. Except this.' He gestured at his wife's body.

'I had no choice,' Creon said. 'She needed someone to help. All the things you weren't interested in. She needed someone to support her.'

'So you're accusing me of failing to take care of my wife?' Oedipus demanded.

'Gentlemen, please,' Sophon said. 'We have all lost someone we loved dearly. Now is not the time for attributing blame. It cannot help, and none of us can pretend that it is what Jocasta would have wanted. Please let's all pause for a moment before we say things we might regret.'

'I have nothing to regret,' Oedipus said. 'Throw him out of the palace and don't let him back in here again. Not while I'm here. Not while I'm alive.'

The old watch commander, who had been standing by the wall in silence, stepped forward uncertainly.

'You aren't in charge of the guard,' Creon said calmly. 'They obeyed your wife, and now they obey me.'

'Don't be ridiculous,' Oedipus said.

'It's not ridiculous,' Creon replied. 'You are not king of Thebes and nor will you ever be. Your wife was the queen, and her son will be the king. Until then, you or I will be the regent. It's perfectly clear in the laws of our city.'

Oedipus sprang at his brother-in-law, panting from the exertion, fingers curling into claws. The guard stepped forward between them, and echoed Sophon's plea for calm. He looked over to the old man for guidance.

'Gentlemen, I'm sorry to interrupt this argument, which you seem desperate to have over the body of a woman who would have loathed it,' Sophon said. 'But if she did have the plague, her body is still contagious.'

Creon and Oedipus faced each other, the guard's hands on their respective chests as he switched his gaze from one man to the other.

'We must bury her,' Sophon said. Oedipus opened his mouth to argue and Sophon raised a finger. 'I know you are sceptical so let me give you my diagnosis. But don't get any closer than you have been.' Oedipus looked over at his wife, whose bloated face told him nothing.

'She had a fever, undoubtedly,' Sophon said. 'You can see her hair was damp around the temples. It's still clumped together now.'

'Is that it?' Oedipus asked. 'You're saying she had plague because her hair isn't neat enough?'

'No,' Sophon replied. 'I'm saying she had plague because I believe she did. I saw the woman you described on my way to the palace. She had a child with her, a girl, I think. They were both dead by the side of the road. I recognized her when you described her hair and her clothing. I'd already noticed the signs of fever in your wife, so your account merely confirmed my diagnosis. Also, and this may be the most crucial point . . .'

Oedipus ran his hand across his forehead. He was burning from the shock and the grief and the anger.

'I think you have a fever,' said Sophon. 'You may be in the early stages of the plague, having caught it from Jocasta before she died. You need to be quarantined, and we need to cool you down as soon as we can. I'm going to send for some ice, as soon as you agree to let me treat you. I don't want you to be frightened. The effects of the disease vary and you may survive it perfectly well. I did, after all. But please believe me when I tell you I hope very much that you will heed my advice and stay away from your children.'

Oedipus slumped forward, unable to argue further. He staggered across the room to a couch and sank onto it, leaning his head back against the wall. Sophon took this as consent, and asked the watch commander to help wrap Jocasta's body. They peeled the sheets off the bed and wrapped them around the queen. Sophon sent another guard to the ice store, and asked him to bring as much ice as he could carry, and place it in the bath. Creon stood back, watching the men in silence. He could not help wrap his sister, but he could attend to the burial of her body.

'There is a grave for plague victims just outside the city wall,' he murmured to Sophon, who nodded. 'We'll take her straight there.' He turned to the watch commander. 'Thank you, sir, for your loyal service in this matter. Will you help me to carry the queen away?'

The watch commander was a widower and childless. He preferred to help Creon than ask one of his men to take the risk.

'Yes, sir,' he replied. 'Now?'

'Now.'

'I'll send word ahead that we'll need to exit the city shortly,' he said, and disappeared through the door. The ice had now arrived, and Sophon wrapped a large piece in a muslin cloth, and persuaded Oedipus to lie down on the couch, before resting the cold block on Oedipus's brow. 'Lie still,' he said. 'The cooler you are, the better you'll feel.'

Oedipus did not reply. Once he knew his diagnosis, he could no longer pretend he felt well enough to stand and fight. But still, he could not tolerate what was happening around him.

'She should be buried properly,' he said, his eyes closed. 'Not like this.'

'There's no other way,' Creon replied. 'The sooner she's buried, the safer everyone else will be. I'm sorry. You know as well as I do that she would never want to put her children at risk.'

Oedipus groaned, but did not speak.

'We need a stretcher to carry her,' said Sophon.

'The men can build a litter,' said Creon, and he left to give the order.

'You can't let them do this to her,' Oedipus said.

'There's nothing else to be done,' replied the doctor.

'What about the children? They'll want a tomb they can visit, for God's sake. They've lost their mother.'

'We'll think of something,' Sophon said. 'Don't worry about it now.'

After a time which seemed far longer to Sophon than to Oedipus, Creon and the watch commander returned with a makeshift stretcher. They laid it down on the bed next to Jocasta, and moved her onto it. They looked at one another and nodded, then lifted her. Sophon held open the door as they made their slow progress. The three men walked together, past the guards who hailed their queen as she left the palace for the final time. There was a scurrying sound from across the courtyard by the kitchens, but Sophon peered at the shadows and could see nothing.

The men continued through the second courtyard, Creon wondering how he would announce to the city that the queen was dead. They were concentrating so hard on carrying her that no one heard the bedroom door, banging shut a second time.

The slaves all knew what had happened. The palace had never contained news or even gossip for a moment. Perhaps he would be too late to make any announcement, Creon thought. This scandal would spread more quickly than any disease. But they came out of their kitchens, their guardhouses and their posts, all saluting the dead queen. Creon's jaw was set hard, but Sophon – who had seen so many die, and so many younger than Jocasta – could conceal his grief no longer. The tears ran down his cheeks, gathering in his damp beard. And still they carried her.

They entered the public courtyard, although the gates were still closed, and it was empty, except for the guardsmen who watched their commander struggling to keep his grip on the wood, and wished they could help. The sky was overcast, but it would not rain today. As the men reached the main gate into the marketplace, the guards opened it and waved them through.

Without speaking, the three of them turned to the left and continued their journey. The market was closed, so no one stood by to see them. They walked until they reached the small gate in the city walls, which led them to the Outlying. The stench of the plague pit was undeniable. Creon wished he could raise his sleeve to his face, to cover his nose. But it was impossible: he couldn't take the weight of the stretcher with just one hand.

No one watched over the plague pit: there was no need.

People brought their dead if they had to. Journeys here were always brief and brutal. The men put their burden down on the ground for a moment, while they decided where they should go. Creon glanced at the contents of the pit and shuddered. Most people didn't have sheets to spare for their loved ones' dignity, so the corpses were covered in the clothes they had died in, or nothing at all. He and the watch commander massaged their shoulders and arms, trying to revive them for one last exertion.

'Over there.' Sophon pointed to the far side of the pit. 'There's a jar of quicklime at the side of the pit there. We lower her in and then sprinkle that over her.'

Creon and the watch commander nodded. Neither had the energy to speak. They bent down, and lifted Jocasta one last time.

'No,' said a voice. 'You can't.'

*

They turned to see Oedipus, raving with anger, or the plague, or both. 'You can't leave her here. You can't.'

Sophon walked back towards him and looked at his fevered eyes. 'We must, my friend,' he said. 'There's no choice.'

Creon and the commander had not stopped walking, and Oedipus screamed when he looked past Sophon and saw they had gone further away. 'No.'

He pushed Sophon in the chest. The old man almost lost his balance, but recovered before he fell, and watched as Oedipus staggered after his wife.

There was no hope of catching them. Two healthy men, even carrying a corpse, could move more quickly than a man running a vicious fever. So by the time he reached them, sweat dripping down his face, they had already thrown the queen into the pit. For a terrible moment, Sophon thought Oedipus was going to hurl himself in after her. But he did not. Instead, he collapsed to his knees and wept as Creon and the watch commander stood catching their breath. Creon patted the commander's shoulder, thanking him for his work. The commander raised his eyebrows in a question, and Creon nodded. He would prefer to do the final task alone. The commander saluted and withdrew, back towards the city and the palace. Creon reached over for a shovel which had been left beside the pit, and began to scatter lime across his sister's body.

Oedipus could not tolerate anything that was happening in front of him. He wrenched himself back onto his feet, and grabbed for the shovel in Creon's hand. The two men teetered for an infinite moment by the side of the mass grave. Creon had to let go of the shovel to steady himself, and Oedipus grabbed it from him and swung it towards Creon's head. Creon dodged the blow, but Oedipus was readying himself to swing again. Creon looked around him for something he could use to defend himself. As Sophon watched him make a decision, he cried out, trying to stop it. But he was too far away, and the wind carried his voice towards the mountains.

Oedipus swung the shovel a second time, like an axe. And Creon ducked, scooping the powdered quicklime into his hardened hands. When Oedipus tried to hit him a third time, Creon flung the lime in his face.

Sophon had treated men in every stage of illness and injury, and he knew he would never again hear a sound like Oedipus made, as the caustic powder ate through his eyes. Creon could not have known what would happen when the lime met damp human tissue. His expression, even from a distance, was one of total horror. He ran from Oedipus, who had finally dropped the shovel so he could ball his hands into his eyes. But the pain was too great, and he could only stand and howl.

The horror was replaced on Creon's face by something else. 'Now you scream,' he said quietly. 'Now you know what pain is. I made that sound too, last summer. Not when I found the message from Eury saying she had the fever and had left. I didn't want to upset my son, you see, so I kept quiet.' He walked back towards his brother-in-law, safe in the knowledge that Oedipus could not see him. 'But when it was time to open up our house again, eight days later, do you know what I saw? I saw my dead wife, lying beside the walls of her own house, mourned but unburied. She must have sat beneath the windows, listening out for our boy, hoping she wouldn't hear him falling ill. Hoping she would live long enough to hear that she hadn't infected him. And she died where she had collapsed, alone, a few feet away from her husband and her son, unable to touch them or speak to them. And when I saw her ruined body, waiting for us outside, then – you can believe it – I screamed as you have screamed. But for another, not myself.'

And then Sophon could hear nothing, but Oedipus's anguished breaths, and Creon's trudging steps.

'Come on,' said Creon, as he reached the old man. 'We must go back to the city.'

Sophon looked at him. 'We can't leave him here.'

'I can,' said Creon grimly. 'I am regent now. Thebes will never accept a blind man, an incomer, as her king. And he will be better dying here than giving the plague to his children. My sister would say the same thing if she were alive.'

'She loved him very dearly,' Sophon said.

'She loved them more,' Creon replied. 'I am ordering you to accompany me to the palace. You will stay in quarantine and tell the slaves how to protect the children. He may have infected them already. In which case, you must tend to them and save their lives. If you prefer to stay here, trying to treat a dead man, I cannot stop you. But you will be throwing your life away. Come back with me. The gates will be closed once I return. They will never be reopened.'

Sophon looked away to the man demolished by every kind of agony, and he looked back at the man who had turned into a king.

29

I put my shoes back on. I didn't think I would ever tire of feeling the grass under my feet again, but I was mistaken. Delightful as it was to feel each individual strand forcing its way between my toes, the pain of treading on the stones which hid themselves beneath the grasses more than balanced it out. Besides, it was easier to wear shoes than carry them, although the leather was so tough at first that it blistered my feet. It has softened now, or my feet have hardened, as we have crossed the stades from the city. This is my first time outside Thebes, up on the mountain roads. We have a donkey to carry our packs. He's young and only occasionally bad-tempered. He limits the distance we can travel each day. After so many stades (the number varies, depending on the hilliness of the terrain), he stops for the night, and no persuasion from me or Sophon has any effect.

I look back to see the lower stretches of the mountains beneath me, and catch sight of Sophon's bald head through the waving grasses, like a large egg in a nest. I am still angry with him, though I feel the rage ebbing away with each step we take. I don't know whether it is the movement which cures my anger, or the distance I have put between myself and Thebes. Once we round the peak of the mountain – later this afternoon sometime – I will be out of sight of my city for the first time in my life. I could not stay there when my sister became queen, and used her first day as ruler to order that Creon be executed in the main square. I understood her reasons – he had turned against her and against our family, he had plotted against our brothers – but she could have banished him instead. Haem may never recover from it, I told her. She said he would learn to, or he would leave. I am not sure she cares which of these things happens. She wants people to know she is unafraid of her power. I'm sure they understand that now.

I plan to return to Thebes one day, but the roads are treacherous, and my plans may count for nothing. We will sleep outside for one or perhaps two more nights. I don't mind waking up covered in dew, my muscles stiffened from the hard ground. But I am decades younger than Sophon, and he struggles to raise himself in the mornings when we have slept on the ground, even if I have wrapped him in all the blankets we have with us. Still, he never complains.

He's coming up behind me, climbing towards me without noticing that I've perched on this boulder to wait for him. He's concentrating hard on the uneven ground; he doesn't want to lose his balance. He has a stick to help him negotiate his way over the rocks, and so do I. I found a branch by a dead pine tree, and I used a small knife to slice off the twigs which covered it. Because the tree is long dead, there is no sap bleeding out of it, gumming up my hands. It's more brittle, but I have been careful with it and it holds my weight when the path is uncertain.

I wave down to him, but he isn't looking up at me. I

want him to know there's a stream right by my feet, which means we can refill our bottles. He worries about water. He says it's from years of living in Thebes, where water was once in short supply. But he doesn't ever tell me I wouldn't understand because it wasn't like that when I was born. He just worries in silence. So I try to reassure him: we won't run out. Travellers used to take this path between the two cities all the time. If dying of thirst was a frequent occurrence, we would have seen the consequences somewhere by now: bodies by the side of the road. But still he worries. So now I just try to go ahead and find water, then wave back to him so he knows. But that only works if he remembers to look up.

He is filled with guilt and I am filled with blame. I don't know if the space between us can be crossed. Why had he never told me that my mother had not killed herself from shame, but that she had been infected with the plague? He says Creon forbade any mention of her, and told him – on the day she died – that if he ever raised the subject with any of her children, he would be banished from the palace immediately. Anyway, we never asked about it because we thought we knew everything already. She hanged herself, and everyone said it was from shame. They spoke about her so quietly and cruelly that we knew it must be so. And yet it was not. I grew up believing that my mother did not love us enough to stay alive. But the opposite was true. She loved us so much, she died to protect us. Sophon used to tell me in lessons that it is possible to change the past. When I expressed disbelief he gave the example of a wound, which might only be revealed as fatal many days after it has been sustained. I never understood it until now.

His head has disappeared from view, as the path curves away beneath me. I cannot hear him yet, but he must be closing in on my vantage point. I lift myself from the boulder, and sit on a smaller rock a little further up the path. He will need the high flat surface of the boulder, to rest his weary bones. The donkey trudges ahead of him, having decided that he keeps a more appropriate pace than I do. There are shoots of new green grass by the side of the stream, which the donkey will appreciate, as much as Sophon enjoys the cool mountain-water.

I have no idea what Corinth will be like. Thebes never did reopen her gates, after the two summers of the Reckoning. Ani has finally opened the city up again and most people are glad of it. But that wasn't so long ago, and word has not yet spread far enough afield for us to see anyone coming towards Thebes. The habit must have been broken years ago: there would have been no point crossing these mountains when you couldn't get into the city.

Or perhaps, as Sophon fears, the plague killed more people outside the city than inside. That happened before, with the first Reckoning, back when he was a boy. The whole world changed, he said, because so many people died. Things which had seemed permanent became temporary. So perhaps we will reach the city and find it inhabited only by bandits or skeletons or wild dogs or nothing at all. Perhaps we'll reach the outskirts and see that it is too late, and that there is nothing there for us, not even information. But I prefer to imagine that it will have survived, just as my city survived, in its own way. I think that people will be carving out their lives, in whatever circumstances remain for them. And I believe that one of them will be able to help me.

One of them will remember a time ten years ago when a blinded man wandered into their city, the place where he grew up. His eyes were gone, but you could see he had been handsome before that. He would have had a beard, I think, and he would have been accompanied by travellers he met near Thebes, who were heading to the city because they didn't yet know the gates had been closed. He would have told them that he had survived a brush with the Reckoning and that he could tell them how to protect themselves. My father was clever, and resourceful. They would have turned on their heels, weary and disappointed that their journey had been in vain. And he would have accompanied them back to his home. He might still be there now. He would be about forty years old.

He won't be able to see me, but that won't matter, because I was a child when he left Thebes. If anything, being able to see me would just confuse matters. It is the sound and the smell of people that doesn't change, even as they grow up or grow old. I know I will recognize him though, and Sophon will, of course. Sophon has survived so much, and for so long, he says appearances are all like masks for him. He can see through them to the true person within.

I know it would be better for him if we spent just one more night sleeping out in the open, but I hope it's two.

Because that gives me two more days of imagining what it will be like to find my father again.

And even though he hasn't heard my voice in all these years, when I say his name, he will know me straightaway.

Afterword

I can't remember when I first read the story of Oedipus (in a book of Greek myths when I was a child? In Greek lessons when I was a teenager, rolling my eyes at the discovery of yet another past tense?), but I certainly read the Sophocles play many years before I saw it performed. Perhaps this was a consequence of growing up in Birmingham, where there wasn't much call for Greek tragedies in the early nineties. Or perhaps they were being staged and I just wasn't paying attention: too busy with homework, or a Saturday job, or an unsuitable guitar-playing boy, no doubt.

I remember being startled to find out there were other versions of the myth: Books 9–12 of *The Odyssey* were a set text in my first term at college, so I was nineteen when I found out that Oedipus' story wasn't (and had never been) immutable. In Book 11, Homer describes the moment when Odysseus catches sight of 'beautiful Epicaste, mother of Oedipus' in the Underworld. Homer's version of the Oedipus myth is sketched out in just ten lines of verse, but it's subtly different from that of Sophocles: there's no mention of the auto-enucleation which forms a crucial climax in *Oedipus The King* (or *Oedipus Tyrannos*, to give it its Greek name. I can't stop you from calling it *Oedipus Rex*, obviously, but since he isn't Roman or a dinosaur, I can't bring myself to do it). And when did Epicaste become Jocasta?

So the Oedipus story was – to me – a book before it was a performance. It is such a relentless piece of storytelling (Aristotle thought it the most perfect Greek tragedy, and you don't want to make a habit of disagreeing with Aristotle. Well, maybe on medicine and anatomy) that it is almost impossible to stop before the story reaches its horrific conclusion. I tell it myself onstage nowadays, and there is something thrilling about being able to deliver the crucial pieces of story in the order they're revealed during the play. If you happen to find an audience who doesn't know what happens already, they invariably gasp at the key moment. It owes nothing to the person telling the story, and everything to the sheer weight of inevitable plot.

But most people don't read play-scripts, and although Greek tragedies are performed with pleasing frequency, *Oedipus Tyrannos* isn't performed as often as, say, *Hamlet*. It's not a school text for many of us. So I have long thought it would be fun to rewrite it as a novel. And if you're going to do that, you might as well retell the bit of the story that you're most closely drawn to, especially if you have always vaguely felt it's part of the narrative which has traditionally been overlooked. For me, that was the character of Jocasta.

Oedipus is famously clever; that's how he solves the Sphinx's virtually-impossible riddle, and earns his right to become King of Thebes. But his cleverness is also his tragic flaw: his quick-wittedness shades into quick-temperedness. This is a man who can solve a puzzle that has baffled all who came before him. But that same quickness explains how a man (who had been warned by an oracle that he would kill his father and was trying desperately to avoid his fate) could be reduced to a murderous frenzy at a crossroads by what amounts to a minor road-rage incident.

Jocasta has about 120 lines in *Oedipus Tyrannos*. People rarely remember that it is she who works out the terrible truth about her marriage, some time before her super-smart husband catches up. That's why she is already dead by the time he has pieced things together. So he is clever, in other words. But she is cleverer. And the earliest version of this myth, those ten lines of Homer I mentioned at the beginning? They're about her, the mother of Oedipus; his story is appended to hers, after Odysseus catches sight of 'beautiful Epicaste'. So I wanted to tell the story from her perspective, and have Oedipus be the more minor character. The myth – as so often – stands up no matter which way you look at it.

Jocasta is intriguingly blasphemous in Sophocles' play; she tells Oedipus that gods and oracles can't be trusted. But when she realizes that something truly terrible is happening, she turns to the shrine of Apollo and begs him for lusis – a release. That interplay between religious scepticism and sudden panicked faith was the key to part of her character. For me, she is and always will be the most courageous, complex character in the Theban story.

As for *Antigone*, it is the earliest of Sophocles' three Theban plays (they're often presented as a trilogy, alongside *Oedipus at Colonus*, but each play is in fact the sole survivor of its own trilogy, written decades apart. Which is why the timeline doesn't quite follow through from one to the next). I have always loved the tension within the play: Antigone is both law-abiding and anarchic, obedient and disruptive, freedom fighter and terrorist. She obeys the laws of the gods and disobeys the laws of men. She is the epitome (to put it in Greek philosophical terms) of phusis over nomos; a follower of natural law over man-made law. Arguing with her is like arguing with gravity. So, obeying the gods, burying her brother: these things simply matter more to Antigone than life itself. It's interesting that when Anouilh wrote his version of *Antigone*, in the early 1940s, he made her the younger sister of Ismene (Sophocles has Antigone as the elder). To Sophocles, Antigone is a dutiful, if excessive, sibling. To Anouilh, she is a rebel.

To me, she shines so brightly that Ismene gets lost in the glare. Sophocles can spare this younger sister just sixty lines. And even Antigone gets overshadowed by her uncle: Creon is the lead role in the play, if you count the number of lines each character has (believe me when I tell you that actors do this. And that the vast majority of them would rather have more lines than share their character name with the play's title). Creon has half as many lines again as his titular niece.

The battle between Creon and Antigone burns up all the oxygen in the room, or on the stage: it's what makes the play so compellingly claustrophobic. But I thought it would make a novel lopsided, so I decided to look hard at the Greek and see where I could find some space. Antigone is wedded to death, we're told, by the (biased, old, male i.e. allies of her uncle) chorus. Their bias aside, she has long seemed to me to be more attached to the glory of her own sacrifice, rather than the rightness of her cause. So I decided to focus on that side of her character, and give Ismene the lead role instead.

Antigone doesn't appear to exist before the fifth century BCE: she isn't mentioned in versions of the Oedipus story before then. Ismene is a good Theban name (there was a

River Ismenos by Thebes, as well as a hill and a village with the same name) but, sometimes in her earlier mythic outings, she isn't part of Oedipus' family. Meanwhile, the two brothers – Polynices and Eteocles – shift lives and deaths: sometimes one kills the other, sometimes they kill each other, sometimes one lives and one dies. The *Seven Against Thebes* by Aeschylus offers a much bigger vision of this fraternal conflict. I scaled things down to two men, boys really, who cannot tolerate each other, and let that stand in for a larger civil war. In other words, I have played extremely fast and loose with their story. But at least they both end up under the earth, which is what their sisters wanted for them.

The version of Thebes which appears in this novel bears some relation to the place you would see now, if you visited Greece. The lake and the mountains are real, as is the distance from Corinth (and indeed the sea – Thebes is a surprisingly long way from it, compared with other Greek city-states in the ancient world). The palace and its courtyards are imagined, and owe at least as much to Mycenae and Knossos as to historical Thebes. If you're a major nerd, you will see Isy and Jocasta using some items which appear in Greek museums. I did tell you I had played fast and loose with the myth, and I have been equally cavalier with the archaeology. But I figured that Sophocles' mythic Thebes owes something to fifth-century Athens, so I'm continuing a noble tradition of reworking the city (and the story) for my own purpose.

If you're wondering about some of the minor characters, Teresa of course owes something to Teiresias, not least her capacity to infuriate Oedipus by speaking what she says is the truth, and what he believes to be a vicious lie. And imagining the character as a woman is not me being anachronistically gender-blind, although I might have done it anyway (who doesn't long to write a female villain?). Part of the myth of Teiresias is that he changed from male to female, and then back again. He reported that women had much better sex. Hey, don't shoot the messenger.

Laius is largely offstage in this novel, as he is in the Homeric sketch, the Sophoclean plays and most versions of the story. He exists only to throw things into chaos with his death (although I did once see a production of *Oedipus* where our titular hero meets his father at the place where three roads meet, and instead of killing him, they have a fascinating chat and then go their separate ways. It was terrific). Laius's lack of interest in women and predatory interest in young men appear in some versions of his story, where he rapes the son of his guest-host (disregarding the bonds of guest-friendship was, to the Ancient Greeks, at least as dreadful a crime as rape). It was a small step from there to the character in this book.

And Sophon, the man with medical knowledge? He is an addition to the story, a modern creation. Though he shares more than just a couple of syllables with Sophocles, who once paid for a shrine on behalf of the cash-strapped Athenians for the god of medicine, Asclepius. Sophocles was an immensely popular and prolific playwright, as well as a skilled military general. So there was a touch of the polymath to him which I was happy to steal.

Sophocles was born in Colonus, not far from Athens, which gives him the setting for the least-performed of the Theban plays, *Oedipus at Colonus*. Because it is performed so infrequently, compared to *Oedipus Tyrannos*, people often forget that Oedipus' story ends much less miserably than it began. A blind exile, he wanders Greece with his daughter for a guide, and eventually settles on Colonus as the place where he will die, and be interred. The gods – so often his enemies – have told him that his bones will bring good fortune to the land which holds them. That is to be Colonus, ruled (at this point in its mythic history) by the Athenian king Theseus, of minotaur fame. After thwarting a last-ditch attempt by Creon – trying to claim the good fortune for himself – to take him back to Thebes, Oedipus dies as he wished: giving a last, enduring gift to the people of Athens. Even tragedies can have a happy ending.

Acknowledgements

A huge thank you to the guys at RCW, especially the quietly magnificent Peter Straus; and to everyone at Mantle, especially Maria Rejt, Lara Borlenghi, and Josie Humber.

Thanks to the crazy-generous writers who read early drafts of this, even though they were busy reading and writing for their own work: Sarah Churchwell and Lionel Shriver. You are my heroes. As is Edith Hall. If you want to know more about Greek tragedy, incidentally, anything she's ever written would be a great place to start.

Thanks to everyone at the BBC who has kept me in gainful employment over the years. Double points to Tanya Hudson and to all those who have worked on *Natalie Haynes Stands Up for the Classics*. You're tremendous.

Thanks to my brilliant friends who have offered unstinting moral support, almost always near cake or gin or both: Helen Bagnall, Damian Barr, Michelle Flower, Kara Manley, Joss Whedon. I am so lucky to have you. And special thanks to Julian Barnes for going to about 900 Greek tragedies with me (one day, I swear, we'll go to something with a death toll lower than, say, four).

A zillion thanks, as usual, to Christian Hill, who still runs the website even though he has a proper job, a family, and impenetrable books about programming to write.

Acknowledgements

Thanks to my mum, Sandra; my dad, Andre; and to Chris and Gemima. If you see Chris, tell him there are spaceships in this one.

And of course, thanks to Dan, for literally everything.

800 645 711